FAIR HAVEN

RED LAGOE

FAIR HAVEN

Second edition 2026 by Death Knell Press
Cover art and interior design by Red Lagoe

paperback ISBN: 978-0-9988531-9-2

DEATH KNELL PRESS

This book is dedicated to all who enjoy
to live,
to laugh,
and to love...
but who also hate those stupid signs.

A NOTE FROM THE AUTHOR

I used to work as a veterinary surgical assistant for several years, and on many drives to and from work, I imagined how my skills might be helpful should the zombie apocalypse happen—as I assume most people do on their daily commutes.

I started *Fair Haven* about ten years ago as a fledgling writer. It was supposed to be a practice novel to get myself acquainted with the art of writing longer works. I didn't plan to take it too seriously, because it would likely (as a first novel for someone with minimal experience) never be published.

But guess what happened...

I took it *sooo* seriously!

Fair Haven became far more than a zom-poc with a love triangle. (They're not really zombies, by the way.) I poured my heart into it and learned so much in the process. So, I pursued publication. I had a lot of help from excellent people along the way. Eternal thanks to Jason, Crystal, Donna, Carrie, and Katie for helping me get my first novel in shape for self-publication.

While I'm incredibly proud of the product I created and published in 2017, I realized after a couple of years how much it needed a heavier edit. I pulled *Fair Haven* from the shelves, and it went out of print.

It took a few years, but it's back from the dead! Resurrected with a new cover and a sharp edit. (Thank you, Gennifer!) I kept true to the original version, doing a little rearranging of the storytelling to make it flow better, creating more distinction between characters, and adding a couple post-COVID adjustments. What I did NOT do was a full-fledged rewrite. This was my first novel, and I love it for what it is.

I almost retitled it to one of my original working titles, "All's Fair in Love and the Apocalypse", but I had to decide against it. *Fair Haven* is not only the name of the small town, but it's a state of mind. It's the end goal—to find a safe and fair haven in a world of chaos and despair.

Enjoy the apocalypse, and try not to take it too seriously.

FAIR HAVEN

To live is the rarest thing in the world.
Most people exist, that is all.

— Oscar Wilde

ONE

Melody

Were it not for the bloodstained pavement in the cul-de-sac, it would've looked like any other beautiful day in Fair Haven. Melody's house sat at the end of Elpis Court, flanked by the other two-story colonials. Her attic ventilation window provided a clear view of the neighborhood to the end of the street, where it met with Mason Drive.

Morning sun squeezed inside, casting slivers of light onto the creaking attic floorboards. She pulled her sweaty, frizzy hair away from her face and tried to suck in some fresh air through the narrow, slatted opening, but all she could smell was the bucket of her own festering waste stewing in the heat. Melody had relieved herself in a five-gallon paint bucket that was still coated with a dried layer of beige paint. The stench made her sick to her stomach, but she was more sickened with herself for hiding, sitting on her ass, and waiting for something to happen, instead of taking action. Venturing down to the toilet on the second floor was too much of a risk, even if she was fairly positive that none of the infected had entered her house.

Last night, the dirge of suffering people bled through her walls. The gunfire that quieted their voices solidified her choice to stay in the safety of her attic.

Her next-door neighbor had been killing the infected. This morning, she spotted him four houses down, exiting the Nickersons' backyard with a hunting rifle slung over his shoulder. He'd been targeting infected, then dragging their bodies into that yard for the past several days. Two shots in the chest, one in the head, with methodical precision.

Military, maybe?

Or serial killer?

With a limp, he cut across the street, wearing a black t-shirt, blue jeans, and a face mask, watchful of his surroundings. Melody had seen him over the summer—before all Hell broke loose—mowing his lawn at sunset with that same limp, so she was sure it wasn't a symptom of infection. But she couldn't remember his name.

He made his way back to his house and sat in an Adirondack chair on the front porch, eyes on the neighborhood. Sunlight trickled through the trees and danced upon the wood of his porch. He removed his mask to expose his facial scruff. His t-shirt stretched across a muscular chest. The rifle rested against the denim of his inner thigh. His presence brought Melody an unusual feeling of security. This stranger next door became Melody's constant in a world of insanity, protecting her neighborhood—protecting *her*—from the incoming infected. It was like having her own loyal German Shepherd dog. She smiled at the thought.

She wished she could remember his name. Her husband, Marcus, had introduced himself to the man a few months ago when he and Melody had first moved in, but the name escaped her. It was Joe or Gary...or something boring. She wished she had gone over there and introduced herself, but casserole-slinging, friendly neighbor wasn't really her style. Melody was more of a dog person than a people person, which was why she was drawn to veterinary medicine.

"Good boy," she whispered to her protective companion next door. She laughed under her breath, convinced she was losing her mind in the heat.

While she couldn't deny that her neighbor had caught her eye as an attractive man, she never felt any substantial draw to him until the world fell apart. From her vantage point in the attic, her mind wandered downstairs, out the front door, and onto his porch. It flirted with him and climbed into his lap, straddling his strong thighs. Energy pulsed between her legs...

Melody snapped back to reality and wiped the sweat from her face. Certainly, the sudden attraction was caused by the stressful, life-threatening situation outside. She was too rational for this kind of primal crush.

Besides, Melody had trust issues, long before there were any cases of the infected in town, or the rest of the world for that matter. Life had been hard on her—a continuous struggle with obstacles so seemingly insurmountable that there had been times when she considered giving up on life altogether. But nobody likes a quitter.

Marcus stepped into the picture during one of those tough moments. They were both in their late teens. He calmed the storm in her life, becoming her haven of trust.

However, time and experience had a way of bushwhacking the hell out of a relationship. A decade had passed since she met Marcus, and while they grew up, their paths seemed to grow apart. Lately, she couldn't seem to recognize him as the friend he used to be. He changed. Or maybe *she* changed.

Considering an epidemic had been bleeding into every nook and cranny of the country over the past week, she would have thought he'd be willing to put their petty differences aside for one day and communicate.

Fucking, Marcus.

A few days earlier, Marcus had been inspecting himself in the mirror, buttoning a crisp blue shirt, while the morning light filtered through sheer curtains in their bedroom, making the fuzz on the new beige carpeting sparkle.

Why did everything have to be beige?

Melody knew it was a bad idea for him to leave the house, considering the reports on the news, but the man's insistence upon doing whatever he wanted trumped her pleas.

"It's just another COVID or something," he argued, rolling his eyes and adjusting his tie in the mirror.

"You've seen the news. It's so much worse." She stood behind him while he continued to inspect his visage for imperfections. There were none, as usual. Melody continued to press. "They reported a case in Madison this morning. Not even a few miles away!"

Marcus put his hands on her shoulders in an attempt to be consoling, "It's not here in Fair Haven yet. You worry too much."

"People are biting each other like rabid animals. This disease is dangerous."

Marcus turned back to give himself a once-over in the mirror. "You *would* say that," he looked over his shoulder at her with a sly smile. "News guy Matt Cunningham says to go about our lives—"

"Matt Cunningham is an idiot," Melody snapped.

Perhaps if the media and government officials were more forthcoming with the information about the early onset of the outbreak, humanity could have stood a chance. But the so-called authorities withheld information, fearful of mass panic and hysteria.

But mass panic and hysteria came anyway. The first images and videos of attacks on social media were accused of being deep fakes. Melody herself dismissed the first viral video she clicked on. A man in a tank top had chased down a woman in full nun-garb on the side of the road in Austin, Texas. The nun screeched in the shaky video, while the crazed man clawed at her with maniacal, swinging arms, biting at her legs.

Then came another video. And another, until the phenomenon finally made world news. By then, it was too widespread for the warnings to make a difference.

"Stay home today. We can ride this out together," she'd pleaded with Marcus.

Marcus's shoulders slumped. He sighed and leaned a little closer. "I wasn't going to say anything, but Greg has a sample of the virus at the lab."

"Of LV01?"

"We're gonna work on a vaccine." He whispered it with a spark in his eyes that looked more like dollar signs.

"But is your company even equipped for that?"

"Mel…" he said. "Do you think I'd try to make a vaccine if we couldn't?"

"So, you *do* think there is something to worry about."

Marcus rolled his eyes. "God, M… Seriously? Think about it from a business perspective. Do you know how much money I could make if I came up with the vaccine for this?"

She fought against the urge to spew out the vitriol building at the tip of her tongue. She took a deep breath. "Do you know how many *lives* you could save?"

"Of course," he said, "it'll save a lot of lives. But if we make a ton of cash on it too, then what's wrong with that?"

"I want to go with you."

"No."

"I have some theories about LV01—"

"No." Marcus walked out of the bedroom and headed downstairs.

"Don't tell me *no*." She hurried after him. "We still have a lot to talk about. A lot to work on between us."

"M." He whipped around at the base of the stairs, stopping her. "Do you really think *now* is a good time for couples therapy?"

"What if it's the only time we have?"

Marcus smiled and kissed her on her cheek with the familiar dry peck of a relative. "Our marriage will be fine. I promise. And I appreciate you trying to help. Really. But I won't bring you out there. You said it yourself. It's too dangerous."

"So, you're leaving me here?"

"Well, you know…HVAC guys are supposed to come today, and someone needs to be here."

"You really think the HVAC guys are going to show up today to fix our A/C?" She nearly laughed, lips twitching into an almost-smile, hoping he was joking.

"I'll be home tonight." He gripped the doorknob. "Promise I won't die on you." He smirked with an arrogance that made her want to throat punch him, and then he was out the door before she could argue.

"Asshole," she said through the door.

After Marcus had left for work that day, Melody stayed glued to the television. Reports of infected were all over the country. Shaky cell phone videos plagued the news and social media. As much as it sickened her to see the violence, she couldn't look away from the screen. The panicked eyes and trembling voices of reporters reached through the television and grabbed Melody by the throat.

In one new video, a woman in yoga pants and a crop top sprinted toward a reporter from behind. The cameraman jerked back, making the image on screen bounce. Before the woman in yoga pants could collide with the reporter, she crashed to the ground, pulled down by a neurological imbalance. The report continued from their news van as they fled the scene.

Melody's pulse pounded as she watched the violence unfold in their own county.

By noon, reports on the television showed that the neighboring town, Madison, had hundreds of infected. Looters. Gunfire. Chaos. It was closing in. Accidents on the freeway jammed the roads. Fortunately for Fair Haven, the sleepy lake town was not large enough to have earned its own freeway exit.

It didn't help that ignorance about the severity of the virus was just as widespread as the virus itself. Melody's boss, Dr. Vanessa Matteo—the owner of Fair Haven's only veterinary clinic—insisted her employees show up to work. Only a few did. Melody was fortunately not scheduled to see patients that day, but she called to check in on her team.

The new young assistant answered the phone. "Fair Haven Veterinary

Clinic. This is Hannah. How can I help you?"

"Hannah, it's Melody."

"Oh, thank God!"

"Can I talk with Vanessa?"

"She left."

"What?"

"Yeah." Hannah's voice soared to a higher octave. "She saw the news and how bad it was getting and just left. Didn't say anything."

"Hannah, you need to leave, too."

"But Milo Gardner's mom didn't pick him up yet."

"Give him some food and go home."

"But what if he's stuck here in the cage and nobody can come feed him?"

"Then…bring him home if you're that worried about it. But you need to leave."

"But he's really sick."

"How sick?"

"Vanessa examined him this morning. She didn't think it's a brain tumor."

"Brain tumor? What are his symptoms?"

"It started with a head tilt. Now he has that weird eye twitchy thing—"

"Nystagmus," Melody said. It was a symptom common in neurologic patients, common in rabies.

"He's falling over and drooling," Hannah said.

"Don't touch him. Leave him in his cage and get out."

"But we don't know how long he'll be stuck here."

"You can't save him."

"I can try," she said with the ambition and naivety of every young animal lover.

"Those are symptoms of rabies." Melody sighed and tried to reason with the girl. "There's no way to come back from rabies once symptoms show up. And for all we know, it's not the rabies virus that we're used to. It could be LV01."

"Do animals get that?"

"We don't know yet. Don't open his cage to feed him. Just get out of there and get home."

Silence prevailed. Nothing but the sound of Hannah's short breaths came through.

"Hannah, I'm coming up there. I'll give you a ride."

"No," she interrupted with nervous breaths. "I'll go." She sniffled, voice cracking. "I'll go home."

The day that Marcus left for work, Melody had spent every second in her bedroom with her eyes darting between the news and looking out her window. She paced, squeezing her fists so tight her knuckles went white. She had to remind herself to breathe. There were no commercials—only non-stop coverage of the horrors unfolding around the world.

Her calls to Marcus's cell went to voicemail. Her gut twisted so much she could have puked. According to the latest reports, Route 28, which ran along the stretch of woods on the outskirts of Fair Haven, was jammed with traffic. Helicopter coverage showed disoriented figures stumbling along the highway. Some circled mindlessly, while others lashed out at anything that moved. People fled their vehicles, scattering in chaos. Their uncoordinated state kept them from climbing the six-foot fence that ran along the highway. They were contained, but Melody was unsure for how long.

Turned out, it didn't take long at all.

Late in the day, after Marcus left for work, a knock at Melody's front door jarred her from her news trance. Mrs. Nickerson, the gossip from a few doors down, hollered at the door. Melody stayed hidden behind the bedroom window's curtain, fearful of exposing her presence to anyone. Marcus had the car, and her Jeep was parked in the garage, out of sight. For all anyone knew, she could've been at work as usual.

"Miss?" Mrs. Nickerson called out. The mid-sixties woman with cotton-candy hair yelled louder. "For Pete's sake, I forgot your name," she said. "The virus is in Fair Haven!"

Melody didn't answer, so Mrs. Nickerson shimmied to the next house. It was honorable of the woman to go out and warn her neighbors like Paul Revere on his midnight ride. But fear kept Melody paralyzed in her home.

Melody's handsome neighbor didn't respond either, but his silhouette could be seen through the glass of his first-floor window as he hammered a board in place. Mrs. Nickerson moved on, waddling as quickly as she could to knock on all the doors.

Once the first siren sounded from the fire station, Melody followed suit with the guy next door and barricaded her door. Without any boards lying around, she opted to push her dining room table to block the front door. The windows were already locked and curtains closed.

Police and ambulance sirens joined in the distance. Fair Haven's streets became riotous. Many neighbors locked themselves indoors, while others packed their vehicles and made a run for it.

The chaos bled into her neighborhood. Men, women, and even children attacked each other, biting into their loved ones in the street like rabid animals. Some of those who were bitten staggered away, but others convulsed and turned ravenous within minutes.

Minutes.

Her neighbor, who had been boarding up windows, sat in a second-story window, firing shots at the feet of people trying to loot his house. Three teens charged toward Melody's house with bricks in their hands, but the neighbor fired at them as well, missing them, and the boys scattered away. Seconds later, one of the infected people—a burly man with a full beard—charged at the looter, toppling onto the kid and tearing into him.

That's when the neighbor began firing shots that didn't miss. Bodies of the infected dropped in the street, and Melody didn't think she could stand to watch any longer, but she did anyway. Her heart raced, pulse thumping against her ears. She gripped a baseball bat in case she needed to defend herself, and she waited.

And waited…

She was ready to unlock the door as soon as Marcus's vehicle came screaming into the cul-de-sac, but it didn't come.

Sirens and humans screamed beyond sunset, so she hid in the attic with the pull-down ladder wedged shut. She figured there was no way the infected could get up here, considering how disoriented they were.

She got one phone call through to Marcus that first night before cell service froze, and he told her something that she couldn't believe.

"I don't think I can come home," he said.

"Don't leave me here, Marcus."

"I'm not leaving you, M. I'm coming home as soon as I can. But I don't know when that will be."

The call went dead.

Her frantic calls back went unanswered, then after several minutes, she couldn't get a call out at all.

She'd waited all night, hidden in the attic, clinging to her small TV that she dragged up from her bedroom for information on the outbreak. She was so paranoid of being found hiding inside that she created a blanket fort to keep light from escaping the attic window.

Breaking news of homicides across the country dominated the broadcasts. Hospitals overflowed with patients. The attack victims assaulted hospital staff. A State of Emergency was declared in every state and then nationally.

Melody slept curled up in the attic on a bed of cushions that she had pulled from the loveseat downstairs. Petrified and alone, she cowered while listening to the pops of gunfire, explosions, and the torturous screams outside.

But she was no stranger to fear and solitude.

After her parents died, she'd spent a short time homeless as a teen. A terrible storm rolled through Fair Haven, and Melody had taken shelter in the chassis of an old Caddy that laid in the stretch of woods between the old railroad tracks and Route 28. The lightning cracked and high winds sent nearby trees crashing to the earth, but Melody had closed her eyes and breathed through the fear, waiting for morning. She had one thing to do for that night in the car—survive.

"Stay alive," she had whispered to herself, and she planned to do the same that night in the attic.

Melody survived homelessness, and she survived that first night in the attic because she stayed hidden. She survived the following nights as well. Survival was all that mattered. She'd figure out the rest later.

She watched from the attic window as new terrors unfolded each day.

Mrs. Nickerson, on a frantic run to her car, fell victim to her son, forty-year-old Daniel with cerebral palsy. He lunged from his wheelchair and bit into his mother before she could get him to the car. Every nerve ending in Melody's body sparked like electric shocks as she listened to Mrs. Nickerson's screams permeate the air. She wanted to rush downstairs, charge out into the middle of the street, and pry Daniel from his mother, but it was too late to save her.

The news began to dwindle, and the sirens waned. The infection swept across the country, plaguing everyone, including police, doctors, firemen, and reporters. Civilization crumbled. The gray static dominating the airways terrified her more than any graphic news report.

When the last surviving news outlet had announced a list of all of the quarantine zones established in the station's viewing area, Fair Haven High School made the list, and Melody knew the perfect route to the quarantine zone—the old railroad tracks. She had run them a thousand times for cross-country practice in high school.

A glimmer of hope flickered inside Melody, but she was reluctant to leave without knowing more about the status of the quarantine zone, and without knowing if Marcus was on his way back to her.

So, she stayed, watching from her attic as the surviving neighbors made a run for their vehicles. Some of them never made it to their cars before being attacked.

On the third night after Marcus left, the electricity failed. The TV and the street lights zapped out, and the neighborhood went dark, intensifying the sound of screaming and inhuman groans. Hours passed in the darkness, the sounds of emergency vehicles dissipated, and the gunshots grew sparse. Death and disease choked Fair Haven into a silence.

The moon fell below the horizon, and the landscape grew black. Melody pressed her face against the ventilation slats, hoping that a glimpse of some stars would bring her some tiny degree of comfort. Her dad had loved the stars. She spotted a bright one, and she wished she could see more. Her mind drifted to her dad's telescope, which hadn't been used since he passed, and she wouldn't get to use it any time soon, either, unless she could find an open roof. And with that ridiculous stargazing pipedream, she clutched Marcus's photo tight against her chest, lay down on her cushions with her eyes wide open and nothing but a drape of blackness before her.

It was time to stop being afraid. Stop hiding from the damn storm. Stop ogling the hot neighbor from her attic. It was time to go out into the chaotic, crumbling world and find her damn husband.

TWO

Melody

She convinced herself that she wanted nothing more than to see Marcus coming home so they could evacuate together up north to her father's cabin in the mountains. But each day that passed brought death to her doorstep and the sickening realization that she may be on her own once again.

Be strong, Melon-Bee—Her father used to say it when she was young.

Dad had sat down with her at the kitchen table one night after she'd been dumped by Mark Gilmore for being "too much of a tomboy."

"I've come to talk to you about love," her dad said, "and look where we chose to sit!" He pointed to the *Live, Laugh, Love* sign and smiled. Mom had hung it despite Melody and her father's snarky remarks.

Melody rolled her fourteen-year-old eyes, still besparkled with glitter eyeshadow, as her father tried to comfort her.

"*Love* should be easy," he said. "If it's not easy, then you're doing it wrong. I'm not saying it won't ever hurt, but if it hurts, either someone died or someone did something wrong. Do you get what I'm saying?"

She didn't.

Dad pointed back to the *Live, Laugh, Love* sign. "*Love* comes easy when you're with the right one. So does the *laughing* part..." He sighed and mumbled under his breath. "It's the *living* that's a bitch."

He had no clue what a bitch it would become. A couple of years later, Mom died after a short battle with breast cancer, and there was no *Be strong, Melon-Bee* from her dad then. Instead, before the funeral for his wife ever took place, Dad took his own life.

But then Marcus came along, and they became inseparable in their senior year. So inseparable that Marcus's mom called them *M and M*. He was her person, so she'd thought.

The heat of the attic became unbearable on the unusually warm autumn morning. The same abandoned cars that had been there for days lined the street—the white unmarked van, the green Volvo with its door open, and the blue convertible.

She spied between the slats of the attic window and drank in a refreshing glimpse of the man next door, wondering if she should reveal her presence to him before she left or if she should slip away unseen. Why she felt the need to let him know she was leaving was beyond her understanding. Her feelings— more like lustings—were downright primitive. Whether she thought he was hot didn't matter anyway, because *Marcus* was the man she had come to rely on. *He* was her constant for the past decade, even if that constant was becoming increasingly toxic.

Then this neighbor-guy—whatever his name was, Joe Rifle (or was it Gary Rifle?)—came along and made her weak in the knees. It had to be the trauma or the heat getting to her.

While she gazed upon him, he stood and ambled toward the porch steps with his rifle aimed at the end of the Elpis Court. Melody's heart raced as a speck of a person shuffled along Mason Drive and disappeared beyond the corner.

Joe Rifle's biceps bulged against his snug t-shirt. He lowered his weapon and returned to his Adirondack chair.

"You're probably a big douchebag, aren't you?" she whispered.

His front door opened behind him, and the face of a young brunette peeked outside. Melody leaned forward, thrilled to see another survivor and curious because she didn't realize the guy next door had a wife—or daughter?

Squealing tires pierced the air from a few houses down, and a Ford pickup pulled out from someone's side yard and into the street, hauling a boat—a Carolina skiff with a red lightning bolt.

The guy next door directed the brunette inside, and he lunged from his porch to flag the driver down. The truck stopped in the middle of the street before the boat trailer had even cleared the driveway. There were two passengers in the cab of the truck, and sitting in the open truck bed was a woman in a yellow dress and a man in a football jersey.

Melody wondered if that boat was her neighbor's ride out of town, and she wondered if they would take her with them. Maybe swing by the lab to check in on Marcus.

The truck's tires shrieked again, nearly running over the neighbor's feet, and the boat with the red lightning bolt was towed away without her or Joe Rifle. The truck squealed around the corner onto Mason Drive at the end of the street, but then came to an abrupt stop. Five infected people staggered behind it in pursuit. The boat and its red lightning bolt could still be seen from Melody's attic.

Joe Rifle stood in the middle of the street watching the scene unfold. Seconds later, screams echoed off the houses, tires peeled out, and the boat disappeared. The woman in the yellow dress, who had been in the back of the pickup, stumbled into view from around the corner.

They left her!

"Do something," Melody said to herself, but she'd been stricken with immobility. The same fear that had kept her from helping Mrs. Nickerson when her son attacked. The same fear that kept her in her attic for days. "Do something!"

Clenching her jaw, she forced herself to move. Melody hunched over and crept across the creaking boards, forced open the attic hatch door, and let the ladder clunk to the floor.

A gush of cool air swept up through the hatch, and Melody stuck her head through the opening to look for danger below.

She sneaked downstairs with her metal baseball bat in her hands, leaving the dank atmosphere of the attic behind. The freshness of the air seemed to offer some relief to the violence of her pounding heart.

Melody peeked out her bay window on the first floor to see the slender woman in yellow, draped in blood, closing in on the end of the cul-de-sac. The bright floral sundress sagged from her sun-crisped shoulders.

Melody feared being spotted, so she backed away from the window. Her neighbor had retreated to his porch and aimed his rifle toward the woman.

Stepping out her front door to help could this person could very well be the end of Melody.

That woman could attack her, or that man next door might accidentally shoot her. She played whack-a-mole with her thoughts of uncertainty while her sweaty palms lubricated the handle of the baseball bat.

The woman in yellow gripped her gushing throat wound with small hands. She was weak and appeared to be desperately seeking help.

Neighbor-guy handed his rifle to the girl inside the house and darted off his porch with a blade attached to his hip. She worried for him, being exposed, especially since there wasn't enough research done about this disease.

"Screw it," she said, pulling her medical bag from the hall closet. She managed to don a plastic shield mask and a pair of purple, latex-free gloves within a few seconds.

Exhaling a steady, calculated breath, she shoved the walnut table that had barricaded the door. She measured the weight of the baseball bat in her hand while her heart hammered against her breastbone. Then Melody cracked the door open, one inch per heartbeat, and stepped out into the infected world.

THREE

Kayla

Kayla Hartford's bare legs trembled within the confines of her tight skirt. She held the handle to the breakroom door and debated whether or not to explore the rest of the building for survivors. The door crept open like some forbidden crypt, and a foul stench of death rushed in.

With her blazing red hair pulled into a tight bun, a death-grip on a broken chair leg to use as a weapon, she tiptoed barefoot down the hallway between the cubicles on the fourth floor. She'd lost her heels in a sprint to the breakroom days ago.

Many of the employees who'd shown up to work on the day the infection spread to Fair Haven had opted to stay within the safety of the building that first night, but by the second day, the building had already been overrun with the infected.

Kayla sheltered on the fourth floor with several others when they got word that the mailroom kid, Nolan, was bitten on the arm. He turned ravenous within an hour of exposure and then lashed out at Sue from accounting. Nolan bit Sue in the neck, then Sue attacked others within ten minutes. Ten minutes was all it took for Sue to lose her mind and go totally bat-shit savage. Many fled the building, but those who remained on the fourth floor were trapped by the infected employees stumbling out of the elevator.

Four of them barricaded themselves inside the breakroom, living on unclaimed lunches and vending machine food for days and washing up in the small bathroom's pedestal sink.

The window in the breakroom allowed a small amount of light inside, but the bumpy privacy glass did not give a view of the outside world. They relied on a nineteen-inch flat screen TV bracketed in the corner to tell them what was happening out there, and the news paralyzed Kayla. There seemed to be nowhere safe to go, so when the list of quarantine zones was finally announced, the other employees lit up with the prospect of being rescued.

Knowing that danger still lurked in the building and outside, Kayla had begged them not to attempt the trip yet. They didn't listen to her. Nobody ever listened to her. What's an eighteen-year-old goth kid from California have to offer the world? Nobody ever took her seriously, even after she removed most of her piercings.

"We're running out of food," Helen had said. Helen was a middle-aged woman with a scant frame and a skin tone that suggested she may have a meth addiction.

"It's only a couple of miles to the high school," Victoria said. She was a fellow intern with whom Kayla had made out with last week. "Please come with us, Kayla."

"Hear me out, though," Kayla said. "Let's stay here where it's safe just for a little while longer."

But all of them were anxious to get moving. Victoria left Kayla with a candy bar and a bag of chips before she kissed her on the forehead and walked out the break room door with the others.

Moments after they left, screaming pierced the thick breakroom door. Kayla swung it open to run to their aid, but Victoria was at the end of the hall, pinned to the ground, being attacked by a man in a white coat—one of the scientists from the lab downstairs. The others, Helen and Jonas, fought through the doorway to the stairwell, leaving Victoria behind.

Kayla screamed and shut the breakroom door, sobbing, gasping for breath that wouldn't come until she almost passed out. She sat against the wall with her eyes peeled open, and her vision blurred from the overflow of tears pouring from her sockets. Immobile with fear and hopelessness, her mind felt like it was slipping into insanity.

When the power quit across town that night, Kayla spent the evening locked within the blackness of the breakroom bathroom, sleeping on the cold tiled floor. It occurred to her that she could just end her life now instead of being ripped apart by teeth, but the thought was fleeting. Besides, there was nothing in the breakroom to do the job. No rope to hang herself with. No knife—unless she could saw through her wrists with a butter knife… Perhaps she should impale herself on the broken wooden chair—and with that morbid suggestion, she came to her senses.

"Mind over matter," she assured herself.

She hadn't heard anyone outside the breakroom door since her coworkers had left. Perhaps it was over, but the rescue teams hadn't arrived at her building yet. Maybe she could find a way out, get help, and meet up with her family back in California somehow.

Sunlight trickled in from behind the gaps in the shades of the tall, skinny windows as she maneuvered around her coworkers' dead bodies. It took every bit of strength she had to keep from screaming or vomiting. This was not how she envisioned her college experience.

She'd gotten as far away from her parents as she could, applying to a small school on the other side of the country where she could claim her independence. Since her arrival at the end of August, she dyed her hair fire-engine red and tattooed a skull on her pale shoulder. Now, her bold move to be her own person was kicking her in the ass. Trapped without family, without friends, and without love, Kayla had no idea what it took to survive in life, with or without the infected gnawing away at humanity. For someone who always considered herself an independent woman, she wanted nothing more than to be with people.

When the stories of the attacks had begun, she was a first-hand witness to a kid on campus attacking his best friend. She ignored the dean's suggestion to go back to their dorm rooms (or to the infirmary if not feeling well) and she got the hell off campus. It felt like the right thing to do. Based on the news reports from two days ago, she was right. The campus had been overrun.

Kayla's parents and everyone else she had left behind in California were not answering their phones. Her daddy gave her an emergency credit card, but there were no flights leaving anywhere. Driving cross-country alone didn't seem like a smart idea given the state of things, so she went to the only other place she knew—her internship in Fair Haven that she'd started two weeks prior.

Blood stained the floors beneath her bare feet; it was difficult to traverse the hall without stepping in it. Helen's thin body lay dead with a metal rod impaling her abdomen—the same metal rod that Jonas had carried out of the breakroom to use as a weapon. Her corpse propped open the heavy door to the stairwell.

Kayla inched closer. The cavernous pit that was the stairwell had devoured all light. A thick, oppressive silence pressed against her ears as she stepped over Helen's body and called into the darkness.

"Hello?"

Her voice echoed off cement walls, plummeting into the inky void. Kayla listened for movement below, but not a single footstep, groan, or rustle of fabric rose from the depths. There was no other way out of the building, so she sucked in a sharp breath, slid her bare toes to the edge of the step, and let the darkness.

FOUR

Melody

Melody stepped onto her porch into a world of chaos and uncertainty. Her eyes were blinded by the flood of sunshine. Her filthy tank top clung to her body as beads of sweat rolled between her breasts, absorbing into the cotton tank. Strands of curly hair, tangled from days of sweat, were glued to her shoulders. Melody's plastic shield was not enough of a barrier to keep out the stench of refuse and death. As her vision adjusted, she squinted toward her neighbor, who had stopped in the center of the cul-de-sac, holding an enormous knife in his grasp. He stared back at Melody with curiosity in his eyes, then he turned his gaze to a second-story window in his house where the younger woman held a rifle in the window.

The man held up his hand, signaling to Melody to stay indoors, but she had no intentions of following his orders.

"Ma'am?" He approached the bleeding woman with his knife held near his hip. The sunlight gleamed off the massive blade.

The lady in the sundress clutched her neck. Bright red blood squeezed between her fingers, dripped down her chest, and seeped into the yellow fabric.

"What the hell happened?" he asked.

She stopped five feet from the neighbor with panic in her large doe eyes.

Melody ticked off symptoms of infection in her mind: The woman was conscious; she was non-aggressive; she was responsive.

There might still have been hope for her if Melody could act quickly enough. She adjusted the strap of her medical bag on her shoulder, but halted on the porch's top step with her baseball bat in hand. Her pulse pounded between her ears, and her gut twisted. She was a fucking veterinarian. She had no business trying to treat a human. Marcus reminded her all the time; whenever she wanted to bandage a cut or suggest medication, Marcus would make sure she remembered what kind of doctor she was.

"Go," she whispered under her breath as her feet remained glued to the top step. "Go!"

She jolted herself forward, taking the impossible steps down to the sidewalk. Thick, humid air fought her, and each step forward felt like she was edging closer to the cusp of death. The infected could come out of any corner. Merely being outdoors was certain to bring death falling out of the sky like a cartoon anvil, but Melody pushed through her fear and approached anyway.

The neighbor's eyes were filled with questions as Melody neared, but before either of them could speak to each other, the bleeding woman wobbled. Her eyes relaxed—lids drooping. She released her hands from her neck, allowing her arms to dangle and her blood to flow freely from the gash on her neck.

Melody dropped her bat, dug through her med bag for supplies, fumbling over gauze and sutures.

The woman in yellow collapsed to her knees.

Melody leapt forward to help, but the neighbor held his arm out to stop her. His black t-shirt sleeve barely stretched over his bicep, exposing a glimpse of tattoos beneath.

Melody tried to push his arm away. "What are you doing—"

"It's too late." He kept his arm firmly in place, forbidding her to get any closer.

Unfortunately, he may have been right. This disease worked quickly. News reports early on were unsure of the incubation period, but most people became aggressive within a matter of hours. Sometimes minutes. At first, they didn't know if the virus was spread by contact or if it had been airborne, but from everything Melody had seen so far, it seemed saliva played a role.

They didn't know much of anything about LV01 other than the fact that it was fast, and once a person was symptomatic, it was all over.

A massive amount of blood still poured from the yellow-dress woman, soaking fabric and pooling onto the ground.

Melody stayed behind her neighbor as the bleeding woman began to tremble. Her eyes snapped to the right, then drifted back to center, back and forth. Nystagmus—the same symptom of neurological dysfunction that Hannah had reported in Milo, the cat.

Those deadened brown eyes repeated the motion again and again. To the right, then back center. Repeat. The woman in yellow collapsed forward onto her hands and knees and vomited splatters of bile and blood onto the sidewalk.

"Lady!" The man looked at Melody. "Where the hell did you come from? You need to get back inside!"

Lady? Considering the situation, she allowed his chauvinistic tone to slide for the moment. Melody moved back a couple of steps, dropped the medical supplies, and picked up the baseball bat.

Her mind pin-balled around for a second, considering following his orders, because being inside was definitely safer. Then to her husband's well-being. Then to whether or not she was about to die. She adjusted her plastic shield at her forehead, then gripped the bat within her gloved palms.

Her neighbor approached the woman with his knife at the ready. She couldn't believe this guy was going to get closer to her without a mask or something to protect himself from infection.

"You shouldn't—" Melody's words barely escaped her as the infected woman became still and tense.

She remained motionless on all fours, as stiff as a coffee table. Her brown hair hung over her face, drenched in blood.

The neighbor took one step closer, crouching with his knife ready. *This guy is nuts.*

A shot whizzed by Melody's ear, and dust kicked up from the bullet's impact on the pavement. Melody ducked. The man shot a glare toward his window, holding his hand up to tell the girl inside to stop firing.

Melody tried not to give a second thought to the gunfire, and it was easy considering the distraction of the infected woman before her.

The yellow-dress woman looked up with dilated pupils. Her head bobbled like a dashboard ornament. She opened her mouth and released an incoherent moan. A string of drool splashed to the pavement as she fixed her eyes on the man in front of her.

Then she lunged at him with an inhuman snarl. With a swift and sweeping arc, he brought the knife into her temple, stopping her in an instant. He pulled the knife from her head and allowed her body to drop to the cement. The quick and calculated motion indicated a level of experience, like the guy had done it a hundred times before.

Definitely a serial killer.

Melody covered her mouth to contain a squeal, but the plastic shield mask obstructed her hand. She staggered back. Blood poured out of the hole in the woman's head and was sucked up by the gray porous pavement that glittered in the sunlight.

Melody had watched him fire shots into the sick ones for days, but never this. She had never witnessed anything like it.

Two more infected people staggered out from behind a house nearby—drawn by the gunfire, she presumed—and impeding any sort of a reaction from Melody. She stood, frozen in shock.

"Incoming," Melody whispered, gripping her baseball bat tight.

An obese man—at least three hundred pounds—wore sweatpants and a loose polo. He shuffled a haphazard path toward them. A scrawny man in navy blue coveralls followed close behind, reaching for the man in front of him like a kid trying to tag his friend. Both had wounds peppering their bodies.

"Where'd you guys come from?" the neighbor said under his breath, then looked back at the brunette with the rifle in the window.

She fired a shot, but it missed.

Melody released a held breath. Her neighbor placed his hand on her arm, startling her, and she yanked away from his touch, readying her bat.

He spoke with a kind voice, "I'm John…"

John!

She opened her mouth to speak, but there were no words ready to come out. She didn't know if she should tell him her name, respond to his stabbing of a woman in the head, or react to the new incoming menace that was walking down their street. All she knew was that *John* was more handsome up close, and only an inch or so taller than her. He must have been about 5'11". His short, dark brown hair was dusted with scattered silvering strands above his ears. At least a few days of scruff grew along his jaw and upper lip, also smattered with silver. John's steel blue eyes stared into hers from under thick, dark brows as he introduced himself. *I'm John.* What an odd thing to do while disease-ridden freaks were heading their way. She tried to gain some control of her thoughts as they crashed through her mind.

Less than a second after he introduced himself, he continued, "You need to go inside now and lock the door."

Melody, still speechless, stood mere feet from the dead woman in the sundress. She ignored John's demand to go indoors—fat chance she was going to listen to this guy—and she shifted her gaze toward the two men heading their way.

"Your funeral, sweetheart."

"Sweetheart?" she scolded. First *lady*, and now *sweetheart?* She should have left him there alone. She could have made it back to her house if she ran, but she committed to holding her stance, especially now that *John Rifle* turned out to be a douchebag. Just as she'd suspected.

A shot fired from John's house again, missing the three-hundred-pound target. John held his hand up to the woman in the window to tell her to stop firing—likely because she was a terrible shot—and she pulled the rifle barrel inside.

John held his bloody knife out to his side and approached the larger man first. Melody held firm to her bat, panting in preparation for a fight, but in doing so, it fogged her face mask. She shuffled forward, staying within arm's reach behind John.

The large, bloody man moved toward them with haste. John stood with a strong and confident stance, like a cowboy ready to lasso a bull. Once within reach of his attacker, he swung his knife with a precise arc toward the man's head, but the infected beast of a man tripped over his own feet.

Before the knife could impale him, the man fell onto John. They crashed to the ground. Pinned beneath the weight of the massive man, John wriggled to free his legs, but the man tried to bite into John's belly. Gnashing teeth were only inches away from him, but John kept him restrained by his hair.

The skinny man in coveralls closed in right behind him.

Melody's pulse raced through her veins, but she charged in to help without hesitation. John had managed to plunge his knife into the head of the man pinning him, but the skinny one had already arrived and collapsed on top of the pile.

John shifted beneath the weight as the small man on top clawed in a frenzy. With his chin drenched in saliva, he ripped into the back of the fat man's neck with his teeth.

Melody lifted her bat to her right ear, unsure if the woman in the window was about to accidentally shoot her. Only a couple of seconds had gone by since John fell to the ground, but it felt like time had slowed down.

Her hands sweat inside of her surgical gloves. She squeezed her bat. Her mask fogged her vision. For a split second, she recalled tenth-grade softball practice. "Clean up!" Coach had yelled to her.

Every fiber of her being screamed not to do it, but she pushed forward, swinging that bat as hard as she could at the head of the scrawny man on the top of the pile.

The crunch of his skull against the bat sent vibrations through Melody's palms.

The little man's brain must have been swollen and surrounded with fluid from the infection, because blood and serous fluid splattered from his head. Bits of cerebral fluid and pus sprayed onto Melody's mask. John was protected by the corpse shield of the man pinning him down. The tiny man's body flung to the curb, motionless.

She ripped off her foggy shield to catch her breath and to improve her vision, checking for more infected. She scanned her body for wounds—anywhere the fluid may have entered her body—but found nothing.

John's right pant leg pulled up while he shifted out from under the large, dead body. A shiny prosthetic lower limb was exposed. He got to his feet and began inspecting himself for injuries.

His black t-shirt had been soaked in blood and drool, and as he was about to pull it from his body, Melody stopped him.

"No! Don't pull that over your face."

John stopped and heeded her warning. "Good point." Instead, he used his knife to slice the fabric down the front of his chest. Fabric ripped, exposing his bare chest. More tattoos and a sparse patch of dark hair. He slit the shirt from collar to hem and slid it over his arms, dropping it to the pavement.

Melody pulled off her gloves and let them fall to the ground. Trembling, she stood near the dead people on the street, but kept her eyes wide open, watching for more infected.

John asked if she was all right, but his voice seemed muffled, like talking through a wall. Not knowing how to answer, she remained silent and looked down at the skinny man on the curb whom she had murdered.

"I told you to get inside." John placed himself between the dead bodies and Melody. Her eyes met with John's, and her teeth began to chatter from what she assumed was shock.

"Hey, you alright?" He reached for Melody's hand.

Her diamond engagement ring shifted within his hand as he guided her away from the dead. Melody yanked her hand away from the stranger, unable to squeeze any sort of verbal protest out of her mouth.

She wondered if she was about to get sick and turn into a rabid freak, because who knows if any fluid got into an open wound...

She headed toward her house, bat held tight in her grip. She reached her front door, and John was right behind her. "Why are you following me?"

"Cool it. I'm just carrying your bag." He held up the med bag she'd forgotten in the street and entered the house.

"I've got it." She yanked it from his hand.

Melody briefly inspected her exposed skin once again for wounds where infection could have entered, but she found none.

John stepped inside with her and closed the door behind him. Sweat and blood clung in droplets on his bare chest.

John moved closer, and Melody adjusted her grip on her bat, prepared to beat the hell out of him if he tried anything stupid.

#

Melody

She aimed the bat toward John as a warning, but there was no time to spare. Her nostrils flared, and she growled as she charged into the kitchen to clean up. Blood rinsed away from her hairline into the sink. Tears tried to form in her eyes, but she huffed out her nose like a bull and chanted under her breath, "Just survive."

"I don't think it's spread through blood." John used a kitchen towel to sop up blood from his chest. "A couple days ago," he explained, "I got some blood in my eye...and I'm still here."

"There was more than just blood that splattered out there!" she snapped at him. "Cerebral fluid, saliva—"

His palms went up in surrender. "You got a bathroom so I can wash this shit off me?"

She pointed to the half bath down the hall, then continued splashing water onto her face, shoulders, and neck. She stood to dry her face with the kitchen hand towel.

John had finished cleaning up in the hall bathroom and entered the kitchen.

"Any wounds?" she asked him.

John shook his head. "You?"

"Not that I can tell. But there are still a lot of unknowns. After being that close, we could be infected."

"Well, I know it's not spread by blood alone," John said. "I would've been sick by now. But if we are infected now after that lovely encounter with Tweedle Dee and Dumber, whether from brain juice or saliva, or whatever, then maybe we should sit tight right here behind closed doors for a bit. So, if we do turn into ravenous assholes, we can't hurt anyone but each other."

John was smarter than he looked. She nodded, then walked past him to enter the living room. He placed his hand against the center of her back as she moved by. She stiffened up, shrugged away, and picked up her bat, aiming the tip toward him with a warning.

His hands went up. "Sorry. I didn't mean—"

"Don't touch me." She believed he didn't mean anything by it. It seemed like more of a gentlemanly gesture than anything else, but it was startling, and she needed to feel in control right now.

Melody walked into the living room with the remnant sensation of John's warm hand still penetrating her shirt. His presence somehow gave her conflicting feelings of both security and warning.

The beige walls and matching carpet reflected the afternoon sunlight as it seeped in through the bay window. Beige… Marcus wanted everything beige.

John followed behind and stopped next to her as she looked out the bay window. He waved his hands to the woman in the house next door, signaling a finger that he was going to be a minute. She gave a thumbs up and sank into the house.

Melody stole a glimpse of his strong arms out of the corner of her eye. A black tattoo of a trident with an eagle adorned his left shoulder. By the looks of it, it was something military-related. Maybe not a serial killer, after all. And hopefully not the uber-conservative type.

From her window, three bodies were visible, bleeding onto the pavement. She wanted to escape this reality. She closed her eyes with the childish hope that she would awake from some dream, but opened them to the same view of dead bodies in her neighborhood and a cocky, shirtless man in her house.

The image of him cutting that black t-shirt from his body while sweat and blood dripped to the ground was something she would likely never forget. She turned her back to the window, and her arm brushed against his. The sensation sent a shocking charge through her entire body, and a sudden urge clawed into her, enticing her to rip the remaining clothes off his body.

"If we aren't infected, which I don't think we are, I'll move the dead to the Nickersons' yard with the others," he said. "It's starting to reek of death out there, so I think I'll have to burn some of the bodies tonight."

"I'll help."

He shot her a strange look. Melody moved to the kitchen.

She scanned her body again for open wounds; any small scrape on her hands could have been an entry point for the infection, but she found nothing.

"You been in here all this time?" John asked as he moved into the kitchen behind her. His voice was intoxicating. This sudden arousal took her by surprise. Melody tried to shake off the shiver he sent through her body. She needed to be sensible about this because she could not be attracted to him.

Her rational, medical-minded self took control. She had experienced a life-threatening situation. When there is a rush of adrenaline and a sudden spike in heart rate due to a traumatic event, it is possible to become aroused in other ways. Melody rationalized that her insatiable need to get naked with John was nothing more than a simple misattribution of arousal. It didn't have anything to do with the fact that he was incredibly sexy.

John stood in the doorway like a shirtless, tattooed Roman god, with denim jeans hanging from his waist. He held a wet towel in strong, capable hands.

"Yes," she finally answered, reluctant to release her baseball bat, as he sat down at the kitchen table with her. "I've been home since this started."

"I didn't even know you were here," he said. A tattoo of crows perched atop a prison wall stretched across his left pectoral muscle. Melody tried not to stare at his body while he wiped away the last bit of blood from his forearm.

"I holed up in the attic. Didn't want anyone to know I was here."

"Smart."

"Cowardly."

He tilted his head. "I wouldn't call what you just did cowardly. And you didn't evacuate with the other idiots in the neighborhood as soon as they announced the quarantine zone at the high school, so I'd call that smart."

Melody's hand began to cramp, and she finally loosened her grip on her baseball bat. "I was going to, but I was waiting for Marcus."

"I was wondering what happened to him."

Melody shrugged. "He went to work and hasn't come home."

"I'm sorry. Do you want to stay with me and Candace? We have room."

"Is Candace your wife?"

"No." He chuckled under his breath. "She lives on the other side of me. Her people were out of the country on vacation before this started, so she came to stay with me when things got bad. You know, maybe you should've talked to your neighbors more often."

"Maybe you should wear a mask when you're out there," Melody said.

"I *was* wearing a mask, but everything happened so quickly I didn't have time to put it back on." He shrugged. "I don't know how much the masks work with this particular disease anyway. It's not airborne."

"Saliva," Melody said.

"I'm starting to think so, too."

"Like rabies—it transmits through the saliva and causes neurologic dysfunction. But this is a thousand times worse," Melody said.

From Melody's seated position, she could see the half-naked autumn trees shifting in the gentle breeze against a blue sky. She released a long, slow breath, like she had been holding it in for the past four days.

John moved in quickly with the washcloth to wipe away a spot of blood that she had missed on her forearm.

"Missed a spot." He pulled away before she had a chance to protest.

She should have kicked his ass for touching her again, but somehow it didn't bother her much.

Definitely in shock.

With a delicate motion, John raised his right hand to her face, requesting approval to clean the specks of blood from her temples, but she backed away.

"I got it." She took the wet cloth from his hand with a guilty conscience, secretly wanting him to touch her in any way he saw fit. Melody stood to look out the window, wondering what the hell was wrong with her, and she wiped her face clean.

"I'm sorry I froze out there today."

John lit up with an impossibly sexy smile. "Froze? Nah. You came through. I'm impressed." He crossed his arms in front of his chest, making the tattooed crows swell and settle.

"Well, if you're impressed with cowardly hesitation," she said, "there's more where that came from." She twirled the bat.

"Not too many people around here have stepped up to help. Most just ran away. And the ones that tried to fight didn't make it. You saved me from a bad situation today." John nodded. "And you're a girl!"

She raised her eyebrows at his remark.

"What?" he laughed. "I'm kidding about the girl thing!"

"You should go."

"You should come with me. You need me," he said.

Melody's jaw dropped. "Are you kidding? You need *me*, as proven by your inability to fight off one man."

"It was a really big man!" John grinned. "Anyway, I had it under control. I was pandering to your need to feel useful."

"Excuse me?"

John failed to fight a sly smile. "Seriously, though. You shouldn't stay here alone anymore. Stay with me and Candace."

"No, thank you. I'm leaving today."

"To where?"

"To find my husband."

The protest that wanted to escape John's agape mouth fell short, and he appeared to stop himself. "Candace and I have been talking about leaving town, too—somewhere more remote. I've been teaching her to shoot from the second-floor window to prepare her. I can teach you—"

"Based on her shooting skills, your offer isn't very enticing. Besides, I already know how to shoot."

It had been years since she fired her dad's old shotgun up in the mountains, but she could remember the kick in her adolescent shoulder. At the time, she was only 120 pounds, but she held her ground and didn't lose her footing. She missed her target—a doe—on purpose.

Since it had been about fifteen years since she had touched a gun, she was confident that her skills were lacking, but she wanted this John guy to believe that she wasn't to be messed with.

A faint voice yelled from outside. "John?" Candace called from next door through an open window.

"That girl is gonna get us all killed anyway." John shook his head and peeked outside. "Neighborhood is clear for now. Lock your doors and pack up some stuff. I'm going to take care of the bodies, close up whatever hole in the fence Tweedle Dee and Tweedle Dumb came through, and I'll be over later to escort you over to my house where we can work on a plan to evacuate."

"I don't need an escort."

John turned to leave her house before she had a chance to debate. This guy didn't know who he was talking to. He bounded down the steps of her front porch with a slight hobble and ran back to check on Candace. Melody's jaw may as well have been on the floor as she watched John jog back to his house, shirtless. She quickly brushed away her feelings as nothing more than a silly crush.

Stay focused on what's important.

Maybe Marcus was out there trying to make his way back to her. She placed an ardent kiss upon her fingertips and pressed them against the window, hoping that Marcus knew she still loved him.

"I'm coming," she whispered.

SIX

Kayla

Ready to dart back to the safety of the breakroom if she heard a sound, Kayla paused at the top step in the pitch black of the stairwell and waited. Silence.

The darkness was a gateway to Hell, trying to devour every bit of courage. It pulled her into its bowels, body tremoring, tears soaking her cheeks. After finding the railing, she placed one toe on the cold, hard step and eased down. One step after the next, her blood rushed to her ears, making it impossible to hear anything but her own pulse and panicked breaths. Her pace quickened, and soon she ran down the steps. One hand clung to the railing, the other swung her wooden chair leg at the darkness, praying it wouldn't make contact with one of the raging monsters.

A small square of light came into view as she rounded the first flight down. She rushed toward it and opened the door to the third floor, tumbling into the safety of the light. Nobody, dead or alive, was in sight.

Panting, she let the door close behind her, not ready to enter the darkness again. Instead, Kayla tiptoed across the rough, gray carpeted hallway between the office cubicles, avoiding dark brown stains that had to have been blood.

Sunlight leaked in below the shades of the wall-to-wall windows. She moved toward it. Behind the roman shades, the bright outside world revealed something unexpected. Calmness. No riots. No swarms of sick people attacking one another. A few dead bodies lay in the street, but there were no upright, wandering infected.

The sun set between the buildings nearby, and its light reflected off shattered glass in the street. She made it.

"Take that, Styles!" A breathy chuckle dribbled out between dry lips.

Styles—the so-called love of her life since she was 16 years old. When Kayla opted to go to college on the other side of the country to study biology, Styles laughed.

"They're going to eat you alive," Styles said one night while he was drunk and getting a little too grab-happy with her breasts. She hadn't been enjoying his company anyway, and he made it obvious that he had a problem with her liking boys *and* girls, so she didn't cry for too long when he broke up with her two weeks after she left for school, via a text message—*Sorry, babe, this won't work.*

She wondered if Styles was all right, or if they ended up eating *him* alive. A breathy laugh escaped her, and she reeled it in, worried she was losing her mind. Mostly, she worried about her parents and her brother and hoped they were safe.

She stalled before a dark, daunting hallway—a stark contrast from the well-lit open space around her. A faint light glowed toward the end. A light from Lab One. She had delivered files down that hallway a few times.

Kayla readied her broken chair leg and slid with her back against the wall toward the ominous light, wondering if she would find survivors in there.

Inch by inch, she made her way through the darkness, panting heavily and praying not to die. Blackness encompassed her. Jagged fibers of the carpeting prickled her bare feet.

She wished her dad were there to keep her safe. He was always there whenever she was scared.

I totally got this, she had said to him before leaving for college.

Her vision blurred from the welling of tears, so she wiped them away with the back of her hand and pushed through the unrelenting dark.

The laboratory window created a shaft of light onto a body. A large man in a white coat lay showcased like a game show prize. She swallowed hard, but the dryness in her mouth made it feel like a brick in her esophagus. The stench of necrotic flesh hit her nose, and she drew her hand over her mouth, trying not to vomit.

She recognized him as Dr. Carter. He was a friendly guy who towered over tiny Kayla when he was upright. She had delivered files to him last week and even tried flirting with him until she found out he was married. He had removed his ring to handle materials in the lab, so she didn't know. She was mortified for pursuing a married man, so she did her best to avoid being the office whore after that. New rule—no more flirting. Until Victoria caught her eye. Kayla couldn't help it. She was a romantic.

She stepped around Dr. Carter's lifeless body with a knot in her gut. Behind the closed blinds of Lab One's window, she spotted shadowy movement.

She tried the handle, but it was locked. After checking over her shoulder, peering through the blackness for danger, she raised her timid hand and knocked on the door.

Someone moved inside. Trying to steal a glimpse through the edge of the blinds proved futile, so she gave a desperate knock again, but there was still no response.

"Hello!"

Nobody came mindlessly raging and banging on the door, so she assumed whoever was in there had to be uninfected.

"Hello?" she called again, a bit louder, voice now trembling.

Still no response.

As she raised her voice and knocked at the door, begging for help, she may as well have been sounding an alarm for the infected to come after her.

Kayla had spent too many hours alone and far too long in the dark. She felt her grip on sanity slipping again and simply wanted back into the light.

"Let me in!"

She lifted her wooden chair leg and smacked it against the glass. The glass held up, but the noise echoed through the halls, stirring the man on the floor behind her.

Kayla wailed against the glass again and again.

"Let me in!"

Still, the person on the other side of the door pretended she wasn't there. She dropped her arms to her sides and rested her face against the window, sobbing, while Dr. Carter stirred with a groan.

SEVEN

Melody

Melody stripped her filthy tank top from her body and pulled one of Marcus's pressed white shirts from the hall closet.

Her blood still surged with electricity from the incident in the street. An unrecognizable face stared back through the foyer mirror as she buttoned her shirt, considering her next course of action.

Shaking hands steadied themselves. Before she rushed out the door to go find her husband, she needed a plan. She caught a whiff of her body odor and cringed.

Shower first?

Help John move bodies out of the street?

She peeked out the window to see him dragging the woman in yellow into the Nickersons' backyard.

Or just leave now and find Marcus...

A thump from her backyard startled her. Melody flinched, then eased toward the kitchen and listened for it.

Outside the sliding glass door to her backyard, there were no intruders, but she could spot movement between the fence slats in the yard behind hers. The thump sounded again—it was close. Maybe right outside her back door.

The idea to get John first for backup cropped into her head, but she pushed it out before entertaining it.

She tightened the laces on her sneakers and pulled her thick hair away from her face, securing it with a hair tie. With her bat in hand and the plastic shield protecting her face, she slid open the door, making as little noise as possible.

The few remaining leaves clinging to the branches trembled under the touch of the breeze while she stepped onto the back deck. The faint smell of death on the air forced her to breathe through her mouth.

With a heightened sense of confidence since her encounter with the infected earlier, she neared the edge of her deck and stepped down to the first step. A clamoring from the yard behind hers drew her attention, but she remained quiet, keeping eagle-eye focus on the privacy fence. She took another calculated and quiet step down, trying to peek through the narrow fence gaps from afar.

She would have to get closer.

As Melody neared the last step, someone reached from under the porch stairs and grabbed her ankle.

A scream escaped her lips, loud enough to draw more of them, so she cut it short. Melody lost balance as she twisted away to see a set of dirty, pale fingers wrapped around her ankle. The earth was unforgiving as she crashed down. The man's second arm clawed out from under the steps. Decomposing flesh dripping from his face, he tried to squeeze himself out from under the porch between the gap in the steps. He wore the same style of navy blue coveralls as the scrawny man whose skull she'd crushed with a baseball bat. A glimpse of his shoulder patch indicated that he worked for an HVAC company. He drooled and snarled, mouth blackening around his lips, teeth snapping shut, trying to bite.

The noise attracted the body in the adjacent yard, and the privacy fence rattled. Melody kicked herself free from his grip, then jabbed at her attacker with the bat, but she couldn't get a good swing in from her position on her ass. She scrambled to her feet and, instead of bashing in another skull, she sprinted away, around the side of the house toward the gate.

While looking back to be sure he wasn't following her, she crashed into a wall of a man. Melody secured her bat in both hands to defend herself, but John grabbed onto the end of it before she could swing. He steadied her against his body.

"Whoa," he said, like he was calming a spooked horse.

She pulled in a gasp and forced herself away from him. "Get off of me."

"You ran into me, lady."

"Stop calling me that!"

John headed toward the backyard and found the man under her deck. He took care of the situation, plunging his knife into his head. The blade entered the temple silently, and sludge-like blood oozed out of the hole after John removed the blade. The infected man fell limp, body slumped on the step.

"I had it under control," she said.

"Obviously."

The moaning continued from the other side of the fence, and John lowered his stance, ready to fight. His shoulders relaxed when he realized the infected person next door was contained. He whispered to Melody and gestured toward her door. "Come on."

They stepped over the dead body between the steps and moved into her house, locking the door behind them.

The fence at the back of the yard rattled for only a few seconds before the infected on the other side gave up and moved on.

"Don't have much of an attention span, do they?" John sat down and leaned back in the wooden chair at Melody's breakfast table as the setting sun's light poured in sideways.

There he was again in her house. Being in his proximity excited her and frustrated her, and she wanted to run her hands along those arms and kick him in the nuts at the same time. John looked to the ceiling and rested his arms on top of his head, releasing a forceful breath.

"You're bleeding." She leaned in to inspect John's elbow, which was scraped and littered with grit and gravel.

"Damn. Guess I missed a spot from when I cleaned up earlier."

"Run your elbow under the faucet for a while to clean it out."

"The wound didn't contact the saliva," he said, more as an assurance to himself than a fact.

"Just run it under water!" Melody left him in the kitchen to grab her medical bag. As she reentered, she allowed her eyes to sweep across his body as he hovered over the sink. He shifted his weight off his prosthetic leg and kept his elbow under the running water.

"Are you a nurse?" he asked. "Or a doctor?"

"I'm a veterinarian."

John's scruffy face held a smile. "I love cats." He inspected his elbow as the water ran over the wound.

"I wouldn't pin you as a cat person."

"They're low maintenance and ninja-like," he explained.

"Cat people are ninja-like?" she asked with a grin. It wasn't very funny, but both of them laughed, exchanging a glance. A moment with a cheesy joke as if the craziness of the outside world didn't exist.

John pulled his elbow from the water, but Melody pushed it back beneath the stream.

"Keep rinsing," she said. "Just in case."

"You're a bossy little thing, aren't you?"

"When I need to be."

John sighed, cheeks puffing out with the slow release of a breath. "You mentioned rabies earlier."

She nodded and leaned against the counter. "It seems to be similar in nature. Neurological symptoms. Aggression and drooling. There's probably encephalitis."

"That sounds familiar," John said.

"It's inflammation in the brain, and this seems to be spread by saliva. These are all symptoms very much like rabies. Even the name they gave it— LV01. I'm guessing that LV stands for lyssavirus, but they never really gave much information—"

"Before the world shit the bed," John said.

Melody nodded. "Rabies is a type of lyssavirus, but it takes days, maybe weeks, for symptoms to show. Whatever this is takes hours, sometimes minutes, depending on the wound. There are multiple types of rabies-like viruses that fall under the category of a lyssavirus. But nothing like this one. Maybe it's some super-mutated version." Melody shook her head and second-guessed herself. "I'm no expert, though."

"You have more insight on this than anyone I've heard."

"Well, I'm sure there's someone more qualified out there than me. Maybe at those quarantine zones…or medical labs." Melody withheld the information that Marcus was working on a vaccine. She wasn't sure why. Maybe because some small part of her believed he was already dead. And another part of her believed that if he were alive, he wouldn't succeed. "If something like a vaccine is possible, the quarantine place might be the way to go."

John stood beside her with his elbow still hovering over the sink. She cut the faucet off and warned him to brace himself before she poured chlorhexidine solution onto the wound.

"It still looks clean," she said. "Pink. No necrosis, so hopefully you're right about no saliva getting in there. The other people out there had some nasty blackening of the skin around their wounds. Rapid-onset necrosis, or something."

The white fabric of her shirt billowed out as she leaned, exposing the blue lace edge of her bra. Her eyes met with John's for half a second, catching him stealing a glimpse.

She let him look, and out of the corner of her eye, she absorbed a glance of his gray t-shirt stretched over his pecs. What would it be like to lay her head against his chest? Her lungs tightened in his proximity. She backed away and packed up her medical bag instead of lingering on the thought. "Let's hope you don't die now."

John laughed. "Sounds good to me. I'm gonna move the rest of the bodies to the Nickersons' and burn them before the smell gets any worse. Why don't you come over and sit with Candace while I do that?"

"Why don't I help you instead?" Melody realized then that she was stalling on venturing across town to find Marcus. She had all day to get out, but she kept making excuses to stay, launching headfirst into danger instead of quietly sneaking away. She was scared to go alone and afraid to admit it.

John looked her up and down as if sizing her up. "You're not going to help me burn bodies."

"You're not going to stop me."

EIGHT

Melody

John got to work moving the bodies in the street, while Melody gloved up and went out back to grab the HVAC man from under her porch.

She tugged on his body, dragging him by the arms, making short bursts of progress across her yard, through the gate, then down the sidewalk. John had already moved the two men in the street. He carried a can of gasoline to the Nickersons' and disappeared behind their house.

It wasn't far, and there were no infected in sight, but fear still coursed through her veins as she ventured outside the house with nobody looking over her except for Candace—the girl with the terrible aim.

She dragged the body past the green Volvo with the door wide open. It was parked at the neck of the cul-de-sac where it had been for days, with two wheels on the curb. Blood stained the pavement beside it, and Melody tried not to think about the gruesome scene that caused it.

Candace peeked out John's window, and Melody nodded as if to say *hello*, but Candace whipped the curtains shut. Melody felt sorry for the girl, locked up in that house and too petrified to face the light of day. That was Melody earlier that morning—too fearful to take a step. Maybe Candace needed some encouragement. She needed to get out of there and see what she was made of.

She hoisted the body little by little past Mrs. Nickerson's roses, which were still in full bloom. As were the gold and burgundy mums adorning the ground below the bushes. Her car door was open, and Daniel Nickerson's wheelchair lay tipped over on the other side of it like a still-life of violence. Neither of their bodies were anywhere in sight.

Melody opened the bright white privacy fence gate to the lush green yard. Mr. Nickerson had mowed his lawn every week, without fail. He was out there every day killing anything that wasn't grass.

The backyard was several days overdue for a mow, creating a luxurious field of plush chlorophyll, speckled with fallen yellow elm leaves.

Eighteen bodies were lined up in three rows of six, and John drizzled each one with gasoline.

"You moved that guy all by yourself?" he asked.

Melody shot him a glare. "I'm stronger than I look. Hell of a cemetery you've created here."

"When the bodies started piling up, I was going to bury them, but—"

"You can't. That would take forever."

John nodded with unease in his eyes.

"Plus, we need to reduce the spread of infection. Keep the virus out of groundwater, just in case. So, you *have* to burn them."

He thumbed the wheel of a blue Bic lighter and sparked it to flame. "You might want to leave now," he said. "This is going to get bad."

She shook her head and held out a hand. "Do you have another lighter?"

John fished one from his pocket and handed it over. They both went to work lighting the dead.

She knelt over the scrawny man's body, whom she had pummeled with the baseball bat earlier that day.

"I'm sorry," she whispered in complete disbelief that any of this was happening. With a flick of her finger, she lit the gas-soaked, raggedy fabric of his clothes.

The corpses went up in flames one by one, as John and Melody worked their way across the yard.

Eighteen human bodies lay neatly upon the vivid green grass, each one engulfed in flames. How simple it was to extinguish an entire life. The flames created a glowing orange light that reflected and frolicked along the surface of the white privacy fence. The smell of burning humans filled the yard.

"It's a strange smell." John held the back of his hand against his mouth.

The heat from the flames nearly singed her arm hair. Melody took a step back. "I'm familiar with the smell of burning flesh."

John turned to face her, his curious stare burned as fiercely as the flames, but she kept her gaze locked on the fire.

She quickly explained with a shrug, "I've done some cauterizing on animals during surgery. It's a smell that can't be compared to anything else."

John kept staring at her, but she refused to face him to acknowledge his unrelenting, come-hither eyes.

"I'm heading out to find Marcus."

"Would it matter to you if I said I don't think that's a good idea?"

She shook her head and turned to leave. "I'm going to take a shower, finish packing a bag, and then I'm out."

"It's gonna be dark soon. We should wait until morning."

"We?"

"Stay with us tonight. Me and Candace. Safety in numbers."

Melody drew in a breath to argue, but she held her tongue. Perhaps she should give Marcus one more night to come home. Perhaps leaving at night was a bad idea. Or perhaps...she was making excuses to spend the night with John.

NINE

Melody

With the scent of the burning bodies lingering in her nose and smoke filling the air over the Nickersons' house, Melody carefully navigated back to her own home with a watchful eye on the street. No staggering infected were anywhere in sight. The sweltering, unseasonable heat and the smoke from the blaze reminded her of her bonfire days from her teen years.

Her first date with Marcus was at a post-track meet bonfire. Even today, Melody wasn't sure why he ever invited her. Rich boy. Silver spoon. Mr. Popular. He approached her in the hall one day and said he had to warn her.

"People have been talking about what happened with your parents," he'd said. "And about what happened with your foster dad."

After Dad committed suicide, Melody had been placed in the hands of foster care. The touchy-feely disposition of her foster father went too far, and she left. She'd rather have been homeless than live with that man.

"I don't care what people are saying."

"Good." Marcus smiled. "Life sucks, huh?"

Melody stared at this guy who'd rarely ever spoken to her, waiting for the punchline—or some twisted prank.

But instead, Marcus invited her to the bonfire.

"I don't go to those," she said.

"I know. You're on the track team, and I never see you at the parties." He leaned in and whispered. "Tyler Marshall is bringing beer."

Things were good between them for a long time. It wasn't until they got married that their relationship seemed to fall apart. For the first few years of marriage, they'd barely seen each other. Work. School. More work.

They lived on meager wages, barely earning enough to pay for their tiny apartment, for Melody's student loans, and for Marcus's need for nice things. Marcus's parents generously covered his student loans, but Melody refused their financial assistance. Year after year, he grew more spiteful. Two years ago was the first time that Melody considered leaving him.

"You get paid salary!" he had yelled when she was rushing out the door on an emergency call. "Whether you go or not, you get paid!"

"This is my career."

"Maybe you picked the wrong profession."

"I picked what I love doing."

"What we *love* isn't always the smartest financial decision."

She shook her head. "I'm not doing it for the money."

Marcus laughed. "Like I said…not the smartest."

Perhaps those past couple of years of bad behavior could be chalked up to the fact that Marcus never had to struggle in life. Marcus's dad had told Melody that *Marcus doesn't get it.* He'd never had to work for anything in life.

He hadn't worked for his education, for his grades, for his job, or this big beige house he had moved them into.

Melody locked herself in that house, leaving the smell of burning flesh behind her.

She fought the sensation of tears behind her lids. If she started crying now, she might not stop. *Fucking, Marcus.* A great divide within her split her heart right down the middle. On one side, she wanted to be the good wife and go rescue her husband. On the other side, she wanted to take the easy way out and give up on their marriage altogether.

Why should she put forth any effort in this relationship when all she'd done so far is give, give, give? She gave it all up for him. She gave up the opportunity to run her own practice out of Mountainview. She settled in their hometown of Fair Haven so *Marcus* could work at his father's company. She gave up her dad's old hunting cabin in the mountains, put it on the market to pay down *Marcus'* out-of-control credit card debt.

That's what married people did. They sacrificed for each other. Someday—

she kept trying to convince herself—he would do the same. Maybe when life stopped being so hard. When she wasn't running from danger or fighting for her life, maybe then she would have the chance to relax on the back deck of that mountain cabin, sipping some tea and enjoying the company of her best friend. She laughed under her breath and snapped back to reality—Marcus was never much of a good friend. He was simply her *only* friend when life was really hard.

Every time she thought about leaving Marcus, she talked herself out of it. She'd been utterly alone before. It was brief, but she never wanted to go back. Back to having nobody. Back to shaking, homeless and alone in the chassis of an old Caddy, wondering if she'd survive another day, another storm. Back to that attic, sweaty and bucket-pissing, unsure if she'd ever speak to anyone again.

She stuffed those insecurities deep inside and told herself that her fears of leaving Marcus were about giving up. Quitting this relationship was not an option.

Love is easy, and if it's not, you're doing it wrong.

A few days ago, when Marcus went to work, she did it wrong. She rolled her eyes at her know-it-all husband, called him an asshole under her breath, and let him go without even a goodbye kiss. As he pulled out of the driveway, she wondered if she had let him exit to his death, and part of her didn't care, at least not until later. The hateful heart she experienced that morning haunted her memories still, and she wanted nothing more than for him to come home safely.

If love was supposed to be so easy, then why wasn't it? What were they doing wrong?

Maybe her dad was wrong. Maybe love is just hard.

Infatuation—on the other hand—comes easily. As easy as John cutting off his blood-soaked shirt with a knife. Unexpected, yet surprisingly welcome. His body lingered in her thoughts, but she shoved him out before she had a chance to explore those daydreams.

She had an important task ahead of her. Marcus could have been trapped out there, needing rescue. The thought of traveling across town terrified her, but Melody couldn't give up so easily.

John was right about traveling at night, though. She'd give it one more night to rest up and leave at daybreak.

With the gas lines still functioning and the town's water supply still flowing, Melody heated some water on the stove to make tea. The warmth of the mug in her palms brought her a brief moment of peace as she moved to the window to get another glimpse of John.

A gentle breeze rustled the leaves overhead as he sat on his porch and turned his attention from the street. He gave her a nod and, with an inviting smile, he waved for her to come over. She held up a finger to suggest she wasn't ready. She still needed to shower and pack after all.

John's front door opened, and the woman, Candace, poked her head out. In a form-fitting, low-cut tank top and booty shorts, she stepped outside. She hugged a casserole in her arms.

John

"Did you put on makeup?" John asked.

"I couldn't stand it anymore," Candace said with the infectious accent of a southerner.

She pulled her chestnut brown hair into a bunch on top of her head and tied it in a messy bun.

"If I go one more day looking like a homeless person, I'll kill myself. We won't even need them infected people to do it, I swear."

She held up a dish and smiled. "I cooked." Candace gave him a flirtatious nudge with her shoulder. Candace had gradually been getting flirtier with him over the past couple of days, or maybe he was reading into the signs. He blew off his concerns as his imagination.

"Did you use the last of the pasta and tuna?" he asked.

"I did. It's not how we do tuna casserole down south, but it's what I had to work with." She smiled.

Her lips were freshly coated with a layer of red gloss. The kind of shiny lips that are supposed to look kissable but are likely to leave sticky marks all over someone's face, or wherever she might put her lips. He kicked that thought out of his head before his dick took control of his brain.

She leaned against the porch railing with her back arched.

John set the dish on the end table and leaned back in the Adirondack chair. He adjusted his prosthetic, which had been irritating his skin for the past few days. He winced as he lifted his leg to adjust.

Candace approached his chair and placed a well-manicured hand against his chest. She eased herself onto the arm of the chair, so close that her tits almost brushed his face.

Definitely flirting.

John leaned as far back as he could, avoiding Candace as she edged closer. He slid out of the chair away from the girl, heart racing, wondering how to avoid whatever the hell she was trying to do. Candace was certainly the kind of sensual woman he'd go for a decade ago, and she was giving him all green lights, but John—for some forsaken reason—wasn't interested.

"How long ago did you say Gavin left on deployment?" He scratched his head.

John had already suffered through the story of how she met her husband, Gavin. She was a sophomore in college in South Carolina. He was in uniform, doing body shots from her belly button at a nightclub. She dropped out of college to be with him. Married after only two months of knowing each other—a typical military couple story—not all that different from John's story. Complete with a deployment that ripped them apart.

When Gavin left, Candace's world shook beneath her feet. They didn't have a home, so she moved in with Gavin's parents in Fair Haven. Gavin's parents had left for vacation two weeks before the world shit the bed, leaving the girl next door alone. They never returned.

Candace's eyes glassed over. She crossed her arms and looked out toward the street. "You must think I'm a horrible person."

"No, I don't. I understand the stress of deployments, but, Candace, you will be okay. And, like I said before, Gavin might be alive and well."

"I know." She crossed her arms, voice trembling with uncertainty.

"He could still be safe and sound on that ship in the middle of the ocean."

"Or there could be infected on the ship." Tears spilled over her lids, and she carefully wiped them away so as not to smear her mascara. "Is that lady over there okay?" She sniffled.

"It was thoughtful of you to make a casserole for all of us." John, despite trying to comfort the girl, kept his eyes on the street, scanning for the infected.

"I'm sorry, John. I don't know what I was thinking."

John shrugged. He didn't know what he was thinking either. He eased his gaze back toward Melody's bay window, disappointed that the other married woman next door was no longer there.

TEN

Melody

Melody stood in the bay window observing as Candace threw herself at John. She wished she had a bowl of popcorn for the entertainment, but mostly wished she could turn up the volume and hear what Candace was saying to him. Probably something about her nail polish, or how she missed the Kardashians. She huffed out a laugh, thinking of all the dumb things the girl was saying, then felt a little guilty for assuming the girl was an idiot.

When Candace leaned her breasts close to John, Melody turned away.

She locked herself in her master bathroom for a shower, thankful that she still had hot water. It wouldn't be long before the town's gas lines quit and her water heater no longer worked. The light of day faded, and the scattered light from the small bathroom window scantly lit the inside of her shower.

Hot water cascaded over her body. Brown and pink swirled in the water at her feet as bits of dried blood washed from her hair.

She ran her loofa across her skin, smothering herself with lavender suds, trying to evict the stench of burning bodies and the sight of brain splatter from her memory.

Instead, she thought about the man next door. She rested her left hand against the smooth white wall of the shower as the water drenched the top of her head, blanketing her face.

She stood for several minutes, simply breathing through the drape of water with her eyes closed. A soapy blue loofa slid across her body, down her abdomen, and along her thigh. John's sexy smile was inches from her face. She imagined leaning into him. Hot breath on his neck. Pressing her slippery, wet body against his, her chest heaved, craving his attention.

Melody opened her eyes only to see her hand pressed against the shower wall. Her wedding band stared back at her.

The sun had already set, and the smoke from the Nickersons' yard had dissipated.

Melody packed a backpack full of supplies, still unsure how she would survive a trip across town. One backpack was all she could carry if she planned on running. An extra set of clothes, medical supplies from her kit, antibiotics and pain medication that she kept on hand for house-calls, tampons...

Finally, she pulled an orchid envelope from her drawer and cradled it in her hands. It was the single most important thing she owned, but she could never bring herself to open it.

Two days after her dad had committed suicide, it came in the mail addressed to her, postmarked the day of his death. Inside the orchid envelope, she assumed, were Dad's bullshit excuses for leaving her behind. For giving up. He had mailed it to her before he committed suicide, but she never had the guts to open it. She couldn't bear to accept whatever excuse he had written inside. She tucked it away, waiting for the right time to read it, but the right time never came. Her dad's writing on the envelope had faded, and the galaxy-themed return-address sticker had peeled up at the corners.

She had a feeling the time to read it was coming soon. She slid it into the outside pocket of her backpack and left her bedroom. In the kitchen, she rummaged through bare cabinets looking for something to eat.

She could tell she had lost weight by the loose fit of her favorite jeans. Her over-worn gray, skull t-shirt soaked up the moisture of her damp hair, and she pulled out a can of garbanzo beans tucked in the far back behind the bottle of vodka. She didn't have much left in the cupboards.

A knock on the door broke the silence with the startling similarity to a shotgun blast. John stood on her porch. A surge of nervousness raced through her veins as she unlocked the deadbolt.

John wore a blue flannel, unbuttoned, exposing a black t-shirt underneath. In his shorts, a curved prosthetic blade, like the kind athletes use, was fully exposed.

"Until today, I didn't know you were missing a leg."

"I miss it every day." John smiled. "The other prosthetic was rubbing my skin raw. This one isn't much better."

"You need anything for it?"

John shook his head. "What's taking you so long?"

"I took a shower."

"And froze to death?"

Melody smirked. "Gas water heater."

"*Hot* water? Lucky…" His jaw hung open, like he wanted to ask to use the shower, but didn't know how to do so without inviting himself in.

"You and Candace can come use the shower here."

"Thank you." John glanced behind him, stepped inside, and closed the door. He stood in the foyer as a tension filled the three feet between them. Something thick and palpable. An energy that could easily be passed through to get to each other, but neither of them would push it out of the way. Neither of them would take the step forward. If he made the move, she might not have had the strength to turn him down.

John broke the silence. "The plan was that you would come to my place. I've got a good setup over there."

"But I've got hot water."

John looked beyond her toward the kitchen. His eyes narrowed, and he adjusted his stance. Focused on the back door, he edged toward it.

"What is it?"

John entered the kitchen and stood before the sliding glass door.

"What?" Melody whispered.

"Lightning bugs!"

Melody's heart lightened for a second. "I thought it was something bad."

Silent laughter made his shoulders bounce.

A childlike feeling took over, and Melody moved toward the door, eager to see them glow. The emotion surprised her, despite its brevity. She didn't think she could have feelings like that while the world was in its current state, but there it was. Something resembling happiness.

The color faded from the grass with the darkening sky, and the fireflies twinkled. They stood so close their knuckles brushed against each other, but instead of pulling away, she allowed the backs of their hands to touch. She should have moved her hand, but every cell in her body wanted to be touched.

John twisted his hand around and embraced her fingers—the same fingers that had clenched the baseball bat and bashed a man's head. His touch surged up her arms and across her back.

Goosebumps invaded her flesh. Fireflies lit up the sky and disappeared. Fleeting flickers of light and hope. John's fierce glare pierced her while she faced forward. Her chest rose and fell heavily with each impassioned breath. If he didn't release her from his gaze soon, she might explode.

She rotated her body to face John. Her fingers entangled with his. A mere inch separated their chests. John reached his other hand behind her, pressing it against the small of her back to pull her in.

Fuck it. Melody gave in to her weakness. She released a sigh along with all her reservations, closed her eyes, and parted her lips.

A startling knock at the front door sent a shockwave through the remaining inch between them. Melody backed away, unkissed, placing three feet of palpable tension between them once again.

ELEVEN

John

"I can't." Melody pulled away.

"You can't what?" John stepped back, wishing he could erase his attempted kiss.

"I can't...kiss you."

John shook his head. "Don't flatter yourself, sweetheart." It was a dumb thing to say, but he couldn't let her think he came on to her. The knock at the door persisted—*Candace.*

Melody shot John a glare as they headed toward the front door. Melody unlocked the dead bolt, and Candace stormed inside, still donning ridiculously short shorts and now high heels. She carried her casserole in her arms.

"John?" She rushed across the foyer to him. "They're coming!"

Outside, three infected ambled across the cul-de-sac. Melody slammed the door shut as John rushed to the dining room table.

"Sorry, Candace!" He shoved against the table to barricade the door.

"You said you'd be right back." Her voice trembled.

"I know. We were discussing staying here instead, and then—"

"Shhh! They're coming." Melody said, peeking through the curtain.

The pounding of drunken footfalls signaled their arrival on the porch steps. John pulled his knife from his belt, and Melody picked up her baseball bat. They backed away from the door, silenced themselves, ready to take on the infected if they broke in.

Candace set the casserole on the floor and retreated upstairs.

He side-eyed Melody. "You should go up there, too. Barricade yourselves in a room. I got this."

Melody glowered at him, as if insisting that he'd better drop the whole tough-guy act with her because she wasn't going to put up with it.

The infected snarled amongst themselves, fighting to get up the steps of the porch. Their bodies banged and thrashed for minutes, but their lack of attempt to get inside meant they'd forgotten why they'd climbed the porch steps in the first place.

Those three minutes felt like ages to John as he awaited a breech. Beside him stood a woman with balls of steel…the kind of woman that wouldn't put up with his shit. The kind of person he needed in life.

After the noises settled down outside, Candace crept down the stairs. With the dissipation of the threat, John noticed that Melody's shoulders relaxed, fingers loosened their grip on her bat, and she let out a steady sigh.

"How long you been holding that breath?" John asked.

Melody turned away from him and didn't answer. He wanted to grab her wrist, twirl her around to face him, and kiss her the way he should have before, but that opportunity was long gone.

"Is everything okay now?" Candace asked.

"No. Everything is not okay! You brought them to my front porch!" Melody's nostrils flared.

Candace turned to John. "You were gone for, like, ever. I saw them out in the street heading this way. I came to warn you."

Through the curtain, John spotted more infected filing down the street, but with the darkening sky, it was too difficult to tell how many.

"I brought dinner," Candace said with a nervous smile.

"But not the rifle?" John said.

Candace held a blank stare.

"My pistol? Not your supply bag?" John continued to question her, but her eyes widened like a deer in headlights, filling with tears. He quickly reeled in his frustration. "It's okay…it's okay."

Melody snorted—a mean sort of laugh indicating that it was, in fact, not okay with her.

"It's my fault," John said. "I shouldn't have left you alone for so long. And I should've brought my gun over here."

With an unknown number of infected in the street and limited visibility, they'd have to stay at Melody's for the night, even if that meant he wouldn't have his guns. He knew better than to leave the house without his pistol, but he did it today, twice—cocky, dumbass move.

They had food, shelter, and hot water where they were, and he could get his rifle in the morning when there was enough light to navigate to his house.

John got a layout of Melody's house, checking for exits and vantage points from the second floor. Candace worked on heating the casserole in the gas oven, and Melody sat back, seeming to keep an eye on the young woman as if she might accidentally burn down her house or invite the infected in for a party.

The three of them sat by dim candlelight over plates of shitty tuna casserole, while thick blankets hung from the windows to obscure the light from view of the infected outside. The soggy noodles had absorbed most of the watered-down cream of chicken soup, and despite the pastiness, it was the best meal John had eaten in a couple of days.

Dinner was awkward and would have been silent, were it not for the sound of forks scraping against the plates. The flame flickered between them. He avoided eye contact with Melody, embarrassed about making a move on a married woman, even if her husband was probably dead.

Candace sat beside John and scooted closer to him. She tossed her hair to one side, exposing her neck and releasing a heavy sigh.

"Mmm…" She slid the fork out from between her red, glossy lips, shifting her eyes to her right to see if John noticed her dramatic display. He noticed—who wouldn't? But his interests had fallen elsewhere.

John, avoiding Candace's attempt to arouse him, wiped some food from the corners of his lips and looked up at Melody. "So, I've been considering evacuation plans for a while now—"

"I have a plan," Melody cut in. "You two have to do what you gotta do. But I have to go find my husband. He could be out there right now struggling to survive, and I'm having…" She dropped her fork onto the plate. "I'm having a fucking dinner party." Melody rubbed her temples with the tips of her fingers.

John took another bite of his dinner. With a full mouth, he said, "We'll come with you."

Melody's eyes lifted to meet his. "I won't be endangering anyone else's life. I can handle it alone."

John laughed. "You against the masses? You're tough, but you ain't Chuck Norris."

"Well, I'm not some helpless *sweetheart*, either."

John shook his head, embarrassed that he'd been such a dickhead. "I don't know if *I* could handle it alone out there."

"Well, you're..." She glanced downward as if to suggest his missing limb would slow him down.

Ouch. That was brutal.

"I'm what?" John stared her down. It'd been a long time since he let the anger over his amputation bubble to the surface.

"Did I hurt your feelings, *sweetheart?*" Melody smirked.

It drew a smile to his face, but he stifled it, refusing to give her the pleasure. He jammed more noodles into his mouth.

Candace grunted, pushing her chair away from the table. She went to the kitchen, leaving John and Melody alone. He imagined Melody crawling over the table, straddling him... He pushed the thought away before his desires manifested physically as an erection. Last thing he needed was to be considered an asshole *and* a pervert.

Candace thumped around the kitchen, opening and closing cabinet doors.

"There's not much in there," Melody said over her shoulder.

"Yes!" she shouted, and came out holding a bottle of vodka.

Melody laughed. "Are you even old enough to drink?"

Candace huffed with the sour face of an irritated preteen girl. "I'm twenty-two." Then, she retreated with the bottle to the dark living room.

John helped Melody clear the table.

At the sink, he leaned close, whispering, "Look. I'm not the type of guy who goes after married women. So, let's just put whatever that was behind us."

"I don't know what you're talking about," Melody said.

"Good."

"And for the record, I don't even know if my husband's alive." Melody's voice cracked.

"What are you saying? You wanna give up?"

"No. It's just... I'm not naïve. I understand that the chances of him still being alive aren't great. But I have to at least try to find him."

He remained quiet as she stumbled over her words of honorable intent. He didn't believe the guy was still alive either. Marcus would have come back for her by now, but that wasn't John's place to tell her that.

"The world is fucked up right now," John said, "and when things get fucked up, it can be hard for people to do the right thing."

"That's not going to be me."

"I know."

TWELVE

Kayla

A set of handsome eyes peered between open blinds on the other side of Lab One's window. The man signaled for Kayla to go away, but she kept knocking, jiggling the door handle, and urging him to let her in.

She couldn't blame the guy; how was he to know if she was infected or not?

The blinds closed, and the lock on the laboratory door clicked. A man with messy, dark hair poked his head out as the infected Dr. Carter climbed to his feet behind her.

"Shit!" He yanked her by her arm into the lab and locked the deadbolt on the heavy door.

Dr. Carter dragged his feet to a standing position and lumbered toward the door, walloping against the glass with dried, bloody hands. Each thud was followed by the sound of his skin streaking against the glass.

The man closed the blinds, kept a hand locked on Kayla's wrist, and hurried to the back of the lab.

He released her, then crouched low behind an island of microscopes

"Thank you." Kayla looked to her rescuer as they sat with their backs against the cabinet doors.

She had seen him working in the back of the lab before while dropping off files, but she didn't know anything about him, other than he was cute. After her flirtatious episode with the married Dr. Carter, Kayla had warned herself to stay away from the guys she worked with.

The man had eyes so dark she couldn't decipher where the iris began and the pupil ended. "You almost got us both killed. You haven't been bitten, have you?"

"No." Insulted, she crossed her arms over her body to protect herself from another verbal assault.

The laboratory was a gray, dull space about the size of her old high school chemistry lab, lined with stainless steel cabinets, counters, and several rows of microscopes and computers. A row of white coats hung from hooks along the back wall near a private breakroom with vending machines. The glass was busted out, revealing empty food slots. Candy and chip wrappers overflowed the small garbage can in the corner.

The overhead fluorescent lights created an even, blinding glow and a suicide-inducing hum.

"You've been here this whole time, too?" she asked.

His eyes drifted downward toward her breasts but corrected themselves quickly. She hadn't given much thought to her appearance. Her breasts were barely contained in a black polka-dot bra, exposed under a button-down shirt. She clasped the button shut to cover her cleavage.

"Been here ever since the building got taken over." He leaned the back of his head against the cabinet.

His shaggy brown hair sat disheveled upon his head. He had a gentle face with a fine layer of sparse beard growth. Tall and lean—the body of a swimmer—wearing stained khakis and an unbuttoned blue shirt, exposing a sweat-soaked white tee.

Dr. Carter's thumps against the door weakened as the two sat side by side on the lab floor, waiting for him to move on.

"Do you have any more food? I was in the break room upstairs, but I ran out."

He didn't answer her question; he just stared upward at the fluorescent lights, now flickering.

"This lab runs on a generator," he finally said. "So, we can't stay here much longer."

"I'm Kayla."

The man let out a sigh and seemed to make an attempt at being pleasant. "Dr. Hill." He extended his hand. "I didn't know you worked here."

She shook the doctor's hand and smiled, biting the corner of her lip. A rush of excitement ran through her body. The scruffy man who saved her from certain death was a doctor, and she was not about to leave his side.

Hell of a step up from boring old Styles Newman and lame-kisser Victoria.

It occurred to her that she had never gotten Victoria's last name before she died.

"I'm an intern. I had nowhere to go when it all happened," she said, relieved to speak with another person again.

Dr. Carter banged against the glass, and Kayla flinched.

"That…" Dr. Hill gestured toward the man outside the door, "…is why I stayed. Dr. Carter and I worked together here in Development."

"I'm sorry." Kayla clutched her hands over her heart.

"Don't be." His face went sour, and he shook his head with disgust. "The moron wanted to get home to his wife."

"Well, that's admirable," Kayla said.

"I told him he was no good to her dead. He didn't listen."

"I'm sorry."

"Nothing we can do about it now," Marcus said callously.

"Did you contact his wife to let her know?" she asked.

"You got a phone that hasn't died yet?" His voice was sharp and cutting. "I don't have a damn charger for mine."

"Oh." Kayla felt stupid for asking, and the lab went quiet, but she couldn't bear the silence. "Do you know where he lives? Maybe we—"

"No. I don't," Dr. Hill interrupted. He shook his head and kept all emotion locked behind his mysterious exterior, which made Kayla want to pry even more.

"Do you have a family?" she asked.

He took a deep breath. "No." He leaned forward, resting his elbows on his knees, and held his head in his hands. "I could hear Dr. Carter screaming out there when he got attacked."

Kayla placed her hand on his back, offering what little comfort she could. Her chipped, black glitter nail polish sparkled beneath sputtering fluorescent lights. She looked up as the humming waxed and waned, then steadied.

The infected Dr. Carter must have given up and stumbled down the hall, because the banging ceased, finally leaving them in peace. Kayla let out a sigh of relief and moved to a swiveling chair in the middle of the lab, folding her legs crisscross and probably exposing a brief glimpse of her purple panties before she tucked her hands in her lap to push her skirt down. She pulled her flaming red hair out of the tightly spun bun and let it fall upon her shoulders.

She didn't know what suddenly came over her, but she wanted to be touched. She wanted to be heard, to be spoken to, to be loved. It was pretty much the end of the world, and all she could think about was sex now.

He took one of the white coats from the hooks and slid his arms in. He adjusted the collar and sat down in front of her in another chair.

He nodded to a microscope. "After that first day, Dr. Carter and I stayed here because we thought we could try to formulate a vaccine," he said.

Kayla's eyes lit up.

"Don't get excited. It didn't happen. We didn't have the supplies we needed—not in this facility." He pulled his dark hair away from his face and let it fall back down over his forehead.

"Wow." Kayla gazed upon her selfless rescuer with her mouth agape. "That's so amazing of you." She couldn't believe her luck in finding the one decent human being in the world. He may have been older than her, but she didn't care. He was perfect in every way.

She wet her lips in case he decided to kiss her, and she didn't care if the romantic in her was taking over. She wanted to be touched, and she was going for it, stroking his ego. "You could've gone to that quarantine place, but you stayed to help humanity. That's saying something."

Dr. Hill shook his head with modesty.

"I looked out the windows today," she said with a hopeful grin. "It doesn't look too dangerous out there anymore. I didn't see any of the infected people inside or out there, other than Dr. Carter."

"Everyone has probably evacuated to the high school, where that camp is set up."

"Maybe we should go there," Kayla said.

Dr. Hill smiled at her. "Maybe. But the sun will be going down soon, and I'd hate to get stuck out there in the dark."

Conversation between Kayla and Dr. Hill flowed effortlessly. The world outside seemed to disappear while she talked about her parents and life on the west coast. Dr. Hill talked about his college experience and how much it made him grow as a person, and she confessed that the college guys were far too immature for her.

"Dating is rough," he said. "Especially when you get closer to thirty."

"How close to thirty?" she asked.

"Twenty-eight," he answered. "I know it's taboo for a gentleman to ask, but—"

"Eighteen," she said with clenched teeth, hoping he wouldn't think she was too young for him.

"Wow," the doctor raised his eyebrows and ran his fingers through his hair again. "I was guessing 25."

Kayla blushed. "Well, I'm more mature than most girls my age."

"I can tell."

An hour had gone by since she had made her way into his lab, and she already imagined their wedding day. She had a habit of doing that with everyone. After she and Victoria kissed, she pictured a beautiful ceremony with both of them in white gowns.

Someday—after everything got better—she pictured Dr. Hill coming home after a long day of being a doctor, needing her comfort. By then, she would be a biologist and an intellectual equal.

They stood in the center of the lab, leaning against an island counter. Kayla hoisted herself up to sit between two microscopes, letting her bare feet dangle. The stainless steel chilled the backs of her legs, and she shifted her short skirt underneath to block the hard surface.

Dr. Hill eyed her bare thighs... She could tell he wanted her. His eyes pierced into her, and she shivered with excitement. As he turned his body toward her in a slow, smooth rotation, Kayla bit her lip and glanced down at his unshaven face. Raw, animalistic emotions enveloped her. She wanted to feel secure. Dr. Hill was perfect for the job, and she figured he was more likely to take her along with him if she latched on now.

He positioned his body in front of her and drifted in closer as Kayla parted her knees. His gaze locked on her inviting eyes as he leaned in to kiss her. Her body melted as he moved his hands to her bare knees. She grabbed behind his ears, pulled him close, and invaded his mouth with her tongue. The doctor slid his hands under her tiny skirt, and his thumbs came to rest at the crease of her pelvis, squeezing her thighs.

Kayla charged at him with fervid intent. They tugged at each other's clothing. Her blouse dropped to the floor. Then went her purple panties. His khakis collapsed in a bundle at his ankles, and Kayla grabbed him by his white coat lapels and wrapped her legs around his waist.

She shrieked from the energy pulsing through her as their bodies smashed together in a furious entanglement of lust. The microscope to the left crashed to the floor in their frantic wrestling match. His fingers worked like magic, crammed between their bodies, circling while he thrusted himself inside until they both writhed in ecstasy. He pulled out last second, like a pro.

After their brief and fervent encounter, she collapsed backward onto the counter. Her pulse throbbed between her legs while she squirmed in the aftermath of his touch. Dr. Hill cleaned himself up, fastened his pants, and plopped into the swivel chair out of breath.

Minutes later, Kayla was getting dressed, longing for them to do that again. She'd only ever been with people her own age. And none of them ever made her feel like *that*.

"Please don't think less of me," she whispered as she slipped her blouse over her head. "I don't normally do stuff like this."

Dr. Hill moved closer and whispered in her ear. "You mean you don't normally scream in delight?"

His words excited her, and she was ready for him again. She released a sharp breath as his lips hovered over her neck.

She trembled. "I don't even know your name."

Dr. Hill took a step back and looked her in the eyes with a smile. "Marcus," he said.

THIRTEEN

Melody

Melody had the strength to do the right thing. She would be the kind of person who would stay truthful to her vows, the kind of person who would risk her life to find her love—even if it wasn't the easy kind of love her dad told her about. Whether the world was fucked up or not, Marcus was all she had left, and she would fight for him.

She carried the candle and a newfound sense of purpose from the kitchen to the living room. Candace sipped vodka straight from the bottle, scrunching her face after each sip. She sank into the couch with her legs crossed and the bottle clutched in her hand. Her other hand held onto Melody's wedding photo.

"Your husband's cute," Candace said.

Melody nodded and sat on the floor with her back against the loveseat. The cushions still lay on the floor in the attic.

"What's he do?" she asked.

"He works at Hill Pharmaceuticals. He's got a Ph.D. in developmental—"

"So, he's a doctor?" Candace interrupted.

"Just like you," John said, entering the room. He stepped over Melody's outstretched legs to get to the couch and sat down beside Candace.

"I'm a DVM, doctor of veterinary medicine, and he's a Ph.D.—developing new drugs." Melody didn't know why she explained the difference in doctors. It always irritated her when Marcus would do it. Someone would introduce her as Dr. Hill, and he was always sure to point out the distinction between the two doctors.

"I called him that night when everything fell apart here," Melody said. The room fell silent as the yellow light from the candle flickered across the ceiling. "He said he was staying to work on a vaccine."

Candace's face lit up.

"It didn't make sense, though," Melody said. "He doesn't deal with stuff like this. He works on antidepressants. Not viral infections."

"And?" Candace's eyes were wide open.

"I argued with him," Melody admitted. "He told me he was going to try to save the world, and I tried to talk him out of it."

"How much progress did he make on the vaccine?" John asked. "Did he say?"

"No. He didn't tell me anything. We got cut off. I don't know what I can do to make things right, other than try to find him."

John nodded. "Tomorrow, we go look for him."

Melody felt horrible about dragging them both into danger on a quest to find someone they didn't even know—someone that might not even be alive.

"And don't try to argue," he said. "We're in this together." John turned to Candace. "And before we go anywhere, you need *pants.*"

"Hey!" She gave him a playful nudge with her shoulder. "It was hot out today."

"Every inch of exposed skin is a target for them—it's another way to get bit. So, put some pants on."

"And good running sneakers." Melody eyed her high heels.

Candace rolled her eyes. "I know you probably think it's stupid that I'm wearing this. But hear me out. I read one time that dressing nicely can make you feel better. And I was feeling sad. So, I thought, what better way to fight depression and missing my husband than getting all sexy? It makes me feel good."

"Fair enough," Melody said. "Maybe save the skimpy outfits and stilettos for when you don't plan on leaving the house."

John laughed. "Could you imagine running in those things?"

Candace held her head high. "I bet I can do better in my heels than you can do on that leg of yours." She cringed. "I'm sorry... I shouldn't... I was just kidding..."

"It's fine." John took the vodka from her and drew a pull, scrunching his face. "That's terrible."

"What happened to your leg anyway?" She leaned forward with her breasts nearly falling out of her tank top.

"It's not a fashion statement, if that's what you mean," John said.

"I heard you're a Navy SEAL. Is that true?" She took the bottle back from John.

"Where would you hear something like that?" He snagged the vodka from her hands before she could take another drink and set it on the coffee table.

"Mrs. Nickerson." Candace laughed. "She tells everyone *everything* that happens on this street. Like how your wife left you last year—"

"I see," John cut her off.

"Oh my God, I'm sorry!" Candace leaned closer, fawning over him, slurring her words into an even deeper southern drawl. "You know, I can't imagine why she would leave you. You are such a nice guy."

John scooted another few inches away.

"Is it true your wife stole your cat?" she blurted.

Enduring the infected outside seemed like a better option to Melody than sitting in that room with drunken Candace. She quickly changed the subject. "So, if you were military, do you have MREs?"

"No," he said.

"What're MREs?" Candace asked.

"Meals ready to eat," John said.

"I thought all you military guys keep that stuff," Melody said.

"I don't eat that garbage. It binds you up. Only hunters and those crazy doomsday people stock up on MREs."

"I bet those doomsdayers are having a celebratory I-told-you-so party now," Melody said. "What about guns? Do you have more?"

John shook his head. "I have a hunting rifle and a pistol. That's it."

"So, is it true?" Candace asked. "Are you a SEAL?"

"Yeah." He pointed to his leg. "I don't see much action these days, though."

"I can't believe I haven't asked you these things before."

"Well, you haven't been this drunk since we've met," John said, taking the bottle from Candace's hands again as she tried to snatch it for another sip. "You should stop drinking. We travel in the morning, and we can't carry you."

"Tell me what happened," she said.

While Candace pried, Melody pulled a blank sheet of paper from the printer in the office, brought it back to the living room, and set it in the center of the coffee table. She started sketching the town.

"Are we playing Pictionary?" Candace giggled.

"She's drawing a map," John said.

She nodded, marking out her preferred route to Marcus's lab.

"Are we driving?" Candace asked.

"No," John and Melody said in unison.

"The roads could all be traffic-jammed with dead vehicles," Melody said.

"Those are the tracks, right?" John asked, pointing to her map.

The abandoned railroad tracks wrapped around the perimeter of Fair Haven, guarded by an eight-foot-tall chain link fence on the city side, well-covered with weeds, and a line of trees on the opposite side, perfect for coverage.

"I used to run them for cross-country and track practice. We could travel through the woods that run parallel here," Melody said, pointing to the strip of poorly drawn pine trees squeezed between Route 28 and the tracks.

"But the highway is right there," John said. "We don't know if the infected are still there."

"There's a fence between the highway and the trees. Then the railroad tracks. Then another fence... It's a fenced path."

"Could be a death trap if any of them got in that corridor."

"Could be all clear too," Melody said.

John studied the map for a moment and looked up. "After we extract Marcus—"

"We go to the quarantine camp?" Candace suggested.

"We're not waltzing into that place without a decent vantage point first," he said, "I want to be sure it's safe."

"I know a place where we can check it out from afar," Melody said.

Hours went by, and the conversation grew sparse with their increasing exhaustion. The night grew black, and the sound of crickets crept through the walls along with the occasional moan or snarl of an infected person. Melody snuck away, leaving John sitting on the couch as Candace cried into his arms, talking about whether or not her husband was still alive.

Melody tiptoed upstairs to change clothes and then down the dark hall toward the floor-length window. She slid to the floor and leaned her head against the paned glass. Fireflies speckled the darkness below. Above, if she craned her neck just right, she could spot stars.

Minutes later, John's footsteps could be heard coming upstairs. His sturdy silhouette moved toward her. He sat against the opposite wall, and his foot met with Melody's in the middle of the hallway.

"She's almost asleep," John said. "She didn't drink that much, but she's toast. Hopefully, she's not hungover in the morning."

"I think we should all sleep up here."

"I agree. We should all stay in the same room. I'll sleep on the floor."

Melody nodded in agreement.

"Do you have a portable radio or boom box? Battery-operated?" John asked.

"Yeah, an old one that used to be my dad's, but no batteries for it. It takes four D batteries. Got any of those?"

"Nope. I couldn't get anything but static on my radio before the batteries quit, anyway."

Melody rested her head against the window and looked to the sky. "I bet if we could get a proper look at the sky, the stars would be pretty amazing now that the power's out."

"You do much stargazing?"

"I used to spend a lot of time under the stars with my dad as a kid, but not since then. I work a lot. Well, I used to work a lot. I guess I don't have a job now."

"Me neither," John said. "So, now that civilization seems to be crashing to a halt, what are you going to do with your time?"

Melody fought a smile. "Hide in attics, of course, and occasionally beat people with baseball bats." She chuckled and contained her laughter immediately, trying not to sound like a crazy person, but John laughed along with her.

"It's good to have a hobby," he said.

Within the darkness, his lips stretched across his face, exposing a gorgeous smile.

"I have a decent telescope, so we *could* look at some galaxies and stuff if we really wanted to," John said.

"Really? Me too. Well, not here. My dad's old eight-inch reflector. It's in storage."

"Eight-inch aperture allows in a fair amount of light. Mine's twelve. But eight's a good size," John bragged.

Melody smirked. "If it's not at least eight inches, a lady's not impressed."

Melody laughed at her perverted joke, relieved that John was laughing too. "The first night the power went off, I thought about how my dad would've taken his scope out to see some dark skies without all the light pollution."

"That would be nice. Wanna give it a go?" He laughed.

"I'm not exactly used to doing defensive battle while I operate a telescope."

"Well, maybe we can team up. Take turns looking through the telescope while the other stands guard."

"Stargazing and stabbing," Melody chuckled maniacally, a little disturbed with herself for cracking jokes.

"Astronomy and ass-kicking," John added. Their laughter bounced off the walls for a second, and then the hall fell silent.

"We should've hung out more before," John said.

Melody let his comment hang in the space between them. She agreed.

Candace

While John and Melody had been giggling in the hallway upstairs, Candace went back to drinking from the bottle of vodka, even though John tried to hide it. She could handle her booze. He had no idea how much this southern girl used to party before she settled into married life. She sat at the bottom of the steps and sipped away, eavesdropping on the two upstairs, but also missing her sweet Gavin. She missed his hugs and needed his comfort.

John and Melody whispered, and soft laughter floated downstairs. It bothered her that John was so readily drawn to some lady he hardly knew. Some lady with ratty hair and ill-fitted clothes came barreling into their lives and stole his attention away from her.

Candace knew it was the booze making her feel this way, so she put the bottle down. It was time to grow up and start helping. Melody seemed nice and was tough as nails. Maybe that was a quality Candace needed to embrace. If she was ever going to make it back to Gavin, she would need to learn to take care of herself. She could take on an infected person if she needed to. It's not like she'd never been in a bar fight before.

Candace needed to start proving herself, or she worried she'd be left behind. The only possible thing she could do right now to make things right was to get John's rifle and pistol.

Even in her drunken state, she knew that her stilettos would make too much noise, so she slid into a pair of flat black sandals by the front door and brandished a stiletto as a weapon, just in case.

She budged the table out of the way, head dizzy and spinning. Candace slowly cracked open the front door. The night was black, and it was too difficult to see much of anything without the street lights on, but she stepped outside anyway and closed the door. She figured if she couldn't see them, then they couldn't see her. She hurried down the porch steps in sandals that were a little too big and tiptoed toward John's house along the sidewalk, but shifting shadows against the houses made her freeze mid-step. It was then that her vision began to adjust to the darkness. Silhouettes of people appeared. They were everywhere. Dozens. Maybe more. Standing on the sidewalk blocking her path to John's place. One of them crept up behind her, staggering closer. Candace realized she'd made a terrible mistake, but her path back to Melody's house was already blocked.

FOURTEEN

Kayla

The humming of the fluorescent bulbs sputtered, and the room became black with the failing generator. They were lucky it lasted as long as it did. Kayla reached for Marcus in the darkness. She found his hand, and they maneuvered their way across the lab, feeling around the counters until they reached the door. Kayla held tight to Marcus's sleeve, and they both sank to the floor once again. He placed a hand on her leg and told her she would be all right. His gentle touch turned her heart into a million butterflies. Or maybe that was the nerves upsetting her stomach.

Marcus checked the digital display on his watch. "It's getting late. First thing in the morning, we have to leave."

"To the quarantine place?"

"Dr. Carter was the only infected person you came across today?"

She nodded, but it was too dark for Marcus to see. "Yeah."

"Okay. That's a promising sign. In the morning, I'll get by him, then I'll go outside and check it out to be sure it's okay to leave the building," he said.

"I'm going with you, right?"

"This place is relatively safe. Out there, we don't know."

"I am not staying here alone."

"I'm just going to—"

"I'm going with you!"

"Okay." Marcus patted her knee. She couldn't see his expression, but his voice indicated a hint of annoyance. "You can come."

She had to admit to herself that she, too, was a little annoyed with him for suggesting they split up. For now, she was relieved that he gave in without too much of a fight. She held Marcus's arm within the blackness of the lab and dreaded thinking about what was going to happen next.

As she stifled her emotions so as not to cry, a violent boom shook the building. It permeated the walls and rattled the door on its hinges.

"What was that?" Kayla braced herself. The whole damn building felt like it might collapse.

She sat upright and alert, waiting for something else to happen, but the rattling was brief.

"Earthquake?" Marcus said.

"That didn't feel like an earthquake. Did something blow up? Was it in this building?"

"I don't know…"

FIFTEEN

Melody

Melody and John had their faces pressed against the glass, looking up at the sky and laughing at each other's jokes, but their brief moment of fun ended, jolted into reality. The unmistakable sound of the front door closing brought them to their feet.

John sprang up and hurried to the foyer. Melody stayed on his heels. He ran outside into the cul-de-sac with his knife at the ready.

Too dark to see anything, Melody listened for footsteps.

"Do you see her?" Melody whispered from the top of the porch.

"Son of a—Stay here." He bolted away, disappearing into the black. He didn't head toward his house, where Melody thought Candace would've gone. Instead, he took off down the street. There were at least five infected that she could make out in the darkness, but none of them appeared coherent enough to see him.

Candace

Surrounded by their groans, Candace had turned away from the infected blocking John's house and headed straight down Elpis Court in the only direction that she couldn't hear them. She searched for a place to hide, but it seemed they were everywhere, other than the sidewalk that led away from the house. Every glimpse over her shoulder, she hoped to see John coming up behind to help her out of this mess, but he was nowhere in sight. It was too dark to see, and it was too risky to shout for help.

Figure it out!

More silhouettes of the infected approached from all directions as she reached the end of Elpis Court. The vague structure of the elementary school on the opposite side of Mason Drive came into view. The building seemed to sway, and her stomach lurched.

The drape of pitch black was broken with pale arms and faces as their sickly bodies staggered close enough, groaning and reaching.

Candace sprinted—then staggered to the side, losing balance. She crossed Mason Drive, hurried along the sidewalk, and into the bus loop of the elementary school.

She dove into the shadowy corner of the school entrance, sank to the concrete, and pressed herself against the doors. Cloaked in shadow and out of sight, she pulled her knees to her chest. The booze kicked in harder, and her head became heavy. Her vision pulsed.

Every decision tonight had been a dumb one. That's all she was, though, wasn't it? Just some dumb girl who let military guys do body shots off her until one of them asked her to be his wife. She was dumb to marry into the military. She was dumb not to do more with her life. And she was especially dumb for hitting on John. And extra-extra dumb for getting drunk during the fucking apocalypse.

Candace's tears spilled over, probably ruining her makeup, which was tragic because she put it on to make herself feel better. Now she'd be dumb *and* ugly. Nobody in the world ever saw value in girls like her, other than the value assigned to her beauty.

Maybe if, while she was growing up, someone ever told her she was kind, or smart, or talented at something, maybe she wouldn't have focused so much on her looks. Maybe she could've grown to be more than just a body.

The infected who had been following her seemed to have lost track. Their incoherent moans and their feet shuffling through the tall grass nearby tormented her. What if they found her? What if they rounded the corner and dove for her? She'd be trapped.

She checked the doors to the school, but they were locked as expected. Head pounding, she shuffled along the side of the building toward a group of work vehicles that must have been parked at the school for maintenance when the outbreak began.

Her dash for a safer location did not go unnoticed. The infected spotted her as soon as she left the safety of the entrance cove.

A yellow ladder was bolted to the side of the school near the work trucks. The bottom rung hung a few feet above the ground and called to her like a beacon of hope. After a staggering sprint to get to it, she grabbed hold of the bars and hoisted herself up with all of her strength. The infected surrounded her underneath.

Candace froze inches above them, barely out of reach, crying as the infected growled and stretched their arms, nicking the bottom of her foot with their fingers.

One of the sick men below bit into the arm of an infected woman. Candace shrieked, desperate for her cries to be heard by John or Melody or *anyone*. But if she kept screaming, more would keep coming.

The woman below snapped back at the man, and the two infected ripped into each other like wild dogs until they were shredded and weak. Candace held on tight and prayed for it to be over while the world continued to spin.

Melody

Melody shoved her feet into her already-tied sneakers and grabbed her baseball bat to follow John. She maneuvered over the side porch railing to avoid the infected near the front steps, then she snuck through the darkest shadows to meet up with John.

The remnant smell of burning bodies lingered on a warm breeze. Aside from the odor of burnt flesh, it reminded Melody of summer barbecues when she was a girl. She thought of her dad standing at the grill with a can of beer in his hand, flipping burgers while her mom lay in a lounge chair under the sun, laughing at one of his dumb jokes. Back when laughing, loving, and even *living* came so easily for all of them. The brief memory brought a moment of levity, but it was stripped away when survival mode kicked in.

John was crouched by the green Volvo as she approached him from behind.

"There are too many around my house for me to sneak by and get my gun. Also…I told you to wait," he said.

Melody scowled, unsure if he could see her disapproval, but didn't stop to find out. She hustled by him, heading down the sidewalk. They couldn't keep lurking around if they were going to get to Candace.

Unlike earlier in the day, when she was too petrified to move, Melody allowed the adrenaline to take over. She charged forward, ready for a challenge with her newfound confidence—or maybe it was more of a death wish.

They snuck through the shadows of the front yards, heading in the direction where they last heard her call out. The moon had sunk below the tree line, barely illuminating a path and making it difficult to see the lingering infected in the dark, but they reached the end of Elpis, where it met with Mason. Already, they'd passed unnoticed by at least seven infected.

Melody's blood pulsed in her ears as she crouched near the last house on the corner, scanning the area where the streets intersected at a T. She followed the movement of bodies near the school across the street, and then Candace finally stood out. Short shorts, long legs. She hugged the brick wall of the school, shimmying along as the infected followed behind.

Melody started to run after her, but John grabbed her by the wrist and pulled her back. In one agile movement, he covered Melody's mouth and pushed her back between the bushes into the mulched landscaping along the house.

A small group of the infected marched by.

John pressed his body as tightly as possible against hers, trying to flatten themselves against the lattice, tight within a narrow shadow so as not to be seen. He slid his hand away from her mouth while pinning her to the house, pelvis to pelvis.

Melody's chest pressed into his with every panicked breath. As the horde of at least thirty infected stumbled along the sidewalk ten feet away, fireflies twinkled in the darkness all around them. The tiny points of light danced around the sickly bodies as the infected trudged forward. Her lips nearly brushed against John's collarbone, sending tiny hairs on her arms to attention.

The infected continued, heading toward the school. Some seemed focused on following Candace, and others were distracted by one another, lashing out as they bumped into each other. Snapping, scratching, they fought in the street, biting and clawing among themselves. Meanwhile, John and Melody had a difficult time releasing themselves from the shadow.

"Do you mind?" She pushed his pelvis away from her and ducked back to the bushes.

As more bodies closed in on Candace, they had to pick up their pace. She wasn't sure if these masses of infected had been around the neighborhood all along, or if the fire or shots from earlier had lured them in, but she knew there were far too many to fight off. They sprinted around the corner of the school as Candace screamed out.

They spotted her on a ladder, with a half-dozen infected snarling below.

"You get Candace from that ladder," John said, "I'll lure them that way."

Melody thought it was a horrible idea, but there was no time to argue. She didn't want John to leave her side, but she nodded and watched him dart toward the work vehicles. She hoped he could run fast enough with that prosthetic leg, because as soon as they spotted him, they redirected their course.

It was like watching Marcus leave her four days ago, unsure if she'd ever see him again.

John leapt into one of the white trucks and started the engine. A miracle that there were keys inside.

She wondered how much of Fair Haven was still untouched. How many other cars were available for the taking, gas in tanks, houses still full of food, and boats on the lake?

The headlights beamed on, then the truck peeled out in the field. Melody focused on her mission—get Candace.

At once, all of the faces of the infected surrounding Candace at the ladder turned their attention to the truck. Even the infected who were lashing at each other stopped fighting and followed John.

Five infected were still close to the ladder, watching the headlights move across the grass. Melody stalled along the wall as her opportunity opened, petrified to take another step and draw their attention back to herself. She clenched her jaw and her nostrils flared as she fought with herself to move.

"Go," she whispered, but her body refused. "Go!" An impetuous jolt forced her into a sprint, faster than she'd run in a long time. She held her baseball bat at the ready. As she got closer, the infected had moved at least ten yards away from Candace, distracted by the truck.

Candace clung to the ladder with her eyes closed tight, unaware that the infected had moved on.

Melody grabbed for the bottom rung and called out with a frantic whisper, "Let's go!"

She held tight, refusing to budge. Melody couldn't keep yelling to her, or she would draw the infected back, so she dropped her bat and moved up the ladder, hugging her body around Candace from behind.

"Candace," Melody said, panting, trying to calm her tone. "I know you're scared, but we have to get out of here."

John's truck came barreling back toward the building, driving parallel with the wall, while the infected lumbered far behind. The truck's pace slowed down.

"Come on!" He waved for them to come down.

Melody shouted now. "Candace. Let's go!"

"Candace!" John kept an eye on the rearview mirror as more closed in, then knocked the gear into reverse and hit the gas.

The truck kicked up grass and dirt as it reared up and crashed into the bodies of three. Two collapsed under the truck, but the third was flung into the bed.

"Get down!" Melody tried prying the girl's fingers from the rung.

Now, every infected body in the area heard the commotion. The field was littered with stumbling bodies coming toward them.

John sped forward with the infected man reaching for him through the small cab window. As he neared the school, he flung himself from the truck. John's body rolled and tumbled to a stop as the vehicle continued along, losing momentum.

"Go!" he yelled as he popped up and ran toward them with surprising speed.

"I think she's in shock!"

"Just go up to the roof! I got her."

Melody edged around Candace and scrambled up the ladder as fast as her limbs would carry her.

John moved up the ladder behind Candace and balanced his weight. He wrapped his left arm around her and lowered his voice.

"Hey. I got you," he said.

Candace turned and wrapped her arms and legs around him as he climbed, carrying her full weight.

Melody spilled onto the roof, but before she could get to her feet, she was met by an infected man wearing a construction hat and coveralls. He crawled toward her. The setting moon pierced through the branches of the trees along the horizon and lit up the edges of his body.

Melody rolled to the side, spitting out an "oh shit" as she got to her feet and searched for a weapon.

His name tag read Paul, and he lunged toward Melody, tripping and falling to his side several times. She managed to duck out of the way, keeping out of his reach. Frantic to find something to defend herself with, she searched the rooftop, but there was nothing. She peeked over the edge toward John, who struggled climbing with Candace. His prosthetic blade slipped off the rung, and he had to readjust, but he was nearly to the top.

Melody stood her ground near the edge of the roof, planting her feet. She let Paul come at her. The man plunged forward with his face distorted and blistered. Saliva strung from his lower lip and connected to his chest.

Melody's heartbeat could've blasted a hole through her chest as he took each step closer to her. When he dove to attack, a thunderous sound caused her to stumble.

An explosion across town.

The flash lit up the horizon beyond the trees while Melody flung her body to the side out of the way of the infected man.

He fell to the edge of the roof and managed to grab Melody's t-shirt sleeve on his way down. She screamed but freed herself from the infected man's grip. The lower half of his body dangled over the edge of the roof. She stayed on her ass, kicking at his forehead, but he continued to hold the ledge, snapping and clawing.

His face seemed inhuman—teeth chomping, eyes devoid of emotion. Filthy fingers bled as he dug them into the edge of the roof, but he showed no sign of pain. Melody got to her feet and balled up all of her panic and rage in the pit of her gut. She ran forward with a lunging kick to his forehead, sending the man's body plummeting down to the ground with a thwack.

John reached the top, and Candace's arms remained locked around him even after he set her down.

Melody pried the girl's fingers from John and dragged her away from the edge of the building, out of sight from those below. She paced, out of breath with her fists clenched, staring at the fire beyond the trees. She could have killed Candace for putting them all in danger, but more than anything, she worried about that explosion and how it seemed to come from the direction of Hill Pharmaceuticals.

John collapsed onto the rooftop on his back.

Melody crept to the ledge to steal a glimpse of the mass of mangy people moving below. They were uninterested in the rooftop inhabitants as they pursued the truck that had rolled to a stop against the side of the school.

The infected man, Paul, lay face down on the ground, still squirming. His arms reached out in front of him, dragging his broken legs behind as he crawled in the direction of the lights on the truck, unconcerned with his injuries.

Candace curled up in a ball and began to sob hysterically. "I'm sorry! I just wanted to help." Her face quivered as she wiped snot away from her nose.

Rage bubbled within Melody. She was thankful she left her bat at the base of the ladder, because she was ready to take a crack at Candace's ribs. She wanted her to go away, and for a moment, Melody thought about how much better it would have been if they had never chased after her. If they let her naturally meet her demise.

She sat down on the roof with her eyes locked on the site of the explosion, still able to feel the sensation of Paul's head against her foot. The image of the infected man's disgusting face was plastered to the inside of her eyelids. Overwhelmed with anger, trauma, and confusion, Melody sat with her arms around her knees and tried to keep a calm exterior.

John knelt before Candace as she concealed her face with her hands. She hated that he was being nice to her after what she had done, but she also envied his patience.

"I think I love you," Candace said.

John hung his head and sighed. "Candace, you're still married."

His words were like a smack to Melody's face. *Still married.* Husband or not, Melody couldn't deny that she was attracted to John. But now she worried her attraction to him was becoming more than just circumstantial arousal. She forced herself to picture Marcus and how happy they used to be, but the memories were dampened by the past two years of disinterest and unhappiness.

Candace lay down on the hard surface of the roof and cried, while John removed his plaid button-down shirt, wadded it up, and stuffed it like a pillow under Candace's face.

John, in his black tee, joined Melody in the middle of the roof, looking toward the explosion.

"Holy shit," he said, as smoke billowed into the sky and the light from the fire waned.

"Marcus' building is over there," she said.

"There's also a gas station over there."

He was right. Melody shrugged, unable to get any other words out. She trapped all of her anger and concerns in an emotional cage and remained silent.

After their pulses calmed, they lay on their backs to stare upon the countless stars stretching across the canvas of the night.

She had a promise to keep to Marcus, and having this guy around was not making it easy. Promises were important to Melody, but how substantial were promises if they were made to an undeserving person? She allowed the starlight to permeate her eyes and permitted herself to steal a glimpse of John's arms.

"I haven't seen this many stars in a long time," John said. "Not since I was in the desert. There's no city glow in any direction."

Normally, there would be some glow to the west and south from Madison and other towns nearby, but the horizons were dark except for a dwindling fire from the explosion. No artificial lights in the city—not even on the other side of town where the quarantine zone should have been.

"Do you think it's gone?" Melody asked. "The quarantine zone?"

"I don't know."

The moon had set far below the horizon, and they lay under the sky with the Milky Way sprawled out before them. The starlight seemed to dance against the blackness of the night. With nothing but the sound of crickets and distant inhuman groans, Melody tried not to think about the difficult road ahead. Her gut twisted, sickened with worry about making the trek across town. Life was always knocking her off her feet, and she didn't know how many more times she could get back up. As her heart began to hurt, her breathing became heavier, and she fought back tears, refusing to cry.

Her eyes glassed over as she stared fiercely into the abyss above. Pinpoint stars turned to blurred splotches of light. John looked away, directing his gaze back to the starlight while she lay beside him, needing the intimacy of a friend. She fought to separate her desire to befriend John from her desire to kiss him. An agonizing attraction lingered between them, but she lay still, knowing she could never act on her feelings.

SIXTEEN

Melody

Clouds had rolled in overnight, draping the town in an oppressive gray shroud. Melody woke with her head nestled into the crook of John's arm, and she hesitated for a moment before tearing herself away from him.

The morning dew clung to her clothes as she stood to stretch. The cool, wet air was reminiscent of mornings at her father's mountain cabin. She and her dad would leave the cabin pre-dawn, while it was still dark outside, so they could be at the summit for the exquisite sunrise.

Marcus wanted nothing to do with that cabin, but she really couldn't blame him. It was on a dirt ATV trail, unserviced by county plow trucks. Living there was not practical for two people with careers, but he wasn't even interested in visiting. It was her favorite vacation spot.

She imagined herself sitting on that back deck, soaking in the view of the distant lake from between the trees, away from the infected civilization.

Instead, she was struggling to stay alive because Marcus practically muscled her into putting it up for sale. As enmity toward Marcus oozed from her heart, Melody mopped it back up with a guilty conscience.

John startled awake, ready to fight, but relaxed when he saw there was no imminent danger. He held his leg above the prosthesis and winced as he stood up. His t-shirt rode up, fabric gripping his abs above his belly button until he pulled it down and approached Melody. He stood by her side on the rooftop of the elementary school while she tried not to stare at his undeniably sexy physique.

"Is your leg okay?"

"I'm not supposed to sleep with it on, but I wasn't about to take it off last night, just in case. I've been leaving it on a lot lately, and it's starting to irritate the skin."

A dense fog smothered the town. Blurry silhouettes of infected lurked mindlessly below. Their dark gray torsos seemed to float across the fog, lower limbs disappearing in the mist like apparitions of the people they once were.

Candace let out a moan and rolled onto her hands and knees to vomit. She plucked a wedgie, groaned, and backed away from her puke puddle. Letting out another vile wretch, she covered her dry lips, trying to keep it in. Mascara tears streaked dehydrated skin.

"I'm so sorry, you guys. I shouldn't have left last night. I don't know what I was thinking!" Genuine sorrow seeped from her.

Melody had a cartridge full of vitriol to fire her way, but she contained her anger, doing her best to understand that Candace still had a lot of growing up to do; she'd better do it fast.

She knelt and held Candace's hair away from her face as the girl spilled her heart out, along with the contents of her stomach.

"We barely knew each other," Candace said about her husband, confiding in Melody while wiping tears from under her eyes. "Even if he makes it back stateside, what're the chances he'll come for me? The girl he hardly knows."

Melody empathized with her feelings of uncertainty. She made some stupid decisions when she was young, too. Hell, she thought it was a smart move to marry Marcus in her early twenties. It seemed like the next logical step in life, but she was still too vulnerable to have made that decision.

"Don't assume he's not coming." Melody paused, trying to think of anything that she could say to give this girl some hope. "Was love easy for you guys?"

"What?"

"Did love come easy between you and Gavin?"

"Oh, yes. We were connected like you wouldn't believe." She held her hand to her chest as if to clutch her own beating heart.

"Well, then I guess you were doing it right."

"What about your husband? Do you think he's out there trying to find you?"

Candace's question was not one Melody wanted to answer. She shrugged.

"I really am sorry," Candace said with tears traversing her cheeks.

"I know. It doesn't matter now. All that matters is moving forward. Let's figure out what to do."

She stood up and approached John, who looked west toward the opposite end of town. Fog and trees obscured the view in the direction of Hill Pharmaceuticals, where a scribbling swirl of black smoke was still rising from the explosion the night before.

"The tracks are just beyond that fence," she said, pointing across the open field, then arcing beyond her neighborhood, toward the smoke. "We follow them around the perimeter of town, all the way to Marcus."

"We need supplies. Let's make it back to the house for our weapons, then we'll go in a couple of hours when she's feeling better." He turned toward Candace. "Can you make it back to the house?"

Candace nodded.

Melody's eyes fell softly upon John again as he helped Candace to her feet. He picked up his plaid shirt from the roof and held it up for Candace to wear.

"There's a lot of fog," John said. "We should be well obscured from their sight. We can go back the way we came, sticking close to the houses."

Melody's pulse began to gallop at the thought of going back down there.

"We're in this together." John put a hand on her arm and rubbed it consolingly for a second longer than what should have been a friendly pat. He peeked over the ledge of the building. Dozens of silhouetted bodies ambled in the field.

"We get our stuff, then go get your husband, then all four of us get the hell out of town." John climbed down the ladder first and touched down on the wet grass. He stood guard with his knife at his hip, peering through the thick fog as the other two followed.

Melody picked up the baseball bat that she had left at the base of the ladder the night before. The cool, wet metal in her hands brought an immediate sense of safety.

They crept along the brick wall of the school, keeping out of sight of the infected, and moved past the landscaped bushes of the school.

As they neared the edge of the school property at the corner of Mason Drive and the bus loop, they spotted some infected ambling by.

They ducked beside the azalea bush. With the thick fog giving them cover, it would be an easy trip back to the house for the rifle and supplies. Or so Melody had thought.

"Wait," Candace whispered, covering her mouth. A loud guttural heave followed, and she hunched over to vomit.

The wretch caught the attention of three infected on the opposite side of the bushes. Their mangy faces turned toward the ungodly sound.

She and John remained crouched out of sight as Candace expelled bile onto the grass.

John leapt up and grabbed Candace by the arm as the infected stumbled toward them. She was barely to her feet, still hunched over and wiping green spit from her lip, as John tugged at her limp arm, dragging her away.

He looked back at Melody, who stayed on their heels, crossing Mason Drive toward Elpis Court.

She readied her bat near her shoulder as they shuffled through the front yards. More infected joined the pursuit, pouring out of the fog. An immense, mountain of a woman in a bathrobe lurched behind Melody, increasing her pace, but Candace's hungover stupor was too slow. Melody pushed on Candace's back to get her to go faster.

"Step it out, Candace," John said. "You can puke all you want when we get to the house."

Melody's throat swelled from the inside as the fear took over, but she turned around to confront the sick, robed lady who closed in.

Clean up. She hurled her bat at her head as hard as she could. The woman stood at least six feet tall. Blood splattered from the woman's mouth, spraying like a Jackson Pollock against the overcast. The robed woman dropped to the ground, squirming, struggling to get up as they hurried away.

Candace hunched over again to vomit, while John tugged on her arm to move forward. She wretched. Melody grabbed her other arm to help her along, but Candace's body fell limp, giving up on the escape. Her knees crumpled beneath her, and she cried in broken defeat.

"Get up!" John shouted.

She folded in half with dry heaves as the infected came from all directions, appearing out of the fog less than twenty feet away, one after the other.

"Move!" Melody yanked at her arms, but Candace collapsed.

Her clammy, cool arms slipped right through Melody's grip as the infected moved in on them.

A medium-built man with round eyes and a buzz cut loomed right behind her now. Melody swung at his head, knocking him to the side, but not to the ground. It sent him off-course long enough to gain a few feet of distance.

John hoisted Candace up over his shoulder. His leg, exacerbated by the extra weight, buckled briefly, but he recovered. With an even slower pace and more pronounced limp, he headed to the steps of the closest house, still far from their homes at the end of the cul-de-sac.

Melody was outnumbered. A horde closed in around her. She swung her bat at one person after another, losing strength, hands sore from the impact.

"Get inside," John shouted at Candace, dumping her off on the steps of the porch.

She scurried over large splotches of dried blood and jiggled the handle of the locked door. Candace, unable to get inside, ducked out of sight on the porch while John rushed to Melody's aid, clearing an opening for her to escape the crowd of infected.

On the pavement of the front walkway, Melody kept her back to the porch and allowed the adrenaline to rush through her veins as she swung her bat into one skull after another.

Her hands screamed in pain with each impact, but she kept swinging. Infected emerged from the fog in all directions. Their moans and growling grew louder and attracted more.

Some of the infected fell over before they could get to her. Others attacked one another, clawing and biting at each other's extremities, but most of them kept a steady pace, closing in.

John managed to plunge his knife into a couple of them, but the method of attack was not fast enough. He gave up on piercing their temples and began to slice his knife through the throats of as many infected as he could manage. His arm arced, blood sprayed. Crimson spilled from their necks. Once the throats had been cut, he knocked them to the ground, and they wriggled like worms on pavement.

The mass of infected was too numerous to fend off any longer. Melody, feeling faint, focused her attention on her next target and struck against the side of his head with as much force as she could muster.

His body dropped, but it was not enough to keep him down.

Her vision blurred, but she kept fighting. She wondered if this was it—if this was how she would die. Fighting tooth and nail, scratching, clawing, and screaming on her way out of a bloody massacre.

She wondered how much pain she would experience and hoped her death would be quick. Excruciating pain was what drove her father to suicide—the pain of loss. Were they the same kind of pain? It was that moment that she regretted not reading the letter he'd sent her in the orchid envelope.

Tears flooded her eyes, poured over her lids, and carved tracks in her dirty face. She sucked up her remaining strength and released it in a screaming fury, plowing her bat into another skull.

Candace

Candace's gut twisted, and she heaved again on the porch, but nothing came out. Drenched in more terror than she could have ever imagined, Candace sought an opportunity to get to safety. The infected in the cul-de-sac had been attracted to the commotion and headed toward the porch where John and Melody kept them busy.

Candace was certain she could make it back to John's house. She had a chance to be the hero—to get the guns. To do something meaningful for once in her life.

She sprang to her feet. The dead eyes of several infected latched onto her as she climbed over the railing, off the side of the porch, and into the street.

Her sandals pattered across the pavement and she held her hand over her stomach, trying not to vomit.

"Candace!" John yelled to her, but she was too petrified to stop.

"I'm getting the guns!" she screamed back as she ran down the street, dehydrated and unsteady. She motioned for the infected to follow her. "Come get me, you bastards!" She'd seen it in movies. The hero draws the attention of the monsters, lures them away so the others can get to safety. And it worked. Many of them had redirected their paths in her direction, including a few who were originally heading toward John and Melody.

She stutter-stepped down the street, unsure which way to run to avoid them as they came from all over. The sick ones had blocked her straight path to John's house.

She froze, just for a moment, to figure out what to do. Whether to sprint between the two scrawny ones, or to cut around the entire throng of infected. But it was too late to consider it any longer.

The bodies swarmed her.

She failed.

Candace was too exhausted and too nauseated to run. Too tired to fight. Cool, morning fog clung to her sweaty skin, and John's plaid shirt was soft against her. These would be the last good feelings she'd have.

She tried not to look at their faces as they charged toward her. Instead, she let her eyes meet with John's for a second through the thickness of the gray fog before the crowd surrounded her.

Melody

"Candace!" John screamed.

Melody didn't have time to think. She stood, petrified, unsure what to do. A hand fell on her arm, but before she could swing her bat, she realized it was John. With the horde of infected temporarily distracted by Candace, John hurried with Melody up the steps of the house. Only a few of the infected followed.

She stayed close behind John, running along the porch and climbing over the side railing behind the bushes. The infected, too disoriented to climb up and over, stumbled and fell over the rail.

John and Melody scrambled alongside the bushes, confusing their attackers with weaving and hiding so they could get away. Melody sprinted ahead down the sidewalk of Elpis Court toward Candace, who was already overtaken.

Her horrifying screams echoed off the houses as the infected mauled her. Screams became gurgled, muffled moans beneath the pile of bodies.

John grabbed Melody's wrist and tugged her away from a sick man, about to bite into her arm. She didn't even see him coming.

She focused on breathing as she stumbled over a body and nearly crashed face-first to the pavement but regained her footing and followed close behind John. They sprinted, dodging the infected, and leapt up the steps to John's porch.

They shut themselves inside. Hands slapped against the front door, blended with the snarling and moaning in the street. The reverberation of Candace's screams joined in.

John locked the deadbolt and dashed to the second floor, while Melody barricaded the stairwell with furniture in case of a breach. First the couch, then the coffee table on top. As Melody scrabbled over to get up the stairs, gunfire popped off from the second floor. John had grabbed his rifle and perched himself in the window, firing shot after shot into the cannibalistic herd below.

Melody stood beside him, flinching with each pull of the trigger. Bodies dropped one by one. Countless infected fell like dead flies on top of Candace. Her screams were no longer audible, and her body was completely submerged beneath the mass of gray flesh.

As John took them out, the mountain of bodies over Candace began to shift from the movement of the living infected squirming underneath. Candace was certain to be one of those bodies beneath, struggling to get out.

The sounds of the hands against the front door, moaning and snarling, pops of the rifle, and Candace's scream played in Melody's head like a hateful song, long after John had stopped firing and Candace had been silenced. Melody's eyes were wide open and bone dry as she stared at the pile of shifting bodies bleeding out onto the pavement of their suburban neighborhood.

Her brain echoed with the song of the attack.

Her pulse hammered through her body, within her neck and ears. Ears ringing and painful from the gunfire. She focused on the mound of dead outside as her vision pulsed in unison with her heartbeat. She couldn't tell if they were still moving or if there was something hallucinatory about the vision of undulating bodies.

She backed away from the window. Her stomach churned, and she held her hand to her mouth, sickened and lightheaded. The thump-thump of her heart banged with violence through her entire body, and her vision narrowed. She staggered backward, trying to maintain consciousness, but the light tunneled into darkness. She focused on simply breathing in and out.

John glanced over his shoulder in time to see Melody backing away from him. He approached her from the side, scooping his arms around her to guide her sinking body to the floor.

She sat with her back against the bed. Her vision faded into blackness, and she fought not to pass out as John hovered over her.

"Just breathe," he said.

Melody stared at the carpeting, taking long, deep, stuttering breaths for several seconds and trying not to pass out. As her pulse began to slow and her vision unblurred, she leaned back to rest her head against the side of John's bed. Then, she curled to the side and puked, heaving up some yellow bile onto the floor.

SEVENTEEN

Kayla

"I'm scared," Kayla said in the darkness of the lab.

Saturated with fear about leaving that morning, she clung to Marcus. They'd eaten the last of their food—a single-serve bag of corn chips—and they needed to venture out if they were going to survive. Whether they had food or not, she couldn't bear to spend another minute within that pitch black room.

The quarantine camp at the high school was their best bet.

"It'll be okay," Marcus said, soft and reassuring.

He stood, tugging himself from her grasp, and used the light of his watch to find the cord on the blinds. He pressed his face against the lab window, craning his neck to see down the hallway.

Kayla joined him, glimpsing a square of daylight which filled her heart with an iota of hope.

"Ready?" he asked. "I guess we slept well."

"Maybe *you* did." Kayla handed her busted chair leg to him so he'd have a weapon. "I was up all night listening to Dr. Carter moving around out there."

He turned the lock on the handle of the lab door. The click of the unlocking bolt echoed through the silent halls. Marcus froze with his fingers grasping the handle, awaiting movement from outside the door, but the hallway remained still. He cracked the door open while Kayla clung to his left sleeve.

He yanked away. "I need to be able to fight off—"

"Sorry." She pulled her arms in close to her body, inching behind Marcus as he stepped out the door.

He gripped the chair leg in both hands and kept it raised above his shoulder, ready to swing. Unable to see much of anything before them but the light at the end of the hall, Kayla shuffled along the wall with Marcus. A distant groan drifted from the opposite end of the hallway—the end that was shrouded in blackness—and Kayla rushed forward, ahead of Marcus and into the open office space at the end, where the diffuse light from the overcast day filled the room from beneath the Roman shades.

Kayla ran to the window and exhaled in relief to be out of the dark. She pulled the cord to the shades, raising the fabric and allowing more light to flood the room. Marcus placed his hand against the window, staring down at the foggy town from the third floor.

The gas station next door had been blackened and destroyed, still smoldering.

"Guess we know where the explosion came from," he said.

Abandoned vehicles cluttered the street, and scattered corpses lay rotting on the pavement. With no signs of the infected wandering the streets, they looked into each other's eyes.

"Do you think it's over?" she asked.

"I don't know."

Kayla looked up to him, thankful that she had someone with her. When the rest of the world turned its back on her, he opened the door. Kayla, always the romantic, wasn't so naïve as to believe that this man could be the one. There was something untrustworthy about Marcus, but she couldn't figure out what. She supposed it didn't matter, considering they could be the last two people on earth. *How tragically romantic would that be?* She stood on her toes, grabbed hold of his lab coat lapels, and pressed him against the floor-to-ceiling window.

Marcus didn't protest the kiss, and despite the danger that lurked within the building, she went for it. The chair leg he'd held for protection dropped to the floor. He grabbed her by her buttocks, hoisted her up around his waist, and spun her around to press her against the window.

The twirling around and rush of the forceful thrust was so hot, she didn't think she could ever stop having sex with this person. Her daydreaming got away from her, and she was pulled back to reality by a deep moaning from down the hall. Kayla froze while Marcus continued to suck on her neck. She stared toward the black opening of the hallway and tapped on Marcus's back, trying to get his attention.

"What?" He released his grasp, dropping her to the floor as Dr. Carter trudged into the office.

Kayla dropped low, crouching out of view as Marcus fumbled for the chair leg. He charged across the office. He tried to dart between Dr. Carter and the cubicle wall, but he was not fast enough. Carter caught hold of Marcus's coat.

Kayla screamed as Marcus fell. Snapping teeth ripped at his lab coat, but Marcus shimmied free, slipping out of the fabric. In the two seconds it took for Kayla to get to him, Marcus had already taken off running toward the stairwell.

"Hey!" Kayla yelled.

He stopped at the entry of the stairwell as if he'd forgotten she was there. "Come on!"

She ran to Marcus, petrified to pass so close to Dr. Carter, but the beastly man was distracted by the lab coat. He gnawed the white fabric, shaking it like a dog's chew toy as Kayla slipped into the stairwell with Marcus by her side.

EIGHTEEN

Melody

A shroud of gray mist draped the neighborhood, and a mound of dead bodies lay in the street with blood seeping out from under, soaking into the pavement. Candace was under that pile somewhere, and Melody hoped she was at least at peace.

She counted eleven of the infected who were upright and wandering the neighborhood. Some were walking in circles, while others lashed out at each other. An infected man in black slacks and a blue pinstriped necktie smacked into the wall of a house at the taper of the cul-de-sac. He backed up and walked into it again and again. Their mindless behavior was mesmerizing. The infected man in the loose necktie thumped into the siding of the house again. His attire—except for the blood and dirt—reminded her of Marcus, and that thought shook her from her trance.

Time to go.

She backed away from the window and went downstairs to John's kitchen sink to wash her blood-splattered arms. His house was minimalist in a way, but not intentionally. It was as if the life and character of the house were stripped away, nothing but empty nail heads where pictures used to hang.

As she dried her arms, she spotted an empty prescription bottle of Vicodin sitting on the shelf over his sink and wondered how long he had been without his pain meds. She could not justify dragging him out into town in pain, obligating him to her mission. With a potential skin infection in his leg, he wouldn't be at his best, and she couldn't let him die out there for her husband.

Besides, John would be fine on his own here. He used to be a damn SEAL.

She snuck to the back door, scouting a route to her house for her bag of supplies. She could get out of the neighborhood before John ever came down those steps. Melody peeked over her shoulder to be sure he was still upstairs, then cracked open the door to the backyard to see if it was clear. Guilt sat heavily upon her shoulders, but it was better for him this way.

"Where are you going?" John startled her from behind.

She tensed up and closed the door. "What are you, a fucking ninja? You weren't there a second ago."

"You're sneaking out?"

"I have to—"

"Eat," John said, holding up an open can of chicken noodle soup with a spoon stuck inside of it. "You need to eat."

Melody shook her head, sick to her stomach. "I need to go."

He pulled out a spoonful of cold condensed soup and shoveled it into his mouth, sucking up a noodle between his lips.

"Calories," he said. "Human body can't do shit without them. Believe me, I know. Weakness, exhaustion, hallucinations…all that shit that comes when you don't eat. We don't need any of that while we're out there."

She gave in and took the damn can of soup from his hands. Each bite slithered down her esophagus and splashed into her empty belly, making her want to vomit.

"I don't have much." He patted his green pack. "But I've got a Camelback of water and some gauze and stuff." John flung his rifle over his back and strapped his knife to his hip. "We should get you a better weapon."

"I want this." She cradled her bat in her hands.

He pulled another knife from the side pocket of his bag and slid it out of the sheath to show Melody.

"Carry this too, just in case."

The blade scraped the inside of the poly-vinyl sheath in a pitch that triggered Melody's memory of Candace's screams. John knelt in front of Melody to secure the seven-inch blade and its sheath to her belt loop on her right hip. She closed her eyes, trying to block out the reverberation of the haunting screams. The ghostly sound of their hands pounding on the door, the gunfire, the moans... The song played in her head.

She worried about what would happen to John out there. She worried for the town and wondered how many people had died. Her thoughts spiraled outward, and her heart hurt for the potentially millions of people who had been infected. Pressure built within her skull from the overwhelming stress.

One step at a time.

One problem at a time.

It was how she survived when she was a kid, and it was how she planned to survive this. She inhaled and exhaled, one breath at a time, and focused on starting with helping one person—Marcus.

"Do you have a dog?" John blurted.

Melody's mind drifted back to the room she stood in.

"A cat, maybe?" he asked, folding his arms across his chest. His questions helped Melody drown out the memory of Candace's screams.

He wore a plain brown tee that hung over the waist of his cargo shorts, which covered his knee where the prosthesis connected to his leg. A holster on his hip held a pistol.

"No," Melody said, appreciative of his attempt to snap her out of the petrifying trance she'd been trapped within. "Marcus was allergic... I mean, Marcus *is* allergic."

"How tragic—a veterinarian without pets." John peeked out the window toward her house. An infected woman lay on Melody's porch, but she couldn't tell if she was dead or sleeping.

"Do *you* have pets?" Melody asked.

"I had a cat, but Jackie—my ex—took her along with everything else."

She nodded, looking around his empty home, and realized that she needed to stop having small talk. Melody rubbed her fingers on her forehead as if she could scrub off the emotional turmoil that clouded her thoughts.

"You don't have to do this," she said. "You don't have to come with me."

John's brow furrowed.

"It's a few miles away, and I plan to be moving fast. Running the whole way."

"I can run."

Melody huffed. Maybe being a little more abrupt would put him off. Maybe, if John was simply interested in fucking her—or whatever he might have in mind—she could make it clear that she wasn't interested. "Are you going to slow me down?"

John smiled and ran his fingers through his short hair. "You know, if you said this shit to me a year ago—back when I was all angry about this stupid leg—I would've been pissed. Luckily, I'm not a spiteful asshole anymore."

For a moment, she felt guilty for saying it, but she kept up her tough façade. "So, this is you *not* being a spiteful asshole? I couldn't tell."

"You haven't been a peach to be around either, *sweetheart.*"

"Look, I don't need to drag anyone down with me while I go—"

"I get it," he interrupted. "But what am I supposed to do? Let you go alone?"

"Yes!" She raised her voice, but quieted herself so the infected wouldn't hear her through the walls. "Yes. I am perfectly capable."

"I'm sure you are a regular Chuck Norris," he laughed. "I've seen you in action. But if you go alone, then you'll be leaving *me* here alone. What the hell am I going to do if you leave?"

She couldn't tell if he was being sincere or patronizing.

"Well, what are you going to do if—"

"Don't argue with me, Miss Chuck Norris. I am leaving, too. Whether it's with you or not. We may as well go together and have each other's backs."

John had checked the neighborhood from a vantage point upstairs. Clusters of infected roamed Elpis Court, but the fenced backyards were mostly clear, so they went out the back door and climbed over the fence into Melody's yard.

She hurried into the house, grabbed her backpack of supplies that she had packed the day before, and changed into a fresh set of clothes—jeans and a tee shirt. Her red "Save the Tatas" tee was purchased at a fundraiser for breast cancer back when her mom had fought the battle. It was the first one she grabbed, and somehow it felt wrong picking a different one once it was in her hands.

She hoisted her pack on her back, and her heart was already wailing against her chest in preparation for their journey.

"Nice shirt," John said as she came down the stairs. "Ready to go find your husband?"

She nodded, but it was a lie. She was not ready for any of this.

NINETEEN

Kayla

Pitch black and silent, with the exception of Kayla's pulse and the pounding of their feet on the steps, she navigated the stairwell, keeping a hand on Marcus.

They spilled out of the stairwell door into the large open space of the lobby, panting. The sprawling lobby allowed overcast light to spill through large windows. The air—though it was still tinged with the aroma of dead bodies—smelled fresher on the first floor.

"My keys were in that coat." Marcus paced before the lobby doors.

"That's okay. Starting a car will only get their attention, anyway."

Marcus's eyes drifted to her bare feet, but he didn't say a word.

She looked around the room as if to find a pair of size-sixes laying around, but there was nothing. "I need shoes."

"I'm not going back up there," he said. "Not for shoes or keys."

The prickle in his voice took her aback. "I don't expect you to. My shoes were heels. I kicked them off intentionally."

Marcus had explained that it was a couple of miles to the high school from the lab by cutting across town, but now they didn't have the keys to the car.

He placed his hands on her arms, caressing her skin and leaning in close to comfort her. "We don't know how bad it is out there. I should go check out the road to the quarantine zone and then—"

"No!" She grabbed his arms, squeezing his biceps and fiercely staring into his eyes.

"I can't risk taking you out there. You could get hurt."

"I'm not a liability. I'm more capable than people give me credit for."

"I'm sure you are, but—"

"I'll get shoes!" She ran to the lobby windows to scan the area outside. A thick fog obscured the view, but she could spot a couple of dead bodies in the parking lot.

"There. I'll get shoes from one of them," she said.

The thought of her prying shoes from a corpse made her sick to her stomach, but she'd do whatever she had to do.

"Fine," Marcus said. "But I don't think this is a good idea."

With no signs of the infected in sight, he pushed open the glass door and stepped outside. The late morning sky was clouded over, and a dense fog released its embrace from the earth. Kayla latched onto Marcus's arm as they walked into the vacant parking lot, inspecting their surroundings.

Marcus checked the few cars that were left behind in the lot, but none had keys. "Looks like we're walking."

Windows were shattered, and burn marks scarred the sides of brick buildings along Horace Ave.

Kayla headed with caution toward a face-down body in the parking lot. She leaned down over the feet of the deceased man, wearing a blood-stained yellow polo shirt and jeans. His shoes appeared too sizable for her tiny feet, but before she had a moment to figure out whether or not they would work, an infected man walked into view from farther down Horace Avenue. His body was silhouetted in the fog as he circled the street by the bus stop on the corner.

"Damn." Marcus ducked beside her. "We gotta go." He pointed toward the man as dozens of others began to appear in the distant fog.

"Let's go!" Marcus grabbed her by her arm before she could get the shoes off the man's body and yanked her in the direction of the old railroad tracks that laid perpendicular to the dead-end street.

As he pulled her along, the stabbing sensation of a million tiny swords shot up from the ground and into the soles of her feet. Kayla stifled a squeal and stopped, but Marcus released her arm and continued forward. In their sudden scramble to get away, Marcus had dragged her through a patch of shattered glass.

He gained at least thirty yards on her before he realized she had fallen behind.

She tried to brush away the shards of glass with her hands, but had to sit down to pluck some of the larger shards from her feet. Blood oozed from the stinging wounds and her eyes flooded with tears, but she got up and tried to catch up with Marcus.

Her parents never believed she could handle life without them. As supportive as they were of her being bi, they had no faith that she could be independent. Her friends thought she was too dumb to study biology. Her boyfriends and girlfriends of the past said she was too flirty to be a serious partner. Too much baby fat for modeling, too little charisma for sales, too this, too that, and never good enough. But she'd always believed in herself.

Maybe they were all right. Despite her drive, she always seemed to fall short of her own goals, always tripped over something, fell in love too hard, crashed and burned too many times. And her friends and family were always standing by to announce "I told you so."

What they didn't understand was that with every failure, she learned.

She couldn't let Marcus think poorly of her as well. She would prove to him that she was capable of surviving.

Learn your lesson, girl! She rolled her eyes at herself.

What Marcus thought didn't matter. Even if he was the last man on earth. She would prove to *herself* that she was capable.

Remnant glass in the balls of her feet fired jolts of pain with each step, so she walked on the sides of her feet, twisting her ankles in a way that was sure to do damage after a while.

Marcus

Marcus hoped she'd work it out on her own and catch up, but she was moving too slowly.

"Son of a bitch."

He ran back to her and helped her brush away more glass from her soles.

"I'm sorry," he said. "I thought they were coming. I didn't even notice the glass. Are you good, Hon?"

"Where are we going?" Kayla whimpered as they walked past the dead-end sign. "I thought we had to go through town."

"The tracks. We can bypass the streets and go around. It's not much longer, and there won't be anyone there, I don't think."

Kayla released Marcus's hand and shuffled herself on the sides of her feet over to a dead body. The half-naked dead man in grey briefs and white crew socks had no shoes to offer, but Marcus helped her peel the socks from his body—at least it was something.

As they were kneeling over the body, a scrawny brown dog trotted in their direction.

"Let's go," Marcus said with the damp socks in his hands, eyeing the dog.

The floppy-eared dog with a smooshed snout and short, muddied fur approached them. He wasn't huge, but he was big enough to do some damage. His wide jaws looked like the kind that would latch onto prey and shake until it was dead. Kayla stood behind Marcus as the dog lowered his head and growled. Marcus took a step forward.

"Do they get infected too?" Kayla whispered.

"Don't know," he said. Melody had warned him about animals potentially contracting this disease. He knew now that she was right, but there was part of him that hated admitting that. When they'd spoken on the phone for the last time, Melody had told him about a cat showing the same neurologic symptoms. Melody was frantic with him that day, saying the disease could be in Fair Haven, but Marcus figured she was overreacting. Her teenage years did a number on her. It had made her paranoid and untrusting, even after all these years. How was he supposed to know?

Marcus picked up a brick. The dog growled again, and Marcus hurled the brick toward it.

Kayla gasped as the brick hit the pavement near the dog's feet. It scrambled away into the fog.

The tracks were not the most circuitous route to the high school, but it was likely less littered with the infected due to the high fences. Marcus used to take walks with Melody along those tracks when they were in their senior year of high school. She would show him all the places that were safe to sleep if one were to find oneself homeless. He laughed at the memory of suffering through the long, boring walks. But it was necessary foreplay back then if he wanted to see any sexy action with her on Make-Out Hill.

Marcus and Kayla made it to the chain link fence along the tracks and squeezed through the gate with ease. The tracks were overgrown with weeds and nestled up against the sparse woods on the outside of town.

Beyond those woods was the highway, which, according to the last news reports, was littered with abandoned cars and chaotic with the infected. A fence ran along the highway and kept most of the infected on the other side of it, so Marcus assumed their passage along the tracks was likely to be clear. Marcus stood beside Kayla and stared down the abandoned tracks at the long, gray road ahead.

"Sit down," he told her.

He took Kayla's feet in his hands and meticulously plucked out the shards of remaining glass, then slid the corpse's baggy crew socks onto her feet.

She looked to him with hopeful green eyes, like she would fuck him right then and there if he made a move.

"It's about four miles to the school this way," he said. "The tracks go around the perimeter of town. There are parts where it runs close to town, and other parts where it runs through mostly woods or shrubbery. Maybe we'll find some shoes on the way, but for now, socks will have to do. I'd give you mine, but size twelve is a bit much for your tiny feet. They'd just slow you down as you tried to keep them on."

Kayla stood and put her hands on her hips. The crew socks were pulled up high around her calves as she stood in knee-high weeds. "I can do this."

Marcus watched her from behind as she moved away from him, beginning her trek. Kayla's tight skirt shifted up as she high-stepped through the weeds with those ridiculous socks on.

She flinched and jumped at every sound they heard. She was adorable and sexy, and made him feel like a real man, unlike Melody, who was always questioning his reasoning.

He wondered if Melody was still alive and if she would be at the quarantine camp when they arrived. If so, he couldn't show up with this redhead on his arm.

His thoughts wandered to the possibility that she may not have even survived the outbreak. Life would be easier to deal with if that were the case. He became sickened with guilt over that thought and shook the terrible idea out of his head.

Whether his wife was at the quarantine camp or not didn't matter. Kayla would slow him down either way. She would need constant supervision and protection, and that could get him killed. He would have to find a way to ditch this poor girl.

TWENTY

Melody

The sleeping infected woman on Melody's porch had thrashed awake. The man in the necktie, who had been repeatedly thumping against the side of the house, broke from his trance and approached her to investigate.

The necktie man lunged, and the two infected began to fight on Melody's porch. She backed away from the window as they hurtled toward her and crashed through the glass.

As the large woman's torso hung inside the house, reaching for them, John and Melody darted out the back of the house and climbed the fence into the next yard.

A light drizzle fell from the sky, and the top of Melody's house began to disappear from her view as she moved from yard to yard. As they climbed the fences between homes, Melody caught sight of the roaming infected in the street. The pavement around the pile of dead bodies in the center of the cul-de-sac was blackened with blood.

Burnt bones laid scattered across the Nickersons' tall grass. The blackened skeletons each lay in a pile of thick, wet ash. Her heart ached, and her stomach twisted. After what happened with Candace, she already wanted to collapse into a ball and give up, but she could not. She pushed forward, trying not to look at the bodies, and trying like hell to stay focused on surviving. There was no time for emotion now. Bottle it up now, let it burst later. She just had to concentrate on getting to Marcus.

The drizzling rain dampened their clothes early in their trip while they crossed the elementary school property. Paul, the construction guy whom Melody kicked off the school roof the night before, pulled his body through the tall grass, allowing his legs to drag behind him.

The field by the school was littered with the infected—at least forty of them—and they began to follow John and Melody, but they made it to the fence line before the infected were able to close in. Melody threw her baseball bat over and began scaling the eight-foot-tall chain link fence. She looked down to John to be sure he could make the climb, but he kept up without a problem. They climbed over and then rushed into the woods beyond the tree line on the opposite side of the tracks, out of sight. The infected lost interest and wandered off.

"That was easy enough," John said.

Melody, riddled with fear, got control of her trembling body. "Yeah. Easy."

John

Melody was a brisk runner, and John kept up behind her with his prosthesis whispering on each step. His already irritated skin screamed for relief, but he didn't ask her to slow down. He knew how important it was to her that she get to her husband as quickly as possible…if the dude was even still alive.

He remembered meeting his new neighbor months ago when they had first moved in. Marcus had a way about him—something he didn't like but couldn't put his finger on. The guy had looked at John like he was an enemy.

John wondered what kind of husband he was to Melody. As far as John was concerned, it was pretty dumb of this Marcus guy to keep her from getting a dog because of allergies.

Melody's wad of messy curls bounced back and forth in a ponytail as she ran.

Marcus… Lucky son of a bitch.

Hell—maybe John was the enemy now, considering he was having inappropriate thoughts about Marcus's wife. But Marcus should have fought his way back to Melody by now, so he was either dead or he took off without her.

They kept a steady pace for well over a mile without incident before John spoke up from behind her.

"So, you run a lot?"

She slowed down and let him catch up.

"I'm sorry." Melody slowed to a stop as he shook out his good leg and bent over to adjust his prosthetic.

"Are you okay?"

"I'm good." He shrugged through the excruciating pain.

She steadied her panting breaths. "I don't run as much as I used to."

"You don't run much anymore. Don't look at the stars as much either. You don't get to have pets," John said. "What do you have time for?"

"Work," Melody said. "You have to work to pay the bills. Work to survive. It always comes down to simply surviving, doesn't it?"

A rumble of thunder in the distance sent a shiver of warning through John as they began walking again.

"It's more than just survival," he said.

John tugged her sleeve and picked up the pace to a steady jog again. Sprinkles turned to a steady rain, soaking their clothes as they went.

They made it another mile before Melody's pace began to slow. She paused with her hands on her hips, trying to muster the endurance to keep going.

"I shouldn't be tired yet," she said.

"Calories equal energy, and we're lacking both."

John offered some beef jerky, and they fueled up before returning to their pace.

They were fortunate to have traveled those two miles without encountering any of the infected, but on the final mile to the lab, they spotted three sauntering silhouettes on the tracks.

John knelt to aim with his rifle, but feared he would attract more by firing. The clouds released a heavy downpour, and a crack of lightning split the sky. Melody ducked and flinched. John could tell that she needed a break, but she'd never admit that. Neither would he. Couple of stubborn idiots, the pair of them.

"Let's go around them," John said.

Through the dense trees, tiny splotches of colors were visible— abandoned vehicles on the highway over a hundred yards away. Distant bodies made sluggish movements around the cars.

They were careful to stay tucked deep enough in the woods to go unseen by the infected on the highway and by the few infected on the tracks. The pines created a canopy overhead, protecting them from the heavy rainfall, while the sound of the downpour concealed the sounds of their footsteps.

The thunder and lightning persisted. John's prosthetic rubbed against the raw, irritated flesh below his knee. Each step sent the prosthetic blade sinking into the muddy ground and shocks of burning pain into his leg, but he was determined to keep up with Melody. There was too much at stake not to.

Melody

A shrieking crack of thunder snapped overhead and careened the path of the infected from the tracks into the woods. Three bodies stumbled between the trees.

"Shit," she whispered.

Physical exhaustion had taken over, but she and John continued to run through the woods while the infected caught sight and pursued them. A tall, thin man with curly hair, a stout apple-shaped woman, and a man in ceil blue scrubs hurried their pace behind John and Melody.

She wanted to rest for a while and knew if she could slip out of sight for a moment, she could hide. Take a moment to catch her breath. Melody knew it was coming up. The place she could go and forget about how hard life was. She recalled the broken-down shell of a Cadillac. She'd spent the night there during a storm before, and she'd visited it from time to time. As she and John climbed over the massive fallen pine that sank into the earth, she peered through the woods ahead to find it.

It appeared like a lifeline, calling for her to come and hide again. It was being absorbed by the surrounding earth, with ivy wrapping it within its embrace.

"Here!" She sprinted toward it and ducked around the shrubbery by the vehicle. Once she was clear of their line of sight, she dove into the musty chassis and waited for John. The floor of the car had been eaten by the earth, and Melody sat on the ground with a dome of jagged rusty metal over her head.

"What are you doing?" he asked from outside the car, hiding behind the vines and shrub growth.

Melody closed her eyes, panting, more terrified than she had ever been for her life. She hoped the danger would pass over her like the storm had over ten years ago.

"I need a minute."

"We don't have a minute." John took Melody's hand.

Her eyes popped open to reality.

"We can't hide here," John said. "They're coming."

Melody didn't care if they were coming… At least, she tried to convince herself of that. She didn't want to fight, or run, or hide, and for a moment wasn't sure if she wanted to keep living.

It felt like her only purpose for existence at that point was to save Marcus, and if she was brutally honest with herself, she didn't know if he was worth it.

She didn't know if her own life was worth it.

John's voice lowered, and he climbed halfway into the chassis with her.

"We're faster than them, but we have to go." He looked back toward the incoming infected that closed in twenty feet away. "Now."

Melody—with the whining defeat of a toddler—smacked her hand to the ground and began to climb out of the car.

The tall man with curly hair and the apple-shaped woman fought one another at the front of the car, but the man in scrubs was not in sight.

As Melody poked her head out of the vehicle, ready to make her escape with John, the man in scrubs had clawed inside the opposite side of the chassis and grabbed Melody's ankle. She tried to pull herself free, but his grip was strong. She unsheathed her knife and twisted her body enough so she could swing at the man's face, but her slashes to his skin did not deter him. Flesh tore open. Blood spilled. Hot, putrid breath filled the chassis. She turned her head and kept her mouth tight so as not to allow any of his saliva to spray as she slashed.

John grabbed her arm with one hand and reached for his pistol with the other. The man in scrubs climbed up her legs, jaw hung open, ready to bite.

Her backpack snagged on the sharp edges of the car as she climbed out. His teeth snagged onto the lower end of the backpack while John yanked Melody free. The metal ripped open her pack along the outside pocket, and the pale orchid-colored envelope dropped into the mud.

"Cover your ears," John shouted with his pistol beside her head.

The man chewed on Melody's pack, and she put her hands over her ears. John fired his 9mm and stopped the infected with a bullet to his forehead.

The other two nearby stopped fighting with each other, attention now drawn to the gunfire.

Despite Melody's attempt to protect her hearing, the bang of the pistol rang in her ear.

John fumbled the straps of Melody's pack down her arms and helped her shimmy out. There was no time to free the pack from the entanglement of the man's deadly clutches, because the other two were staggering toward them.

"Leave the pack. Let's go!" John's muffled voice urged her through the high-pitched hum in her ear.

Melody snagged her dad's envelope from the ground and ran alongside him, shaking her head in an attempt to free her ear from the ringing.

They sprinted through the woods and back out to the tracks, leaving the other infected far behind. Melody's body surged with adrenaline, and she powered forward faster than her energy levels should allow. She left her pack behind. Her food, her antibiotics, the medical supplies, her underwear... everything.

John was right beside her. She looked back frequently to be sure they were nowhere in sight, but the infected were not able to run as fast without falling over.

She slowed down and looked to the sky as the rain continued to pummel her head. She wished it would wash her away.

"I would've been fine there," she said, but she knew otherwise.

He looked at her with an odd concern—the way Marcus' parents looked at her on that first night she stayed at his house—like she was a charity case.

"I freaked out," she said, digging a finger in her ear as if it could free her from the ringing. "It won't happen again."

John sighed. "It's okay... We're okay."

But she didn't believe him.

TWENTY ONE

Marcus

Progress was slow as Marcus and Kayla navigated the railroad tracks. Concealed within the tall weeds and rocky bed were more broken glass and sharp rocks. Kayla's bloodied feet took further beating and slowed Marcus down.

With every passing minute, he silently schemed a plan in which he would arrive at the quarantine camp without her. He could lag behind, then sneak into the woods and leave her, but he was certain that she would see him running off. He passed by an opening in the fence between two brick buildings where he could slip through and duck behind the buildings, but when it came right down to it, he couldn't bring himself to leave her out there alone.

After about a mile of travel, a rumble of thunder rolled across the dark clouds, and rain droplets began to fall from the sky. Kayla's head dropped, defeat in her eyes, and Marcus tried to encourage her to keep pushing forward.

The rain turned to a steady downpour as they crossed over a steel rail bridge. Lightning lit up the sky, coupled with an ear-piercing crack. Kayla ducked and hurried to the other end of the bridge to find cover.

She sought out a dry patch of gravel beneath the bridge where Marcus joined her to wait out the storm.

Torrential rain plummeted to the earth for over an hour while they sat beside each other. The creek water rushed past them faster and faster, threatening to flood them out.

Several infected could be seen over the bank on the other side of the fence, but they were not aware of Marcus and Kayla's hiding spot. Marcus leaned back and allowed Kayla to rest her head against his chest. Her soaking wet hair fell across his shirt, and he caressed her head with a gentle hand.

"That's a cop, isn't it?" Kayla said, looking toward two of the infected beyond the bank.

"I think so." The heavy rain made it difficult to see. The man in the dark uniform bumped into the railing of a loading dock over and over again.

Kayla sighed. "Yikes. We don't have guns, and we managed to stay alive."

"Maybe he hesitated. You hesitate, you die."

"It makes it even scarier, doesn't it? To know that even someone with professional training didn't make it."

Marcus nodded. "My grandfather was a cop. He used to take me up to the lake for shooting practice, but he stopped letting me shoot when I was about twelve."

"Why?"

"I found an old metal ammunition box he had from his days in the Marines. I thought it looked cool, so I opened it and found a pistol. It was right there on top of all his military and cop stuff. So, I picked it up. I was just looking at it. Wasn't even loaded. But he didn't trust me not to play with it. Sad, when you can't trust your own family."

"Well, if it means anything, *I* trust you." She stretched and yawned, lying against his chest, and Marcus wasn't sure how to break it to her that she'd have to go solo soon. They could've been at the quarantine camp by now if it weren't for this storm and Kayla's damn feet.

The rain continued, and her head became heavier against his chest. The hush of the falling rain lulled her to sleep, and Marcus's opportunity to slip away presented itself.

TWENTY TWO

Melody

"That old car in the woods… I used to climb onto the roof when I was a kid. I played there, and then for a short time, I lived in it. It used to be my place. My safe place. I thought we could hide…"

There was no excuse, and she couldn't find the words to explain why she crawled inside, but she didn't need to, because John seemed to understand.

They approached a gated portion of the fence along Horace Avenue while the rain continued to dump on them.

"I had a place like that," he said. "But as an adult. It was a small vacation house in a little hamlet in upstate New York. Dark skies. Great observing."

She stood with fingers curled through the fence gate at the dead end of Horace Ave. There were four dead bodies face down on the pavement between the tracks and the charred, blackened remains of a gas station. Smoldering remnants of the explosion had been snuffed out by heavy rain. The top two floors of Marcus's building were visible behind it, appearing to be undamaged.

Melody sighed with relief.

"Told you it was probably a gas station." John smirked.

Confusing feelings of hope and dread overwhelmed her, and she found herself stalling with conversation. "So, what happened to your little place in

New York?"

"After this happened," he gestured to his leg, "Jackie talked me into selling it and moving here."

"Sounds familiar," Melody said.

"She claimed it was so I could be around more people, that it'd be good for my PTSD or some bullshit, but it wasn't. What she really wanted was to live near some guy out in Madison that she had an online thing with."

"You gave up your place for her, and she took everything?"

"Yep. And to top it all off, she claimed I had psychological issues that she couldn't handle anymore. I don't know... Maybe I did. I'm certainly not the same person she married, but I wasn't some axe-wielding psychopath either. She got the money from the sale of that house in New York. She got almost all our stuff and even took Norris."

"Norris?"

"My cat."

"Like Chuck Norris?"

He nodded.

"I'm sorry."

John shrugged. "I've been wondering how she's doing through all this. If she made it or if..."

"Your ex or your cat?" Melody shot him a devilish grin.

John laughed. "Mostly the cat." He manipulated his prosthetic leg to give his sore flesh some relief.

"How's it feeling?"

He shook his head. "That's not a *now*-problem." He gestured toward the building. "How many people worked in there?"

"I don't know. But the day Marcus went into work, a lot of them stayed home because of what was happening. He said that he and Greg Carter were staying, but I don't know about anyone else."

The street was barren. Vacant buildings and cars lined the path to the lab, and the blood stains from the bodies washed away with the heavy rain. Melody's heart was already pounding within her chest from running, but it intensified as she looked through the downpour toward the lab.

They slinked through the creaking gate and crept down Horace Ave.

A parking lot stood between Melody and his building. Marcus's car was one of the few left in the lot. Seeing it conjured both fear and hope.

The eerie emptiness put her on guard as she moved across the lot to the front doors. She pressed her forehead to the window and cupped her hands around her eyes to see into an empty lobby.

They left the pounding of the rain behind them and moved inside, dripping puddles onto the floor. The tiles were smeared with dried, bloodied footprints, but there were no people. The desire to scream out for Marcus was quelled by rationality. She had to search the building in silence. As their shoes squeaked across the floor, John rectified the position of his rifle across his back, and unhooked the strap on his pistol holster. He readied his knife in his hand.

"He works upstairs," she said.

"Let's sweep the whole building," John said. "We'll start with these hallways down here, then head up the stairwell."

They worked their way through the empty first-floor halls with their flashlights, but found no one who was still alive.

John opened the heavy door to the stairwell and shone his flashlight inside and up the stairs. He closed the door.

"What's wrong?" she asked.

He contemplated the door for a moment and sighed. "It's really dark in there."

The corner of her lip twitched into half a smile. "Is the Navy SEAL afraid of the dark?"

He shot her a playful glare. "Only when there are monsters in it. Plus, I know you scare easily, and I have to warn you that there are no cars in this stairwell for you to hide in…"

"Hey!" She gave him a sour face.

He smirked, then readied his pistol and opened the door.

"Hello." His voice echoed off cinderblock walls, which triggered the imagined sound of footfalls stampeding toward them, but Melody controlled her fears, and the false noises ended. It was silent.

"Ladies first?" John said, gesturing for her to go. Melody stepped into the stairwell, and he held out his arm. "I was kidding."

John controlled the closing door as it clicked shut behind them, then led the way. Climbing the black stairwell with nothing but a flashlight beam to guide them brought a new level of fear. Melody held her breath and stayed close to John for the seemingly endless ascent. Each of their footsteps was a sound and a vibration for the infected to follow. But no one came hurtling down the steps toward them.

Once they were on the second floor, the stench of death became stronger. They worked through a maze of cubicles, finding four dead bodies along the way. Their faces looked familiar, but Melody didn't know most of the people with whom Marcus worked. With each corpse that she approached, her heart thumped a little harder in anticipation of finding him.

By the time they made it to the third floor—Marcus's floor—hope slipped further from her. They entered the open office area with the floor-to-ceiling windows, and anxiety took hold.

A white lab coat laid crumpled on the floor ahead, and Melody approached it with trepidation. It was torn and smeared with blood. She held her breath as she knelt to pick it up with trembling hands. The embroidered name on the pocket read, Dr. Hill.

The floor shifted beneath her, and reality spiraled. His lab was down the hall, mere steps away. She held onto the coat and sprang up, dashing down the pitch black hall, shining a beam of light in search of him.

"Marcus?"

"Damn it," John cried out behind her.

The hallway reeked of necrosis as she jogged with her bat on her shoulder. This time, she wasn't freaking out—she was prepared to fight, fully aware of her surroundings and ready to pummel skulls.

She found the door to the lab and slowly cracked it open as John rushed up behind her.

"Marcus?" she whispered and shone her flashlight into the blackness of the lab, sweeping the light across the counters and microscopes. There was no response.

John placed his hand on her shoulder to hold her back from entering, but she pulled away.

She stormed through the lab, searching for him and calling out his name. Her white column of light shone on every wall and every corner. The vending machine was busted open, and candy wrappers overflowed the wastebasket. He had been there for a while. A sign of a struggle—the microscope was busted on the floor.

In an instant, she imagined all the scenarios that could have led up to him being attacked, wondering if he had fled to the roof for safety.

Melody rushed back toward the lab entrance and tripped over a rolling chair in the middle of the room. She regained her footing, but John had grabbed her. He held her by the arms while she struggled to get away. Heavy, panicked breaths escaped her.

"I have to find—"

"I know," John interrupted with a calm voice, "but you're losing your shit."

Her own violent breaths muffled his words, but she understood what he'd said. John was right, and she hated that. She needed to calm down. This kind of frantic behavior would get them killed. John's steady flashlight beam shone beyond her as he watched for intruders while she regained her senses.

"I'm good," she said, nauseated but ready to move on.

John kept his stance in front of the lab door.

"This is as calm as I'm going to get," she said as John inspected her face with his flashlight to be sure.

"You can't just run off on your own. Like I said, you ain't Chuck Norris. We do this together. *Communicate.*"

John opened the door, aimed his flashlight into the hallway, and a large body lunged at him out of the darkness. The man in the lab coat had necrotic skin around his collarbone. Melody recognized him as Dr. Greg Carter. He grabbed at John, growling as he attempted to bite.

John gripped him by the throat and shoved the beast of a man against the wall in one swift, methodical movement. Melody held her flashlight on Dr. Carter as John stabbed his knife into his chest.

Dr. Carter was unfazed. He chomped his teeth at John, despite having a knife in his heart. John kept him pressed against the wall, then pulled his 9mm to blast a hole into the side of Dr. Carter's head. The tall man was instantly immobilized and dropped to the floor.

"Did you see that?" John asked, pulling his blade from the man's chest. "Right in the heart. It didn't even slow him down."

They made their way through dark rooms, up to the fourth floor, and all the way to the roof, but found no sign of Marcus or anyone else. The four-story building was clear.

Melody sat against the floor-to-ceiling window in the corner office on the top floor, manipulating the fabric of the torn, bloody white coat between her fingers. A long, candy-apple red strand of hair was attached to the coat, and she pulled it away.

She searched the pockets and pulled out his car keys. His wedding band fell to the floor. She snatched it up and stuffed it in her front jeans pocket, wondering who the red hair belonged to. It was not the first time that Melody questioned his fidelity, but this time she didn't care enough to let it bother her.

She held the coat up to her nose in an unlikely hound-dog attempt to catch a scent of some woman, but she could only smell the necrotic odor left behind from the infected. She dropped it to the floor, brushed off her knees, and stood up to look out the window.

"I knew that guy back there," Melody said about Dr. Carter. "I only met him once, but he seemed like a good guy."

She'd met him at the company picnic over the summer. Dr. Carter ran around with the children in a water gun fight while his wife confided in her that they were trying for a little one of their own.

"What if it isn't his blood? What if he survived and went to that quarantine camp?" she said.

John crossed his arms, ready to protest.

"I know," she interrupted before he could speak, "It's not likely that I'll find him."

John hung his head with obvious discontent.

"I have to try." She was desperate.

"Is there a reason your husband wouldn't be wearing his ring?"

"He has to scrub before handling certain materials sometimes. He takes his ring off occasionally. That's not unusual. What are you getting at?"

John sighed. "That quarantine camp might not even be there anymore."

"I know."

"We couldn't see beyond the trees on the roof to get a look at it from here, and based on what we saw last night—no lights coming from that direction, it's likely gone, or overrun." John's words were sharp and to the point.

"I know," she snapped.

"If he's alive, do you think he would've gone there?"

"Maybe."

"Without coming to get you first?"

His words sliced through her, but he had a point. Marcus was either dead or he had left her behind. All of the potential things that could have happened to him whizzed through her mind.

"He may not have had a choice," she tried to make excuses. "He could've succeeded with the vaccine and taken it to the quarantine zone." But she didn't believe that was the case.

John turned from her to look out the window. "We should get out of here," he said. "We need to go somewhere more remote...maybe the mountains."

"I'm not an idiot," she whispered.

"I don't think that you—"

"I know we shouldn't be running around town in search of someone that is probably not alive. I know that we should get the hell out of here, but I won't be able to live with myself if I give up on him."

"Certainly seems like he gave up on *you*."

"Then that's on *him*, but *I* can't do that."

"Are you fucking serious?" John put his hands on his head and paced.

"I have to try," she said.

"You did try."

"You know what? You should go on. I'll stay in town and look for him. We can meet up with you somewhere later. You mentioned the mountains, and I sort of have a place up there."

"That's not happening. I'm not leaving you here."

"After we find out what happened to Marcus, we can take a boat," Melody said.

"There's a good chance that all the boats around here have been taken out of the water for the winter, and those who had boats still in the water are probably already gone," John said. "If we stumble upon a boat in the water, that'd be great, but I'm not going searching for one. How far do you think our neighbors made it towing that Carolina skiff? They couldn't get around the corner without that lady getting her throat ripped out."

"Almost everyone pulled in their boats a few weeks ago to winterize. But I know for a fact that Marcus's parents did not. They were certain we'd have a warm spell, so they left the boat in the water."

"Someone could've taken it by now. Hell, Marcus could've taken it."

"He wouldn't do that," she said, unsure if that was true.

Nervous and hopeful, she grabbed a pen and notepad from the desk to draw another crude map of Fair Haven.

"To get to the lake from here, we would have to either go straight through town—which is no good for obvious reasons—or we could continue to follow the tracks to the outside of town and cut through Gilmore's fields."

She spoke fast, without giving him a moment to argue. "These tracks lead right to the high school."

Her eyes met with John's to gauge his response—he appeared leery of her plan, but she continued talking. "We can check out the quarantine area from afar…" Melody drew a U-shaped bump on her map. "…from Make-out Hill. We hop off the tracks just before the school and climb the hill to—"

"Make-out Hill?"

"Mariner's Hill to most people. If the quarantine zone looks bad from up there, we can move on, cut through Gilmore's land toward the marina—it's only about a mile or so from there—and hope the boat, or any boat, is still there. Then, we can boat to the northwestern-most point of the lake up near the mountains. Like I said, I have a place up there."

John looked up from the map to make eye contact. They were both hunched over, and their faces were close enough to smell the rain on each other's skin.

"You were serious? You have a house up there?" His voice was skeptical.

"It's a cabin way up in the mountains—very secluded. It should be safe. It was my grandfather's, and then my dad's…"

"Why didn't you say anything about it before?"

"I couldn't trust you."

"And you do now?"

"Not really, but what the hell do I have to lose?"

John smiled and fist-bumped her shoulder. Melody knew that he had no interest in checking out the death camp that authorities were calling a quarantine zone, but he at least understood why she needed to swing by before moving on.

She stood up before the window, soaking wet, triumphant in her negotiation with John, but the glass reflected a broken woman staring back at her, barely holding the pieces together.

Marcus was likely gone for good, but until she checked the quarantine zone to be sure, until she saw a body, she was not ready to grieve.

John, in an attempt to comfort her, placed his arm around her back and held her from the side.

Awkwardly giving in to the intimacy, she leaned into him and allowed the side of her face to rest against his strong shoulder. Melody was never one to hug, but that partial embrace was a powerful one—the true embrace of a friend who had her back.

"I'm okay," she insisted, stepping away from John. "Don't get all sentimental."

John grunted. "I don't do sentimental." He stared into her with smiling eyes, and she knew he was kidding.

Despite the levity, those steel blue eyes pierced through her, and that was all it took. She thought she had gotten over her crush on John, but there she stood with her entire body screaming for his attention. Her sudden attraction to him again shocked her, and she imagined throwing all of her reservations to the wind and charging at him with a kiss, but she couldn't.

In a few miles, maybe she would know for certain what became of Marcus. She didn't know what would happen between John and her, but there was one thing she was certain about. If she found Marcus alive, he'd have some fucking explaining to do.

TWENTY THREE

John

John was eager to get out of that dreadful building and move on. Wet clothes clung to his body as he stood outside the building with Melody. Twenty minutes sitting in that fourth-floor office was not enough time to recuperate, but they had to get going. The rainfall eased up, and a feeling of warning settled upon him. There was nobody in sight except for the dead bodies lying in the street.

"Ready to move, Chuck?" he asked Melody, whose lip twitched in a half-assed attempt to smile at the nickname he'd given her.

She really was the toughest woman he'd ever met.

A brown boxer dog trotted along the edge of the parking lot, coated in filth. Toenail clicks cut through the sound of the drizzling rain. Its small floppy ears perked up at the sight of John and Melody as they crossed the lot toward the tracks.

As the boxer followed, John watched its approach, seeking any sign of infection. Melody knelt as the pathetic, emaciated dog got closer. His tail nub wiggled excitedly, while he lowered his head and pinned his ears back nervously.

"Leave it," he told Melody.

She glared at him, indicating that she was going to do whatever the fuck she wanted.

"Hungry?" Melody whispered as the dog gyrated with happiness beside her. "Come on."

She patted her leg for the dog to follow, and he was quick to obey.

John squeezed through the gate to the tracks and knelt to pull some jerky out of his backpack, while Melody petted the dog along his protruding spine. He wiggled, dancing in circles and licking at Melody's hand as she loved on him.

Melody broke her attention from the dog to look up at John. "You've been limping. Don't think I haven't noticed."

"Don't know if you've noticed, but I *do* only have one leg." John smiled.

"Do you need to rest?"

"I'll be fine." John looked to the dog. "He looks sick."

"He doesn't appear to have any symptoms." Melody scanned the boxer's entire body, feeling his ears for fever, checking for swollen lymph nodes, and palpating his abdomen. She tugged at his skin between his shoulder blades, then opened his mouth and pressed her fingers against his gums. "He's a little dehydrated."

She drizzled some water out of John's camelback and let the dog lap at the stream.

"Can we keep him?" she asked with a cheesy grin.

John shook his head and laughed, "Not a good idea."

"I wasn't actually asking permission."

"He could draw attention to us—"

"Don't care."

"If he causes problems, we'll have to leave him."

"You're coming with us," she said, like she was talking to a baby, and the dog shook his tail nub and danced in a circle again.

The tracks led them over the steel rail bridge, and John's pace began to slow. The gravel crunched beneath their feet, and the dog lowered his head to growl into the woods. John and Melody heeded the dog's warning and ducked.

A lone woman with black hair hanging in her face was drenched to the core, stumbling between the trees. She tripped over the branches and fell into the mud, struggling to get back to her feet.

"She hasn't noticed us. Just leave her," John said, sheathing his knife and moving forward. "I'm tired of killing people today."

He recalled plunging his knife into the doctor's heart at the lab. "I mean, how does a person not die after you stab them in the heart or slice their throat? These people get injured and keep going like the wounds don't bother them."

"It has to be some kind of malfunctioning of the pain receptors."

"Yeah, but the heart?" John said. "Can't live without that."

"I've been thinking about that. The brain can keep functioning for a few minutes after the heart stops," Melody said. "Maybe Dr. Carter—though he was stabbed in the heart—maybe his brain kept driving him until it stopped getting oxygen from the blood. The heart got stabbed. He didn't feel it due to the lack of pain reception. His brain kept functioning because it still had oxygen being delivered from the blood. I wonder if we gave him a few more minutes for that blood to stop pumping to the brain... I wonder if he would have died. Have you shot one in the heart and then waited to see if he died eventually?"

John couldn't hide his dumbfounded expression. "No... I never conducted that science experiment. I shot one of them in the heart, but when I saw him getting back to his feet, it was pretty fucking scary. So, I shot him again...in the head."

"Are you sure you got him in the heart? You didn't miss?"

"I considered that at first—that maybe I missed. Look, I'm not so arrogant as to say that I don't miss, but... Fuck it. I don't miss."

John walked alongside Melody, trying to take each step lightly as his prosthesis rubbed against his raw skin. Sharp pains shot through his knee, across his thigh, and into his hip with each step. The dog weaved back and forth on the tracks, sniffing the ground.

"There've got to be people—experts—working on this somewhere," she said. "CDC or something. Maybe they've got something set up at the quarantine areas."

John's heart became heavy, and his words came out with reluctance, "What if they find a cure? All those people that I've put down. What if I shot them before they could seek treatment?"

Melody turned to him and stopped walking. "Those people... There's no cure for them. The extreme neurologic dysfunction indicates that the brain is too far gone. This is going to sound really shitty of me, but once you're symptomatic of a disease like rabies, there's no hope. If you have symptoms, you're good as dead. This disease is a hundred times worse. It transmits and presents so quickly, even a post-exposure treatment—if there was one— would be impossible to administer in time. There was nothing that could have been done for those people. That, I'm sure of."

"A vaccine, though?" John asked, with hope in his voice.

"If this is a lyssavirus like rabies, then yeah. A vaccine is theoretically possible."

John stopped, holding out his arm to keep Melody from moving forward. An aggregate of infected blocked their path ahead, forcing them to go through the woods.

While high-stepping through the mud and fallen branches, an infected man appeared ahead of them between the trees. Clothed in a three-piece suit that was coated in a layer of mud, the man tripped over branches as he traipsed along.

John crouched as Melody pointed out another up ahead. A girl—possibly a teenager—slathered in mud. A third came from the left, then a fourth appeared behind them. Along with the movement of bodies from the highway and the mass of infected on the tracks, they were surrounded.

With four of the infected nearby, and dozens more in the distance, Melody patted her thigh to have the dog follow closely as she and John snuck through the woods. The teen girl spotted their quick movements first and lunged toward them with a moan. With that sound, the others turned their attention.

The dog growled but kept up with John and Melody, while they prepared to fight. John pulled his knife from the sheath and was ready to take on the girl up ahead, while Melody readied her bat above her shoulder for the man in the suit. The four infected scrambled toward them from all directions, tripping and falling in a chaotic shuffle toward the sound of the infected girl's moans.

Then, a sound more terrifying than any of it made John's heart stop. The dog barked...and barked again.

All four of the infected maintained their direction, eager to get to the dog, while Melody and John tried to slip away. She called to him while running, but the damn boxer stayed back, barking at the infected and luring them closer.

"Come on," she whispered, desperate not to lose that damn dog, but he fell farther behind.

John tugged at her sleeve to keep moving.

The mass of sick people on the tracks heard the commotion and, seconds later, their bodies staggered off the tracks and seeped between the trees toward the dog.

John grabbed Melody by the wrist to get her to hide with him near some thorny bushes.

"I don't think they see us," John said.

The boxer gained at least twenty yards and let out a low-toned bark. All of the infected—the four from the woods and the horde from the tracks— were heading toward the scrawny thing.

The dog took off, chased down by the horde. He zoomed between the trees as bodies flung themselves toward him. Many kept a slow, stumbling pace, and others sped forward in short sprints before tripping over fallen logs. The infected from the highway were roused by the commotion, rattling the fence between them and the woods.

"He'll be okay," John lied.

John tugged on Melody's t-shirt sleeve, and they snuck away from the infected, unseen. Melody's eyes flooded with tears as they left the heroic dog behind and made their way back out to the tracks, free of the infected, heading toward the quarantine camp.

TWENTY FOUR

Marcus

Marcus figured Kayla would be safe enough under the bridge for the time being. He could sneak away from her while she slept and run to the quarantine zone to seek out Melody—if she was even alive. He would find a way to get some supplies and get the hell out of town before Kayla could find him and fuck everything up.

He slithered his body out from under her head, trying not to wake her, and laid her head—blood red hair dirty and soaking wet—gently down on the ground.

As he backed away, Kayla opened her eyes and stretched. Marcus plastered a charming smile on his face and held his hand out to her.

She looked up to him with stars in her eyes and accepted his hand, like he was some damn knight in shining armor.

Kayla picked up her busted chair leg and stepped back onto the soggy trail while the downpour eased to a light rain. Marcus was torn about the way she looked at him with such admiration. Part of him liked it. Melody never looked at him like that, not even in the beginning.

Though it was still raining, they moved forward with wet gravel crunching beneath Marcus's shoes. He kept a watchful eye on the woods to his left and the city to the right. Kayla kept her delicate feet in the tall weeds close to the trees, trying to avoid the rocks and jumping at every noise that she heard coming from the woods.

After another mile of travel, they were only halfway to the school. Two hours had passed since they left the lab. At this rate, they'd be dead in no time.

They approached a bend in the tracks and could see numerous figures a hundred yards ahead in the gray, drizzling mist. The silhouetted bodies traipsed along in the haze before them, and Marcus and Kayla crouched down while deciding where to go.

"Should we go through the woods?" Kayla asked.

"See that?" Marcus pointed to two of the infected who were deep in the wooded area.

They would have to get off the tracks. With the highway and an unknown number of infected in the woods—and possibly nowhere to escape to once they got in there—Marcus opted to go on the other side of the eight-foot fence, along the backs of the buildings facing Jackson Street. The thick shrubbery and weeds along the fence could obscure them from the horde on the tracks, but they would need to be careful not to expose themselves to the infected that were wandering the streets.

After squeezing through an opening in the fence, Kayla dashed ahead without warning. She rushed up to the body of a woman in an olive green jumper—it was headfirst in the bushes. A pair of slip-on black flats was falling off her dead feet.

"Keep up," Marcus demanded.

"Hold on," Kayla whispered, and she bent over to slide the shoes from the woman.

The size nine shoes were far too big for Kayla. She was unable to pick up her feet without the shoes falling off, so she scuffed them along the gravel to catch up with Marcus.

They crossed onto the broken pavement behind Hank's Auto.

Out front, a thin man in gray coveralls circled the lot. Tyler Marshall—Hank's son, who had taken over the auto shop. The same kid who couldn't get beer for the post-track meet bonfire. Tyler had stayed in Fair Haven and worked at the garage after high school. Melody always brought her car to him when there was an issue, even when they lived out in Madison. She claimed it was because she trusted him not to rip her off, but Marcus wondered if there was something more. It's not like Marcus never strayed from time to time, but never with the same person. He never got personal.

Tyler Marshall—what was left of him—continued to circle to the right, dragging his left foot, eyes focused on the ground beneath his feet. Marcus could never prove anything was ever going on between Melody and Tyler, but Melody seemed far too comfortable around him.

Marcus felt a hint of relief when he saw Tyler staggering in circles outside the shop. He felt the corners of his mouth try to pull up in a smile, but he forced them down. At least he didn't have to worry about that asshole anymore.

They moved along the back of a small apartment complex, and a large horde of the infected was in the parking lot out front. Most were unaware of the others, staggering around without cause.

Marcus shuffled from the apartments to the next building, the Thrift Safe Storage Units, keeping a watchful eye on the infected.

Within the crowd, a deteriorating man with torn flesh and blackened wounds turned his gaze toward him. The man with blood-crusted dreadlocks let his heavy shoulder pull him forward, and he stumbled directly for him.

"Faster," Kayla insisted with a whisper. Despite her new corpse-reclaimed shoes, every step Kayla took was still excruciatingly slow.

Marcus moved faster, just like Kayla demanded, but he left her limping behind, struggling to keep up.

"Marcus," she called in a whisper. "Not that fast."

As she called to him, more of their grungy heads turned.

The panic in her voice broke his heart, and he did everything he could to prevent himself from looking back at Kayla while she fell behind. The moaning intensified, and several bodies that had been wandering aimlessly leaned in to head toward Kayla's voice.

Marcus let his conscience run awry for a moment as Kayla lagged. She had told him to go faster. This was his chance to leave the girl. Survival of the fittest at this point.

She hobbled with the uncomfortable urgency of a person trying not to piss themselves on the way to the bathroom. Slow, but as hurried as possible. The infected man with necrotic skin and gnarly dreadlocks moaned behind her. Her soaking wet clothes clung to her body, and she scuffed her feet like a little girl wearing her mom's enormous shoes.

"Fuck," he blurted.

He ran back to Kayla as the dreadlocked infected man approached with his arm stretched out to grab her. His mouth hung open, allowing a line of drool to cascade from his lower lip, but Marcus got to her first and yanked her by the wrist.

"Lose those shoes!" he snapped at her. "You're faster without them."

He jogged toward the storage sheds as Kayla stumbled, still clinging to her chair leg. She kicked off the oversized shoes, and her socked feet scraped along the pavement. She could barely move faster than the infected who were after them.

More of them poured out of the alleys between the storage rows.

Upon seeing the size of the incoming crowd, Marcus froze—his mind went blank at the sight of so many infected. It felt like cement filled his throat and he couldn't breathe. He saw familiar faces—nobody he knew by name— but townspeople that he had seen before. Maybe some people he went to school with. Some of the infected were fast, sprinting in short spurts that sent them crashing to the ground or into a wall. Marcus flinched as each one fell, but he remained still. His feet were anchored to the pavement.

"Go!" Kayla screamed, but Marcus couldn't move. She pulled at his arm.

A thin man with a maroon t-shirt gained proximity, and Marcus couldn't help but stare at his mangled face.

Kayla's chair leg smacked against the man's jaw, making him tumble to the side. And with that, Marcus snapped out of his state of shock.

Kayla screamed. Marcus regained his senses and sought shelter. Leaving her in this mass of infected was not an option. He couldn't let the poor girl be torn apart by those things, so he held her hand and ran as fast as he could force her to.

While running by the rows of storage units, Marcus caught a glimpse of a door ajar.

"Come on!"

There were four of the infected wandering in the row of storage units where Marcus intended to hide. All four leaned in, moaning and lumbering toward him. Marcus pushed on the open door in the alley of units, but it was blocked by a large desk on the inside. He pushed harder, screaming and grunting to get the door open wide enough to squeeze through.

One of the infected closed in. She was an elderly woman with white hair and varicose veins cluttering her pale legs. Her lilac nightdress was soaked through from the rainfall, exposing her braless, sagging breasts. She snarled and fell over in an attempt to get at them.

Even more bodies began to filter into the storage row. Kayla helped Marcus push the door with all of her strength.

It finally budged, and Marcus dove inside, flinging himself on top of the desk on the other side of the door.

"Get in!" he screamed at her.

She shifted her body through the crack of the door and onto the desk, wiggling inside as the infected old woman thrashed at them.

Marcus jabbed the chair leg at the woman's head, knocking her backwards. Despite his racing heart and nausea, he kept fighting. When the woman was on her ass, he leaned across the desk and closed the door, entrapping them in the dark once again.

Kayla pressed her hands against the heavy desk, pushing it back against the security door while she heaved out of breath.

The sick ones outside pounded against the door with wild thumps, growling among each other, fighting and thrashing with the door and each other.

As Marcus's eyes adjusted to the darkness, light seeped in through the edge of the blinds on the door's security window. Despite the men banging against it, the sturdy glass did not break.

The small amount of light exposed an office space with a green comforter spread out in the corner. A milk crate sat against the wall with an unlit oil lantern and a lighter. An orange floral blanket laid wadded on top of the comforter, like it had been used as a pillow. The putrid smell from the small attached bathroom filled the office.

The thuds of the infected waned as minutes went by. Marcus and Kayla stood with their backs against the far wall, flinching with each thump.

Gradually, as the infected gave up on their attempt to get in, Kayla slid down the wall to the floor, and Marcus paced the room, devising a plan to get themselves out of that office.

"You stayed with me," she said.

She combed her shaking fingers through her red hair in an attempt to brush it out, and Marcus wondered if she knew that he had been considering leaving her behind.

He placed his hands in his pants pockets, tilted his head to look at the trembling redhead, and sat down beside her on the comforter.

"Of course," he smiled, "I couldn't leave you."

TWENTY FIVE

Melody

Melody's heart broke over the dog she didn't even know. Her eyes still stung with tears, yet she couldn't seem to shed a drop for her own husband. She and John walked another mile in silence before easing back into the woods on the path that led to Mariner's Hill.

The drizzling rain became a fine mist, and Melody's drenched clothes were glued to her body. Her t-shirt was suctioned to her chest, and her old jeans barely hung onto her hips. Her sagging pants drooped lower, and she struggled to keep them up as they ascended the muddy incline.

John winced in pain with each step, but she figured he wouldn't want her to ask about it. The prosthetic blade slipped and stuck in the mud, making the upward climb difficult for him, but he plowed through the pain without a word.

Thinning trees exposed more cloudy sky as they neared the top of Mariner's Hill. Then, the sound of snapping twigs behind them forced her attention down the hillside. She froze, on guard, holding a thin sapling for support.

There were no infected in sight.

Beyond the whisper of the rain through the pines, a low hum of voices rose from over the hill. The murmur from the quarantine zone pierced the air.

"Do you hear that?" Melody asked, looking back to John.

He nodded.

Driven by the prospect of hope, eager to find refuge, to find out what people had learned about the disease, and to find Marcus, Melody quickened her pace, sinking into the mud with each step up the hill.

Perhaps Marcus was there, close to success with a vaccine. Maybe he couldn't get back to her because there was more important work to be done. Maybe life was about to get easier. These were all the naïve thoughts of a raving idiot, but she didn't care. She still had room for hope. She powered to the top of the hill, frantic to see, but as she approached the summit, the murmur of voices morphed into something far less human, and her ephemeral dream unraveled before her.

John and Melody looked in each other's eyes, knowing what they were about to see. They both lay down on their bellies at the top of the hill so as not to be seen from afar. They crawled forward with dread within their guts.

She first spotted the tops of the tents in the football field below. The large white tents were ripped; some were burned. She edged closer to bring the entire field into view. The fenced-in football field enclosed thousands of people. Their colorless flesh and filthy clothes blended into a massive grey throng of bodies. Each person moved individually, but from afar, the crowd undulated like a swarm of locusts.

At least half of them were not moving at all, lying in the mud, dead. Beyond the football field and the fallen quarantine zone tents was the high school, windows busted out with blackened burn marks on the brick. Cars were overflowing the parking lot into the street and onto the grassy fields beyond.

Closer to them, before the fenced mass of bodies in the football field below, was the set of soccer fields at the base of the hill with at least a dozen infected wandering free outside the fences.

Melody released a heavy, sharp exhale and rolled onto her back to look to the sky.

"That's gotta be the whole damn town," John said. His tone softened. "You okay?"

Marcus is gone.

And with that thought, her heart sank deeper into her chest cavity as if gravity tugged it so hard toward the earth that it could rip out her back.

Tears welled, and she covered her sour face with muddy hands, while John sat with reverence beside her. She would never know where Marcus was or what happened to him, and the unsolved mystery did not sit well with her. She squeezed her temples within the vice of her hands, trying not to let her brain explode from the trauma. Tears broke the dam of her eyelids and streamed down her cheeks.

Her body had been deadened from the events of the day, and she would have liked to stay hidden with the tall wet grasses for all of eternity, staring into the gray nothingness above. She wiped her tears away with the back of her hand, smearing mud, and she scowled at the sky in an attempt to stop crying.

She pulled her orchid envelope from her back pocket and ran her finger along the seal, debating whether or not it was a good time to open it. In that fleeting moment, she would've liked to give up. Cash in her chips and quit just like dad did, but she couldn't do that yet. She couldn't leave John out here on the hill alone. She tucked her depressed feelings into the deepest corners of her being and tucked her envelope back in her pocket. She'd deal with them both later.

They lay on top of the hill in the fading daylight, with baritone voices groaning from below.

"It's getting late," John said.

"Now what?" Complete and utter lack of hope tainted her tone.

John stood and held out his hand to help her up.

"We find that boat and get the hell out of here," he said.

TWENTY SIX

Melody

Melody was drained, unsure if she had the stamina or willpower to carry on, but there was still a spark within her. Some kind of primal drive deep within the core of her anatomy that forced her to her feet to seek shelter. Her drenched clothes hung heavily from her body, like she carried an extra fifty pounds, but the weight of her grief was far worse.

Survival instincts trumped her overwhelming sense of demise, and she and John navigated down the grassy side of Mariner's Hill toward the open soccer fields. The fenced-in football field was far enough away that the infected within the fences were unaware of them as they crept down. A couple of dozen infected souls peppered the soccer fields nearby. An infected man ensnared within the soccer goal net tossed and turned in the grass while others walked in tight individual circles, falling to the side and scrambling back to their feet, just to fall over again.

John and Melody cut a diagonal path down the hill toward a stretch of privacy fencing along the backyards of the houses on Carlisle Road.

She squinted toward the football field, trying to make out faces within the crowd, but it was too far away. If Marcus was in there, she wouldn't be able to pick him out among the mass of muddied bodies.

She hunched over and followed John, who hobbled forward with his pistol ready. Ahead was the school's old outdoor equipment shed—another spot she'd taken shelter in back when she was on her own for a while.

It called to her, like the car chassis had called to her earlier. She wanted to crawl in through the window and hide for the night, but hiding had never done her any good. As they approached the back of the shed, she heard growling from the opposite side and then the slow groan of a man.

John motioned for her to follow him around the back of the shed, but Melody fell back and went to the front.

There was something about the sound that forced her to look. It wasn't a man at all. It was the same damn dog from earlier that day. The skinny boxer was face-to-face with a pale, grotesque man in a gray tank top. The man's left arm suffered severe injury at the elbow—skin torn, muscles and tendons exposed. His forearm dangled from the joint, and his blood had clotted and crusted at the wound.

With a deadly groan, the man lunged toward the boxer, who was backed against the entrance of the storage shed.

"Hey!" John whispered to her when he came out from behind the other side of the shed.

The heavy, sick man charged at the dog, forcing it to bark in defense. The sound of barking roused the attention of the infected in the soccer fields.

"Melody!" John yelled.

Melody snuck up behind the infected man with her baseball bat over her shoulder.

The man's jerking, staggering attacks were dodged by the barking dog.

The moaning from behind the football field fence intensified, and the metal rattled and creaked as infected clamored to escape. Melody whaled the man in the back of his head, sending him to his knees as the dog cowered and retreated with a whimper.

The grotesque man was quick to get back to his feet and fly at Melody, so she dropped her bat and groped at her hip, searching for her knife.

John sprinted toward her, hampered by a severe limp, as Melody whipped the knife from its sheath and drove the blade into the man's head.

Melody flinched, lips closed tight as his face came within inches of hers. Inhuman rage oozed from his eyes as the blade punctured the surface of his temple. It popped through the soft tissue, then slid with ease the rest of the way into his head. She cringed at the sensation and released the knife as the man's body dropped to the ground. She placed a foot on the corpse's shoulder for leverage, and she forced the blade out of his skull with a gag.

"Damn, Chuck! You okay?" John's concern was laced with a sense of admiration.

Melody winced as she wiped the blood from her knife onto the tank top of the dead man. She nodded with a violent shiver.

The dog barked and paced nervously as more of them approached, so John and Melody hustled to the privacy fence and raced as fast as their tired legs could carry them. John's limp worsened, and Melody's legs by then had turned to rubber.

Infected were approaching from all sides, and the property was too long to run without getting trapped by them. The quarantine camp's chain link fence continued to rattle in the distance. If it busted open, they'd be swarmed by hundreds, maybe over a thousand, rather than just a dozen.

They had to go over the privacy fence and into one of the houses.

John leapt up, hanging onto the top of the wooden fence to look into a yard. Once he was sure it was clear, he knelt. Without saying a word to each other, John gestured for her to use his knee as a step stool. He hoisted her upward, and she swung over the fence. Melody grabbed a plastic lawn chair from the other side and set it against the wall.

She climbed up as John lifted the dog. He was no more than sixty pounds if she had to guess. Once the dog was safely behind the fence, he quit barking. Melody held out her hand to help John over, but instead, he stepped back, sprinted a few steps toward the wall, and leapt up, swinging himself over and landing in a crouching stance with apparent ease. He growled in pain as he landed, and his prosthetic sank into the muddy ground.

The moaning and snarling continued on the other side of the fence, and the smacking of their hands against the wood warned Melody to keep moving. The haunting sound joined the memory of Candace's screams, the memory of gunfire, and the sound of her world ending.

"I need to stop," Melody panted, resting the weight of her upper body upon her knees, becoming lightheaded. "I can't make it to the boat."

John nodded with understanding and didn't ask any questions. He ran— limp worsening in severity—to the back door of a two-story house to peek in the windows. The lace curtains were wide open, and there was no sign of anyone inside. The fading, overcast sky barely illuminated the rooms.

"Looks empty," John said, and went to work looking for a key.

After checking under the doormat, above the door frame, and under the multitude of potted plants lining the back deck, they found one. They walked inside, ready to fight, and hoping to find refuge for a while.

To lure out any infected that may have been lurking inside, Melody swallowed her fear and called out, "Hello?"

TWENTY SEVEN

Kayla

Within the confines of the dark office, Kayla leaned her head on Marcus's shoulder, curling her body close to his.

"At least we have water." Marcus smiled and pointed toward the water cooler in the corner that was less than a quarter full.

"You're an optimist," Kayla said with a chuckle. Her heart hadn't stopped racing after their close encounter with the infected, who seemed to have forgotten Marcus and Kayla were inside. They still loitered in the row of storage units outside, though. Marcus periodically checked between the blinds only to find they had not moved on.

"I really need some shoes," Kayla said as she held her swollen and sore foot in her hands.

"I agree. We didn't' get too far today," Marcus said, "but with this weather and your feet, let's just rest here for now, and we'll get moving again when the assholes outside clear out."

"I'm hungry." She didn't mean to complain, but that's all that could come out of her.

"I know," he nodded. "But nobody ever died from going a couple days without food. We should wait here for a while until they clear out."

"I don't know," Kayla said, unsure of Marcus's plan. She felt like it would be better to keep moving, but she also wondered if he'd leave her behind if she argued with him.

"First chance we get, as soon as they're out of sight, we'll go."

Kayla limped around the room, searching the cabinets for something to eat, but found nothing. Her stomach growled. Her bloodied feet left tiny red footprints on the cream-tiled floor. She rummaged through the desk drawers and found nothing but a butter knife, an empty peanut butter jar crawling with ants, and some candy wrappers.

"I can't open this one." She jiggled the handle on the top desk drawer that was locked. Starving and scared, she sat beside Marcus with the butter knife in hand.

"That little thing isn't going to do much damage."

"It's not for them." She used the knife to saw through the fabric of the threadbare comforter, working at it until she created a tear. She ripped a few narrow strips of material free. Kayla used some water from the cooler to wash the blood and dirt from her feet, and began to wrap them with the strips of fabric.

"That's pretty clever," Marcus said.

"You'd be the first person to ever say that about me."

"I doubt that," Marcus said.

Kayla talked Marcus's ear off in that small office. She went on and on about her life growing up on the west coast. She had to keep talking or her thoughts would get the best of her. Sickened with the thought of what may have happened to her parents and her little brother, she kept talking. She talked about her little toy ponies when she was a young girl. She talked about her high school sweetheart. Marcus was quiet and listened to her as she yammered on and on. She talked about volleyball and bike races with the neighborhood kids when she was younger.

"We did that too," Marcus finally spoke up, "My grandparents had a cottage on Barton Road. You know, off Barton Harbor on the lake?"

"Yeah?" Kayla was relieved he was finally talking.

"It was my grandfather's lake house, but he left it to my parents. I haven't been there in years. It lost its appeal as I got older. The other kids and I would race bikes down that gravel road. I always won. I earned the title Baron of Barton Road." Marcus laughed.

Kayla smiled and rested her head on his shoulder as he talked about his childhood.

"They still have that cottage. You know, when I was a teenager, I'd ride my bike right from high school to the cottage on weekends. I used to go there and get high with my friends."

"*You* used to get high?" Kayla laughed.

"Surprised?" Marcus asked with a smug grin.

"Yes! So, you went to high school here in Fair Haven?"

"Yep."

"And the high school you went to is now the quarantine zone?"

Marcus nodded. "Just a couple more miles away if we take the tracks. As soon as the fuckers outside the door wander off, we'll get moving again. We'll head back toward the tracks if it's clear. A little way farther down, these tracks arc out away from the town, where it's a little more secluded, then they arc back right to the high school."

The sound of moaning from outside the door waned, but the infected continued to wander as if they had forgotten why they were there. Kayla could still hear them moving around and tried to block out the sound with conversation.

"Do your parents have a boat at that lake cottage?" Kayla asked.

"What?"

"Most people with a lake home have a boat. Do they have a boat, because we could—"

"What? You wanna sail off into the sunset with me?" Marcus laughed.

His comment took her aback. "Well...not because it's romantic or anything. I thought maybe it could be an option if something goes wrong. Like a backup plan. I'm not asking you to marry me, man. I'm just—"

"They winterized their boat with everyone else in town a few weeks ago. The boat's not even near the water right now, unfortunately."

Kayla had begun to believe that if they didn't get moving soon, they'd die in that office, but every time they checked outside, there were still infected people ambling around. She filled up on water as the light of day faded, and the darkness of night enveloped them again.

The scuffing of deadened feet along the pavement waxed and waned, while Marcus and Kayla remained whispering inside. He lit the oil lantern and set it on the milk crate in the corner.

"We'll prepare to get moving in the morning," he said.

"I don't think we should wait any longer than that. Even if they're out there, I think we need to make a run for it in the morning, no matter what."

"Deal."

"I am glad we at least have a little light tonight," she whispered as the flickering lamp danced across her body.

Her damp clothes still clung to her, chilling her flesh. Kayla unbuttoned her shirt, slid the sleeves down her arms, and draped the blouse on the back of the chair.

"Don't mind me. I have to get dry." She bent over, tugging her skirt down around her ankles, and hung it beside her blouse.

Marcus

Marcus leaned against the wall, watching the peculiar girl undress and then wrap her body with what was left of the blanket.

Marcus took a step closer and paused, knowing it wasn't right to string her along like this, but considering they could both die horrible deaths by morning, what the hell did it matter?

"You should get out of your wet clothes, too," she said, and that was his green light.

He stepped closer and put his hands on her waist. "Can you help me with my clothes?"

While Kayla unbuttoned his shirt, Marcus tugged gently on her blanket and made it fall to the floor. She shivered, standing in her bra and panties, then slid his shirt down from his shoulders.

Marcus charged at her, wrapped his arms around her, and kissed the girl. If he was going to ditch her, he might as well let her feel good for a while first.

She jumped up, squeezing her legs around his body in a boa-like grip, and drove her pelvis against his. Her scraggly, red hair hung in her face as they entrenched each other's mouths with a long, invasive kiss.

With Kayla still latched onto him, Marcus moved to the comforter. He held onto her back with one arm as he lay her down on the floor. Their bodies rocked, entangled in the comforter as the lantern's light flickered across their naked skin. Her toes curled, and her chipped black fingernails dug into his back. There was a groan outside, and a thud against the door, but it was not enough to stop them from one last embrace.

TWENTY EIGHT

Melody

The clip-clip of the dog's claws tapped along the kitchen floor, breaking the silence of the stale house they'd broken into. John and Melody surveilled the house for signs of danger, working their way across the first floor; it was clear. The décor reeked of the late 1980s. Doilies lined every wooden surface. Gold touch-lamps with floral prints on the glass lampshades adorned the living room set. The house was peppered with Bible scriptures on the walls and cross-stitched into pillows and oven mitts.

Once they were certain the house was empty, Melody found the master bedroom upstairs. A row of decorative candles lined the dresser—some adorned with biblical imagery and others had cute animals. She lay down on the downy blanket of the bed with her head on the pillow. The dog jumped up, muddied the bedding, and curled up beside her.

Marcus is gone. She would never know what happened to him.

"I should be crying, shouldn't I?" she whispered to the dog.

Perhaps it was because she didn't care enough to cry. She considered that her seemingly emotionless state may be due to shock, but a tiny part of her felt relief that she didn't have to look for him any longer. And with that thought, guilt crept in.

John stopped in the doorway and braced his arms in the frame, holding weight off of his prosthetic leg. The sweet distraction of seeing him kept her from thinking about how she was supposed to feel.

"You should take that leg off for a while," she said.

"The leg? Well, I'd prefer to remove the prosthetic," he joked, and Melody was able to let out a brief chuckle.

"Seriously. Are you okay?"

"Are *you*?" he asked. His stunning eyes stood out in the color-faded room. Unsure how she felt about anything, she simply looked down at the hands in her lap—they were coated in mud and blood.

"I'm not strong enough," she admitted.

"I don't believe that. You're a tough son-of-a-bitch."

"I used to think I was, but look at me—traipsing around town, endangering lives so I can hold onto a marriage that was doomed anyway. I'm good at hiding from problems, not facing them."

Melody inhaled the earthy scent of her muddied clothes and stood up. "I'm gonna shower," she said, "if the water still works."

"It works," he said. "And guess what? Gas water heater is still working."

"Hot water?" She almost smiled.

"I'll take the hall bathroom," John said.

She closed the bedroom door and removed her soaking wet, disgusting clothes, and dropped them to the floor. The dreary, rainy day allowed a small amount of gray light through the window over the toilet in the master bathroom. She peeked out the tiny window to look down at Carlisle Road; it was desolate, but she could spot five dead bodies in the street.

More of them are dying off.

She turned the faucet handle. Water sputtered out of the shower head and came to a steady hiss.

Melody allowed it to drench her body, washing away blood and filth. Clumps of mud dropped to the bathtub floor and diluted around her feet.

Melody tilted her head back to soak the top of her head. She wasn't even sure if Marcus had loved her anymore. They had been arguing constantly and even discussed divorce a few days before the town fell apart.

She pulled a bottle of tea tree shampoo from the shower rack and began to lather herself from head to toe, trying to scrub away her memories along with the filth.

She shut off the water and stepped her bare feet onto the plush bathroom rug. It was a tiny bit of luxury in a living hell. *Finally, something nice.* Everyone deserved a chance to have something nice from time to time. Something like a good marriage. Something like a loyal dog, a hot shower, and a fluffy bath rug. Something comfortable. *John* was something comfortable.

She opened the bathroom door to see her dog sitting patiently on the other side, wagging his nubby tail, leaving brown paw prints across the pale blue carpeting.

"Come on." She waved him in. "Your turn."

She washed up the dog, then her clothes, and rummaged through the drawers of hideous old-lady clothes for something dry to wear.

Pink jumpsuits. Yellow silk blouses. Large royal blue sweatpants. She pulled out a bedazzled kitten blouse that read, *Hang in There*. She laughed at the ridiculous shirt and put it on.

John's bathroom faucet down the hall shut off. Melody grabbed two of the candles from the dresser, walked down the darkening hall, and stopped outside the open bathroom door. The warm, moist air spilled out of the bathroom and clung to Melody's skin.

"Do you want a candle?" she asked.

"That'd be great," he answered, "but avert your eyes, I'm indecent."

She entered, looking away, holding up the unlit candles for John to see.

"Your choice," she said. "Kittens or Jesus?"

John laughed, and after a moment of contemplation, he said, "Jesus."

"Really?"

"Well, it feels wrong burning kittens," John snickered.

"And burning Jesus doesn't seem wrong?" she asked.

"Jesus can handle it."

Melody lit the wick of the Jesus candle, protected the wavering flame with her hand, and set it down on the edge of the sink. She tried to respect John's privacy as he was soaking in the tub, but Melody stole a glimpse of his strong, tattooed body out of the corner of her eye. Glistening orange and yellow sparks of light danced around him.

"Are you taking a *bubble* bath?" she asked with her eyes on the candle.

"Are you looking?"

Melody turned to leave.

"Hey."

She froze in ecstasy in the doorway, awaiting him to summon her back to him. Ready to climb into the tub with him on his word. "Yeah?" her mousy voice cracked.

"Nice shirt!" he said.

A genuine smile stretched across her face.

Melody ventured downstairs alone and rummaged through the cabinets, which had been mostly cleaned out. She found a stash of about a dozen cans of pork and beans, cracked two open, and fed herself and the dog while John bathed himself upstairs.

John

John pulled himself out of the tub. He wondered what to do about Melody. He wanted her more than he had ever wanted any woman but warned himself not to pursue her so soon.

He wrapped a small white towel around his abdomen. He carefully blotted dry his residual limb. The skin was irritated and too sore to put the prosthetic back on, so he hopped out of the bathroom, supporting himself on the walls.

He braced himself in the dark hallway with his prosthetic in one hand, fresh out of the tub. His body was wet from the bath, and his thigh bulged from the constraints of the towel as Melody climbed the stairs.

"Do you need some dry clothes?" Melody said. "There are some in there." She nodded toward the master bedroom behind him.

"Are they going to be as cool as yours?"

"If you're lucky." She tried to squeeze past him, but he barely stepped to the side, making her slink around his body. Her breasts grazed his ribs, and he inhaled the scent of tea tree shampoo as she passed. His towel was so skimpy, he worried an erection might make it drop to the floor, so he curtailed his wandering thoughts and gave her space. It was too soon after learning of her husband's death—or abandonment—for him to make a move anyway. Downright sleezy.

She went through the drawers in the master bedroom and pulled out a plain white undershirt and a pair of plaid pajama pants.

"Nothing better?" he asked.

"It's this, or the God Camp '99 shirt with the unidentifiable stain." Melody shrugged with a smirk.

"Dangerous yellow stain? It could be mustard."

"Could be urine," she said.

"Plain white tee it is," John agreed, taking the clothes from her hands.

Melody slid her arm into the crook of his elbow and helped support him as he moved toward the bed to sit down.

"Your leg doesn't look so good." She looked at the red, raw flesh at his limb.

"It's okay. It happens sometimes. I powdered the hell out of it this morning, but all this moisture and running irritated it. I have a balm for it in my bag."

John slid the t-shirt over his head and noticed Melody looking at his chest.

"You have any tattoos?" he asked.

"Yeah."

"Let me guess. A butterfly."

"No," Melody sounded offended.

"Sorry. I assumed you had a girlie tattoo. Then what is it, Chuck?"

She laughed and repeated, "Chuck."

"Better than calling you sweetheart, right?"

She rolled her eyes.

The fact was, if he said her name—*Melody*—it was like a song on his lips, and that made him want to kiss her. But Chuck was just a cool dude's name. He didn't want to fuck a *Chuck*.

"So, what's the tattoo? A skull? Dragon?"

"It's a dolphin," she said, trying not to laugh. She tugged down the front of her jeans to expose the pale blue dorsal fin of a dolphin on her pelvis, but left the rest to John's imagination.

Melody turned to leave as her cheeks were blushing, but before she was out the door, John stood up; his towel broke free from his bulging thighs, dropping to the floor. John froze, wondering if he should scramble to pick it up or if he should wait for her to turn around and *accidentally* catch a glimpse of what he was carrying.

She didn't turn around, but the sound of the towel dropping made her pause with her back to him.

"Pork and beans?" she asked.

"Excuse me?"

"Do you want some pork and beans? I found some downstairs." She said it with a cool disconnect, like she wasn't interested in him at all, still facing the hallway.

"Sure," he answered.

She left him alone in the bedroom, pantsless, and feeling ridiculous for assuming his tactics would work on someone like her.

Melody

Once downstairs, the light of day was nearly gone, so Melody lit a candle while they ate some canned beans. She settled into an old man's recliner, but was too on edge to kick her feet up.

The moans of the infected outside began to permeate the walls of the house, so she lowered the candle to the floor and tried to obstruct the light so as not to attract outsiders. Melody and John rested in the living room while paintings of Jesus and inspirational word art surrounded them.

Perseverance was printed beneath a photograph of Mt. Everest, but it did not make Melody want to persevere at all. The thought of climbing anything right now was daunting. It made her want to give up. She leaned back as the wet dog nervously climbed into the recliner with her.

"What are you going to name him?" John asked with a sleepy, deep voice.

"Good question."

"Too bad Chuck and Norris are already taken by you and my cat."

"Something else bad-ass, then."

"I got a bad-ass name for you. Harkness."

"Who's that?"

"He was as bad-ass as they come. He got hit by the same explosion that took my leg. His face was burnt, and he took a bullet while pulling one of our guys out to safety. That guy was the epitome of badassdom."

"*You're* kind of bad-ass, though, aren't you?" Melody said.

John shook off the compliment with modesty.

"Not like Harkness. Besides…my last name is Myers. What kind of name is that for a dog?"

"Well, Harkness it is."

A thump at the front porch startled them.

Melody jumped up and blew out the candle. Paralyzed in the darkness, she awaited another sound at the door. The shuffling of feet played on the wooden planks, but the infected were not trying to get in. Melody watched the movement of shadows beyond the lace curtains in the windows. Harkness growled at the door, but quieted down on Melody's whispered command, "Hush."

She and John slid the couch across the carpeted floor to barricade the stairwell, and they moved upstairs for the evening. They sat on the edge of the steps, with weapons in their hands as the moans and clunking of the infected persisted.

"I don't think I can take this anymore," Melody admitted. Her fingers were barely strong enough to hold the baseball bat. "At least not tonight. I can't fight anymore tonight."

John led her into the master bedroom and locked themselves inside. Harkness jumped on the bed and curled up near the pillow, while they listened to the ungodly groaning sounds outside.

"But you will," he said. "You'll fight if we have to. If they get in here, and all we have is an ounce of strength, then we will use every last drop to survive."

The thought of it exhausted her.

"You got that?" John's voice was urgent and forceful.

Several infected were crawling about on the street below.

"I don't think it'll happen tonight, though," he said. "They don't seem to realize we're in here. They're just making noise."

John stood with his back to Melody. The thin white tee clung to his muscles as he peeked through the lace curtains. She could scarcely make out his body through the darkness of the room.

He shuffled himself to the door to move a small chest of drawers in front of it, and Melody got up to help him. They stripped the muddied white down comforter from the bed to expose a clean, green quilt beneath.

"It's been a long day," he said, "and honestly, I don't think I have much more strength in me either, but if it came right down to it, I would run. I would fight… You and I both would. We'll fight our damn asses off."

"Okay, okay. I don't need a pep talk," she said.

He smiled. "Whatever you say, Chuck. But neither of us are in this alone. We'll do this together as long as we can. And even then, even if we're separated, we keep up the fight."

John

John looked at the woman in those silly blue sweatpants. That ridiculous cat shirt hung off one smooth shoulder. Her damp hair laid heavy on her back. He was tormented by her, but she had just lost her husband. Grieving. He could not rightfully make a move so soon, but every second with her was torture. Perhaps the same rules didn't apply in this environment. Maybe, with the volatile state of the world and their futures, it didn't matter. Did the standard rules of engagement apply here?

He relit the candle and set it in the master bathroom doorway so the light couldn't be seen from the street.

"Do you want me to sleep on the floor?" he asked, desperate for her to decline.

Melody froze for a moment, considering the question, but didn't respond.

John interrupted before she decided. "I would offer to take the bed in the other room, but—"

Melody shook her head, and John sat down beside her, inches away, as her fingers explored the fibers of the bedding. The candle's flame frolicked, and Melody sat still as she faced the door to the bedroom, unresponsive to John.

He gave her a moment to figure out what she wanted. Minute after minute passed, and Melody remained still. A damn statue frozen in time and contemplation. He shifted closer, trying to read her. John placed his hand on her back between her shoulder blades, and he noticed the fine hairs on the back of her neck stood to attention. He was under her skin.

This was his chance. He gently rubbed her back, and she released a deep sigh.

"We'll be all right here for tonight," he whispered as he placed both hands onto her shoulders, massaging her aching body. "We'll keep each other safe."

John's hands drifted down her arms, while his breath skimmed the nape of her neck. She released an ecstatic breath of relief. John knew she wouldn't be able to contain her passion any longer. He knew she wanted to be with him as much as he wanted her.

Melody turned her body to face him. He smiled, waiting for her to tell him to stop, but she stared at him with longing eyes.

Melody

She relaxed in the comfort of his touch. John's handsome, scruffy face gazed back at her with kind, worried eyes. She closed hers as he inched so close that the warmth of his breath and the scruff of his beard tickled her skin.

Melody fought to keep from kissing him. It was too soon. It was wrong. He leaned closer but would not close the gap between them with a kiss. He awaited her to make the move.

And Melody caved. She collapsed into him, allowing their lips to meet. It was a passionate and gentle kiss. The electric tension in his body radiated through her skin. Melody surged with a wave of ecstasy as John held the back of her neck and simply kissed her.

With that flow of passion in her blood as she reveled in his touch, guilt crept in and coursed through her veins. She leaned into him, tugging the fabric of his white t-shirt while he held onto her waist and lay her softly back on the bed.

John hovered over her, one muscular arm holding him above, the other hand on her waist. She lay with tussled, wet hair on the pillow, gazing up at him. He was as beautiful and calming as a starry sky. John's hand crept from her waist and came to rest with his thumbs barely grazing the cups of her breasts. Her body pulsed with temptation, ache swelling between her legs to have all of him against her and inside of her. Their eyes met again, and he smiled. She saw a trusted friend in that gorgeous, friendly gaze—maybe someone she could trust more than Marcus. She worried she had moved on too fast. She wasn't even sure if Marcus was dead.

John's thumb explored the underside of her breast, and before she realized what her body was doing, her right fist swung up and clocked him in the jaw.

John retreated with his hands protecting his face.

"Fuck!" he shouted, then quieted himself.

Melody briskly shifted herself out from under him, "I'm sorry!"

She backed up against the headboard, vagina still screaming for what it had been denied. She covered her mouth with both hands. "I can't."

"You could've said 'no' like a normal person!"

Harkness perked up with the excitement and huddled close to Melody.

"It was like an instinct. I didn't mean to—"

"What the hell, Chuck?"

And with him calling her Chuck, she cracked a smile and knew it was okay.

John lay down on the opposite side of the bed, pawing at his face.

"It's wrong," she whispered, "Isn't it?"

"Yeah, it's fucking wrong." John adjusted his jaw. "You punched me!"

"Not that..."

He sighed. "I know what you meant. I get it. I do."

"I just need time."

"That's okay. I don't know how much time you need. That's your call." He sat on the edge of the bed and pushed himself to a standing position. "I just hope we have time left."

Melody scrunched her face, "Really? End-of-the-world sex plea?"

John laughed. "Damn! That won't work?"

Melody blushed. "Maybe in time."

John stretched. "Well. I can try to survive a couple more days for you." He threw a pillow on the floor.

"Don't sleep on the floor," she begged.

John paused with his back to her. He picked up the candle from the bathroom floor and blew it out, leaving them in the dark.

"I'm right here," he said as he hopped back to the bed and slid under the quilt.

Melody lay face to face with John, bodies separated by Harkness and awkward tension. She felt ridiculous, like a teenager reluctant to give up her virginity. There was no valid reason not to give in to her desires, but she couldn't make her brain shut up about Marcus. Guilt prevailed.

She lay with her head on the pillow, looking at John's face through the failing light as he closed his eyes. His beard, with silver strays speckled throughout, had thickened since the day before. She wanted to touch it—to trace his jawline with the tips of her fingers. She wanted to do a lot of things with him. If she had a less sensible mind, she would think she was falling in love, but she knew better.

Civilization was dying, along with the rules that governed humanity, so she wondered what difference it made. Perhaps her vows meant nothing at this point, and she should do what felt good and right to her in this moment.

Her combatting thoughts were interrupted by the moaning sounds of the infected piercing the walls. Melody covered her ears and closed her eyes, trying to gain some peace. The tick-tick-tick of the grandfather clock in the corner cut through the silent bedroom and sounded as loud as someone knocking at the door. Fortunately, John and Melody were both exhausted enough to fall asleep through the sounds of the clock and the moaning voices outside. Between them laid the odor of a wet dog, but it didn't diminish the desire.

TWENTY NINE

Marcus

Marcus had known Melody since elementary school. She was a nobody up until her dad killed himself in some tragic Shakespearean story that made headline local news. Then the rumors got around that she ran away from her foster family and lived on the street. As a teenager, it intrigued him. He would watch her at her locker down the hall, wondering if living on the street had made her an easy lay, but it didn't seem that way. She was reserved and mysterious—an impossible catch. But he always knew how to lure in even the most difficult of prey.

They started dating, if that's what you want to call it. At first, it was nothing but long walks and talking. It took over two weeks before she finally kissed him. That was back when he was young and stupid and thought the thrill of the catch was worth the hard work. It didn't pay off, though. Once his parents found out that she had been living on friends' couches and sometimes in the woods, they insisted that Melody move in with them. From that point on, he was trapped.

He can't deny that she was in some ways good for him, and good *to* him, but he was too young to be picking one girl and settling. Even during college, when over a hundred miles separated them, she still visited him frequently. They always met up during their summer break, and despite mostly enjoying her company, he got bored.

The intrigue vanished, the thrill of the catch was nothing but a carcass on his plate, and he was full.

However, he stayed with her. She was a good person, and he needed that in his life. That's what his dad always told him, and for the most part, he believed it. She loved him, and in a familial way, he loved her back. His family, especially his dad, practically held him at gunpoint to make an honest woman of her. Leaving her would make him look like a monster, so he did what seemed like the logical next step in life; he proposed.

Marcus pulled himself out from under the orange floral blanket, leaving Kayla asleep on the dirty office floor. He stared at the side of her head as she slept. So peaceful. So young and naïve. He couldn't rightfully leave her behind to fend for herself, but he couldn't let her tag along either.

Marcus—the magnet for tragic females—jimmied the butter knife into the locked desk drawer that Kayla could not manage to open the day before, hoping to find something of use. The drawer bowed open at the top, and the frail, rusty internal mechanism snapped easily under the pressure. He jerked the drawer open, dropping the knife to the floor. He froze, hoping the noise wouldn't wake Kayla, but she was not fazed.

A chocolate bar laid neatly on top of an empty bank envelope. *Jackpot.* He scarfed it down as fast as he could. As he took each bite, he peered over his shoulder to be sure she remained asleep. With the last quarter of the chocolate bar remaining, he considered leaving it for Kayla, but he had to be smart. He needed strength and energy for the trip to the school, and one candy bar was barely enough calories to do it.

He had sacrificed enough already, spending the last decade with a woman whom he didn't really love. He sacrificed his dreams to stay with her and to keep her from falling apart. It was time to stop helping the people who couldn't manage to help themselves. Kayla would have to fend for herself. He swallowed the last of the chocolate and hid the evidence at the bottom of the drawer.

The morning light began to creep through the blinds of the office door, and Marcus peeked outside at the vacant storage alley. The infected people had moved on.

His plan was solid and honorable. Kayla had enough water for a couple of days, and she could venture out on her own when her feet healed. Marcus had to get moving.

THIRTY

Melody

Sunlight shone through the white lace curtains while John and Melody were still asleep in the house on Carlisle Road. The big hand on the grandfather clock jerked to the twelve, and a tiny bird poked its head from a hole, screaming out "cuckoo."

Melody bolted upright alongside John.

He jumped from the bed to stop the alarm as Melody ran to the bedroom door, still blocked by the dresser, prepared to stop anything that might try to enter. John tried ripping the bird from the clock, then grabbing the pendulum to keep it from moving, but it kept sounding. The alarm finally silenced after six cuckoos. It was eight o'clock in the morning. They'd slept later than expected.

They ate canned fruit and saltines they'd found in the garage and barely spoke to each other as Melody stirred her fruit cocktail with a spoon.

She was disturbed by her impassive state, surprised that she hadn't cried yet. Maybe she was in shock. Survival mode. She watched John as he attached his prosthetic leg. The muscles in his arms flexed and rippled as he leaned down to put it on.

"Let's see what else these people have," John said, heading to the garage. He scanned the shelves, moving dusty boxes and fishing gear until he found a small portable crank radio.

"No way," he said. "I haven't seen one of these in a while." John turned the tiny hand crank several times, arm growing tired after a minute, then switched hands to keep going. After it had been cranked, they hovered over it, turning the knob millimeter by millimeter, waiting for a station to come in. With each turn, the static remained steady until finally a voice came through. Melody pulled her hand back.

"…refuge can find it here." A man's voice crackled in the static. "…best minds working on a vaccine…" Static continued to interrupt the message, "Fort Drummond National Guard…LV01…causes abnormal behavior, aggression…violent tendencies…death within five to seven days…all persons seeking refuge can find it here." The message repeated itself, broken and full of static.

"Fort Drummond?" Melody tried to contain her excitement.

"That was a recording. Who knows how long it's been airing?"

"It could be overrun by now."

"Maybe," John said.

"That's just fifty miles or so north of my cabin," she said. Nervous energy ran through her as she went back to rummaging through the house for more supplies.

"We'll bring the radio and keep listening," said John. "If it stays the same, we'll assume it's overrun."

"Did you hear what they said? They die within five to seven days after infection. Is that accurate? Can we confirm that finding?"

"I don't know."

"It *is* similar to rabies."

"So, if people can hunker down for a week, nobody else will get infected? This could kill itself off?"

"Only if everyone, I mean *everyone*, keeps from getting bit for a week. The infected could die off."

THRITY ONE

Marcus

Marcus pulled the heavy desk centimeter by centimeter, trying to move it without making a noise. Each brief scrape across the floor shrieked through the small office.

Kayla yawned and stretched, and Marcus winced, kicking himself for moving so hastily. A little more patience, and he could've been out of this situation.

"Eww, I need a shower." She slipped her socks over the makeshift foot bandages.

Marcus scowled and considered making a run for it. He should knock her out and go. She'd never see it coming.

Kayla rubbed sleep from her eyes and poured more water from the corner cooler.

"We should get moving." He clenched his jaw, unable to do what he knew was necessary for his survival.

"Let me help." Kayla, barely awake, shuffled to the desk. He turned his head away from her, gritting his teeth as they shoved it away from the door.

"How much farther to the school did you say?" Kayla asked as Marcus stepped outside first. The road between the storage units was empty.

"Maybe a couple of miles."

Kayla clutched her wooden chair leg and followed him out.

They traveled close along the backs of buildings that ran parallel with the railroad fence. They crossed a construction site next door to the Fair Haven Plaza Shopping Center, and Marcus picked up a metal rod he'd found on the ground to use as a weapon.

Kayla struggled to keep up with his brisk pace as he moved around dumpsters along the back of the strip mall. It was time to stop caring. Time to fend for himself.

Then a miracle happened. As they crossed the space between buildings, they were spotted by the infected. About seven people, including two young ones, tripped and staggered from the street. Their eagerness sent them falling to the ground and crashing into each other, slowing their pace, but this was Marcus's chance.

He sped up.

Straight ahead, behind the next building, the space between the brick wall and the eight-foot fence narrowed. On the other side of the fence, a horde of the sick crowded the tracks and pressed against the chain link. They grabbed at the fence, pawing over one another to get closer to Marcus as he approached.

"Marcus?" Kayla called from behind.

"Keep up!" he snapped without so much as turning his head to look back. He couldn't bring himself to turn around. He was too weak to see her fall behind and not do something to help her. So, he kept his eyes forward and pushed onward toward the back of the next building.

The mass of people behind the fence snarled and moaned, lunging and snapping at each other. Marcus flinched, trying not to look at their faces as they scrambled along the fence to follow him. The noise had roused other lone infected people on the streets, and they closed in from the other direction.

"Marcus?"

He wished she would tire out and give up, but Kayla pushed on. He turned his head, and out of the corner of his eye, he saw the space between them growing.

"Marcus?" Her voice became distant.

Marcus approached the back of Barton Plastics Factory, where the long brick wall of the building backed up against the fence along the tracks, creating a narrow passage just wide enough for one person to walk through.

The fence gyrated, and their bodies pushed against one another to get to him. The daunting passageway caused him to pause and reconsider going around the front of the building, but another group of infected was staggering toward him from that direction.

"Please," Kayla said in desperation, falling at least forty yards behind.

Marcus turned around and looked at the pathetic redhead stumbling toward him, barely able to walk. She looked like one of them with her grungy clothes, scraggly hair, and sickly stance.

"I'm sorry," he whispered, tears biting at his eyes.

He rushed through the narrow passage, leaving her to fend for herself and freeing himself of the burden of protecting her. Guilt stabbed him in his heart, but his conscience needed to focus on survival.

The mass of bodies pressed against the fence, forcing it to bow inward, and Marcus kept his back to the brick wall, shuffling sideways. The bodies leaned toward him, oozing through the chain link. Bits of their flesh were getting caught in the rusty fence as he side-stepped along the wall. They pushed in closer, squeezing within inches of his face.

Kayla

Kayla's heart dropped to the deepest cavity within her as she watched her rescuer flee like a coward. Her world blurred out of focus, but she continued to push through the blinding pain of her wounded feet, faster and faster to catch up. However, the small group of the infected from the street had made it to the narrow passageway and blocked Kayla from following Marcus through.

The sun peeked out from behind the trees and poured rays of golden light across the infected. Sunlight glinted through the strands of their hair. She felt paralyzed for a moment, then let her anger take the lead. She tightened her grip on her chair leg and darted toward the front of the building, dodging the staggering infected. Most of them were incapable of walking in a straight line, falling over themselves, and smacking into the walls.

Cold, dead fingers swiped across her back as she arched out of the way of an attack. He fell to the cement and squirmed to get back up.

Kayla sprinted through the shooting pain in her feet that radiated up her shins. With tears welling in her eyes, she ran to the front of the building and pulled on the door handle. It was locked.

A group of them came up behind, so Kayla took off toward the opposite side of the building. She ran to the fenceline and leapt in front of the passageway where Marcus was still shuffling sideways toward her. She blocked him from exiting.

"You left me," she screamed, shaking.

"I…"

The fence creaked as it leaned in with the weight of the infected pressing against it. The pungent odor of the rotting flesh was right under their noses. The fence bowed further and was about to collapse.

"Get out of the fucking way!" He pushed past her, getting to the open space, but came face to face with more infected.

Kayla put her back to the brick wall of the factory and watched as Marcus swung his metal rod at the head of a drooling man in a Yankees shirt.

The blow knocked the man to the ground, but he immediately worked on getting back on his feet.

The growling, groaning, and the rattling of metal roared as dozens of manic infected pushed and clawed against the fence.

Another man, freckled with black sores, lunged toward Marcus, but Marcus jabbed him with the metal rod. Despite the blow, he kept coming at him. Kayla nearly leapt in to save him, but Marcus outmaneuvered the man. He spun around, positioning himself behind the infected man, and grabbed him by the shoulders.

Without hesitation, without a moment of contemplation, Marcus shoved him toward Kayla.

She screamed, and Marcus took the opportunity to escape.

Her arms trembled under his weight as he leaned heavily into her. Beyond his snarling face, she watched Marcus run off, dodging the infected and heading farther down the fence line.

A deep creaking sound of metal overpowered the noises of the infected. The chain link fence groaned like a sinking ship and snapped under the weight. The mass of writhing bodies plummeted to the ground along with the fence. Infected spilled onto the pavement into a pile, while Marcus vanished in the distance.

Kayla held off the black-splotched infected man with the chair leg pressed against his chest. She was pinned to the brick wall as the throng of fallen bodies began to rise to their feet, climbing over each other.

She released him long enough to jam the chair leg into the man's mouth. She plowed forward, shattering his teeth and sending him back, but she was already overtaken by the others.

Marcus

Marcus turned around as the crowd of bodies fought with each other and closed in on Kayla, trapping her against the wall. She sank below the sea of bodies. Her ungodly screams echoed in his mind as Marcus took off in a sprint.

At least five of the infected followed him. He didn't try to count. He just ran. He ran without thinking about anything other than survival. He focused on his loafers hitting the ground as his body plowed through the rays of sunlight beaming through the trees. He ran. That was all he could do.

He made it farther down the fence, scaled it, and kept running through the woods. Tripping over branches and sprinting through the trees as fast as his legs would carry him, he ran until he couldn't breathe.

Marcus stopped, panicked, whipping his head from side to side in search of incoming infected, but there was no one other than scattered dead bodies lying lifeless in the woods.

Panting, Marcus sat for a moment on a fallen log as he pulled in enormous gasps of air. His feet were heavy on the wet, mossy earth. Sweat ran down his back as he hung his head between his knees and pulled at his own hair.

What kind of man had he become? He could still hear the snarling and screaming, but it was in his head. Covering his ears didn't help. Marcus smacked himself against his skull repeatedly, trying not to fret over what *had* to be done.

"Damn it!" He whacked himself against the temple as her screams played on repeat. Dr. Carter's screams outside the lab joined in.

He had left them both to die. He could have saved Dr. Greg Carter when he had banged on the lab door to get back in, but he didn't. Greg made his choice to leave, and Marcus couldn't risk opening the door to let him back in.

He let them die to save himself, because he had to. It was necessary. Marcus stood up with a twitch in his eye, trying to catch his breath and keep his sanity.

This was how it had to be now. This was how a person would survive. Anyone who slowed him down would have to go.

He stayed close to the trees, following the tracks toward the school, gripping the metal rod in his sweaty, shaking palm, and ready to kill anyone who got in his way.

It was more peaceful now that he was alone. He didn't have to worry about whether or not she could keep up. He would make his way to the quarantine zone and finally get some food and rest, then he could move on.

Melody crept into his thoughts. He wondered if there was any possibility that she was there at the quarantine zone. He hoped not. He hoped that she got out of town or at least died quickly. His head spun, wondering how he could be so heartless, but he silenced his conscience. Melody would slow him down, just like Kayla did.

THIRTY TWO

John

They stared at each other for a long time, as if the world had just given them an opportunity but neither of them was ready to believe it.

They'd continue on with their plan to go to the lake house, get a boat, and go to the secluded cabin in the mountains to ride out the storm. There were far too many infected wandering Fair Haven, and they couldn't stay any longer. The school on the other side of the fence was so overrun, they feared it wouldn't be long before the infected stumbled into the yard, lured by a cuckoo clock or Harkness's barking. Getting on the boat was their best option. And then maybe Fort Drummond beyond that.

John found a school backpack in the hall closet packed with notebooks and trigonometry homework. Before he allowed himself to think about what happened to the kid who owned it, he dumped out the contents and got to work filling it with supplies. Knives, rope, lighter fluid, matches, and bungee cords were among the things he stuffed into the bag. He set the portable crank radio in the pack along with some canned food and was ready to go.

The lake cottage was not far. John stepped out the front door with Melody, and they began cutting across yards with Harkness trotting alongside them. A cold front had moved in the day before and brought relief from the sweltering heat. It felt more like autumn again.

Bodies lay dead on the sidewalks, and no signs of living people were in any direction. It made the world feel bigger. Like they were the only people remaining on the planet, until John saw the curtains move on the second floor of a house at the end of Carlisle.

"Did you see that?" Melody asked.

"Yeah." John kept an eye on the curtain and spotted the faint movement of a shadow backing away. "Let's keep moving. We don't want any trouble."

John scanned the other houses, wondering how many others could be alive, finding haven in the safety of their homes, and that thought brought a newfound sense of optimism.

"We can beat this," Melody said, passing another body. "Look. This person doesn't have life-threatening injuries."

She knelt over the short, round, dead woman, curled in the fetal position. "There are some minor lacerations—just the bite wound to her arm and some scratches. She got infected and died from the infection. Five to seven days. If people can stay inside, stay away from the infected, they can ride this out."

"If…" John said. "Look at us. We had to move. Getting frightened people to stay put is hard."

"But if there's a place like Fort Drummond—"

John interrupted, "*If…*"

"If they're studying the disease, they're working on a vaccination. We can beat this."

"That's a lot of *ifs*," John said.

They didn't encounter many of the infected on their way to the lake house, but they did see plenty of corpses, many swarmed by flies.

They hiked across the open fields through the Gilmore Farm on the outskirts of town, passing more bodies decomposing in the field with crows pecking at their flesh. Occasionally, they'd see a person lumbering along in the distance, but they were far enough away to avoid a fight.

John's leg was still sore, and Melody was exhausted, even after a full night's rest, so they were relieved to have a break from battle.

As they marched through a field of tall, golden grass, the low rising sun skimmed across the surface of the blades.

"Hey, Chuck, about last night…"

"Nope." Melody picked up her pace to move ahead of him.

"What do you mean, *nope*? I just want to talk about what happened between us last night."

"Don't flatter yourself, sweetheart," Melody said.

John smiled and tried to speed up behind her, but his swollen leg kept him back. He considered reaching for her hand, pulling her against himself, and lying her down right there in the field, but maybe that was too abrasive of a move right now. She would probably whack him upside the head with that bat of hers if he tried anything stupid again.

"I want to apologize for—"

"Don't apologize." She turned around to face him and smirked. "It was nice."

"It was nice?"

"Yes." She blushed. "It was a nice kiss."

"Oh, you thought I meant the kiss? No. I'm apologizing that you missed out on all this." John gestured to his own body sarcastically.

Melody rolled her eyes and stormed ahead, but he could tell she held back a laugh.

Ahead, they spotted the lake in a clearing between the trees. Thick dark clouds hung low on the horizon—a stark contrast to the bright, orange sunrise to the east.

Ahead, a Ford pickup's front end was lodged into the wall of one of the lake homes. Hitched behind it was the boat with the red lightning bolt that had sped out of their neighborhood two days ago.

"They didn't make it," John said.

"If we can get that truck backed out of the house, we've got a boat."

Harkness lowered his head to growl as an infected man staggered out from behind the house. John stepped in front of Melody. His shoulders dropped, and he held his hand over the knife at his hip. He was not up for the challenge today. Melody readied her bat and moved in front of John to approach the elderly infected man, snarling at them.

"I got it," she said.

"That's all right, Chuck," he argued and stepped in front of her.

As the infected man rushed forward, John realized he shouldn't risk the fight. Neither he nor Melody had the strength for combat.

"How close are we?" John asked.

Melody pointed down the gravel drive. "Close enough."

He pulled his rifle from his back and fired a shot into the man's head. The guy dropped in an instant.

John slung his rifle on his back. "Better hurry." He could barely walk. The prosthetic ground into the raw end of his leg.

"We're almost there," she assured him and started running.

The sunlight to the east had disappeared behind the fast-moving clouds, and a rumble of thunder rolled across the late morning air.

They arrived two minutes later in front of a tiny pink house with weeds already invading the landscaped front yard. The little cottage was no more than five hundred square feet. Out back, the land sloped down into a steep hill that led to a dock with the pontoon boat tied to it. The sight was an instant balm to all worries.

We have a boat.

A sprinkling of rain began to pepper the dock, and the sky became electrified over the lake. Melody tilted a canoe that leaned against a tall oak tree behind the cottage and pulled out the hidden house key.

She unlocked the back door, and they walked onto the furnished screened porch that overlooked the lake. Beyond the porch was an inside door that led to a musty, dark living room. The stale odor inside indicated that her in-laws had not been there in a while. The cottage was no more than a kitchenette, tiny bath, and living room, with an open loft bedroom above.

John sat down on the green tweed couch on the screened porch and lifted his prosthetic leg onto the coffee table. A spectacular view of the lake sprawled out before him, with nickel grey clouds creeping above it. He removed the prosthetic to expose his swollen flesh. The skin around the wound was discolored.

"Holy shit," Melody said.

"It's okay." John leaned back on the couch and winced from the pain. "I have that balm."

"Balm, my ass!"

"Well, if you say so…" He shot her a playful sneer.

"You're going to need more than just a balm for that." Melody hurried to the kitchen. "My mother-in-law is always on a prescription for something."

John could hear her rummaging through cabinets.

"But it looks like all she has here is Tums and Tylenol." She shook a couple of Tylenol into her hand and brought them to John. "The vet clinic is right down the road, though, so I can get you some antibiotics and better pain meds."

"Dog drugs?"

Melody smiled. "Amoxicillin. Cephalexin. It's the same as human drugs. I had them in my pack, but that's gone now."

She tried to get John a glass of water from the kitchen, but a grinding sound came from the faucet, then nothing.

John called to her from the porch, "I take it the water tower doesn't supply these old lake houses?"

"I guess not," she said. "I'll get some water from the lake."

"That's okay," he said and popped the pills in his mouth and swallowed. "Let's wait out this storm—"

Melody, without warning, ran outside with an empty glass jug in her hand. John jumped up to stop her, but she was already halfway down the stairway to the dock by the time he made it to the door. John's heart pounded within his throat. He worried he would not be able to act quickly enough if she needed help. He readied his rifle.

"Chuck," he whispered, while he propped himself in the door frame on one leg and kept an eye out for the infected.

She lay down on the dock and scooped up water from the rough waves, then hurried back to him without incident. He peered in all directions outside as she came back.

"Don't do that again," he insisted.

His concern shocked him. He didn't realize how important she was to him until, in that brief moment, she left. He imagined what would happen if he lost her. She kept him sane, and she kept him laughing, but she also kept him *safe*. He would have been dead under a pile of infected if she hadn't stepped out of her front door the other day. She was exactly what he needed in his life, and he was certain that she needed him, too.

Melody

Melody raised an eyebrow. "Don't do that again?" she mocked him.

She knelt beside the couch and held up a brown bottle of hydrogen peroxide that she had found in the bathroom.

He sat down beside her and held out his leg while Harkness curled up beside him. She poured it onto his irritated, raw skin and watched as John clenched his jaw and gripped his own legs. A white foam bubbled up as the peroxide invaded the wound. Melody rinsed it off with lake water.

"Peroxide isn't the best choice because it'll kill good cells too," she explained. "But I didn't see any soap in there, so peroxide it is—just once—

to kill off any bacteria and stuff, and we'll keep it clean with just water from here on out."

She didn't have much gauze left to wrap his leg, so she suggested he let his skin air out until they needed to get moving. She would have to get to the veterinary clinic for more supplies, but first, she sat down beside John on the couch to look out over the lake and give her body a much-needed break.

"You shouldn't wear your prosthetic until your leg heals."

"I don't exactly have a lot of options, unless I hop around on one leg."

"That won't be necessary." Melody left his side and went to the small bathroom. She pulled open the shower stall curtain and found Marcus's dad's walker. Melody carried it out to the screened porch and set down the gray, shiny walker with three tennis balls on the feet. The fourth ball was missing.

"Tada!"

John looked at it and shook his head. "No."

She rolled her eyes and picked it up. "Look, it can be a weapon too." She laughed and jabbed it at the air. "It's here in case you need it."

"I'm not using that thing."

"Well, that would be stupid of you."

The rain fell. The landscape turned gray as the thunder cracked. Waves on the lake crashed against the dock, rocking the pontoon boat as a tall, thin infected man crossed into the backyard. He dragged his feet through the grass, kicking up mud as he stumbled along. The rain poured upon him, and he trudged on, unaware that John and Melody were sitting exposed within the screened porch, close enough to see the detail of his pineapple-printed necktie.

They sat still with their breath held as he moved on. Lightning streaked across the lake, followed by a piercing crack of thunder. The man turned toward the sound and lunged as if picking a fight with God above. He reached the edge of the slope and tumbled down to the bottom of the hill. The lanky man scrabbled to his feet, walked in circles, biting at the sky with every rumble of thunder, then he dropped off the edge of the bank and into the waist-deep water. Waves knocked him around until he was swept under and out of sight.

Melody's mouth hung open. She turned to John, who had an equally shocked look on his face, and they both started laughing. Melody covered her mouth, trying not to, but couldn't help herself.

"We shouldn't be laughing." She whacked John in the chest with the back of her hand while they both tried to contain their laughter.

That brief touch of her hand against John's chest lingered on her skin. She wanted to touch him again. John leaned back into the arm of the couch, resting his head in the crook. His posture practically invited her to touch him, so she let herself in. She invaded his space, crawling closer to him, until her head came to rest against the cotton fabric clinging to his pecs. Her arms rested around his waist, and she closed her eyes. As she inhaled, her breasts pressed against his abs.

John raked her tangled hair away from her face and let it fall behind her back, then he rested his arm on her.

This feels easy.

That brief moment of comfort and solitude with a friend was worth all the fighting it took to get there.

Melody wanted to stay with John every step of their journey, but she couldn't let him risk the trip to the vet hospital on that leg. Once he was asleep, she would sneak away to get the supplies he needed. However, her body had other plans, as she accidentally drifted to sleep instead.

They both slept for a couple of hours on that couch as the storm moved through. A cool wind blew through the screened porch, bringing in splatters of rainfall onto the cement floor as they napped.

THIRTY THREE

John

John woke to the sound of gravel crunching beneath tires. He slid out from under Melody while she slept and heard the vehicle rolling to a stop. There was no time to remove the bandages and put on his prosthetic, so he grabbed the old man's walker.

The sudden jump upright made him dizzy. Blood rushed to the end of his residual limb, and it throbbed as if the sores might burst open with each step.

Through the small kitchen window, he saw a blue Toyota screeching to a stop out front with at least eight infected trailing it.

He rushed out the front door, shifting the tennis-ball walker beneath him, pistol in hand. A tall, lean man exited the vehicle in front of the cottage—a familiar-looking man.

"Keep it running!" John shouted as he pointed toward the incoming infected.

"Who the hell are you?" the man asked, putting his hands in the air at the sight of John's gun.

John recognized him and couldn't believe it. "They'll follow the car. Move!"

Marcus backed away as John took a few enormous leaps with the walker, as fast as his body could go. He leaned into the car, put it in drive, and pressed on the gas pedal with his hand. He pulled his body out of the vehicle as it jolted forward, but not without the door frame whacking him in the right shoulder as he backed out. The blue vehicle crept down the gravel road and veered slowly into an open field.

John signaled for the man to follow him.

"You're my neighbor, aren't you?" Marcus asked, scurrying alongside John to the back of the cottage where they waited in silence for the mass of infected to stagger by, uninterested in John or Marcus. They followed the car as it rolled to a stop in the field.

John and Marcus entered through the screened porch. His chest tightened as he closed the door, and Marcus moved toward the kitchen. John waited a moment longer to be sure nobody followed them.

Melody

Melody had heard the commotion, so she went to the kitchen window to see the scattered group of infected as they stumbled down the road toward a blue car. Before she got a chance to see where John had gone, the back screen door creaked open and a familiar voice came through asking John, "What the hell are you doing here?"

Melody's heart plummeted to her gut, and she wanted to puke.

"Marcus?" she said.

There he was, standing in the same room with her. The man she had given up on. He made it to her. So many questions whizzed through her head as they stood separated by a mere seven feet.

"Melody?" Marcus opened his arms, smiled, and tucked her into a snug embrace. "I'm so glad I found you."

She hugged her husband and squeezed her eyes shut tight, thinking that when she opened them, she'd be back on the couch with John, with the cool lake breeze misting their skin. But when she opened her eyes, Marcus was still there, pressing his body against her. John stood in the doorway, watching as she and Marcus held each other.

THIRTY FOUR

Kayla

Kayla Hartford had been backed against a brick wall and surrounded by
infected as she watched Marcus run for his life. She slunk down, accepting her
fate as the horde toppled the fence and came at her.

Her life flashed before her eyes. Until this moment, she believed it to
be a figure of speech, but—in an instant—she saw it all. Her dad teaching
her to ride her bike. Mom sprinkling white flour onto a cookie sheet. Playing
rummy with her brother on their bellies in the den. Her prom dance with her
girlfriend beneath the glitter of the ballroom lights. All of it was revealed to
her in an epic one-second flash.

On the ground, with her heart wailing, she screamed in terror, looking
away from the infected and awaiting her demise. But as she turned her head
to look away, she saw that the crashed fence was pressed against the wall,
creating a tunnel.

A way to crawl out. She could reach the opening with her hand.

Their hands fell upon her body, and she crawled beneath the fallen fence,
squealing as sickly fingers grabbed at her legs and pawed at her body.

She scampered on her belly along the pavement under the chain link
as the horde piled on top, darkening her path. Bits of gravel stuck to her
forearms and knees.

The metal pressed against her back and the top of her head, pinning her down, but she stayed close to the wall and managed to squeeze through. They snarled through the fence, grabbing and biting, pulling her hair and scratching her back.

She screamed out in excruciating pain but continued to crawl out to the other side, where she got to her feet and ran.

Blood dripped down her back and legs as she followed the fence as fast as her sock-footed, injured feet could move. The horde of infected was not far behind.

She had to keep moving forward, away from the infected, even if she backtracked in the wrong direction. There was nowhere else to go. She kept a steady pace, but was slowed by the nauseating pain encompassing every inch of her body. Afraid to stop and inspect herself for wounds, she kept going.

She wanted her mom and dad. She wanted Marcus to be a good man. She wanted her teeth to stop chattering and her eyes not to fill with tears, blurring the world around her.

When she was far enough ahead of the infected, she slipped back through the fence at one of the gates and went into the woods.

Kayla lay down on the wet, muddy earth beneath the tree canopy. The cool mud on her body relieved the wounds on her back. She stared above as the sunlight decided whether or not it would stick around. She wanted it to. Her body was tired, weak, and in more anguish than she'd ever experienced. She wished she had let the infected kill her. A few minutes of pain would have been better than the horror she experienced now.

"I can't do this anymore," she cried in a sputtering whisper.

The camp was nearby, back in the other direction—where Marcus had fled.

Fucking Marcus. She would kill him if she found him there.

Rage filled her heart, and she drove herself back to her feet. If she fought a little longer and a little harder, she could soon have sanctuary at the quarantine camp.

She moved slowly, lurching through the woods, wanting to collapse with every step. Her scraped feet were numb compared to the throbbing pain in her legs. Her back wounds stung, and her own blood dried, gluing her shirt to her skin.

She was starving, dehydrated, and ready to die, but her mind zoned out as she plodded along. All she had to do was put one foot in front of the other.

It was as if she woke up from a nightmare as she realized she stood in front of the high school. Hope prevailed, and her heart lightened as she saw the goal posts of the football field through the trees ahead. The agony lifted as the gentle push of angels seemed to propel her closer to the school. The clouds above parted, allowing sunlight to spill before her feet, and the gloom lifted. Her god spoke to her, telling her it would be alright, but the sound of moaning ahead stopped her.

Muddled voices slurred and groaned. She inched forward to the bend in the tracks, staying hidden within the trees as the gated fence near the school came into view. It held back hundreds of them. Maybe more. The quarantine zone was gone.

Kayla backed out of sight around the bend and collapsed to the ground in defeat. The sun had been swallowed by the fast, incoming clouds. Rain began to fall, and she curled into herself while all of the other lost lives roamed about in the fenced enclosure.

She gave up. She let the rain drip-drip-drip onto her body while she lay in the mud. All hope of survival seeped out of her wounds and into the ground.

The moaning around her grew louder, and the shuffling of bodies in the woods nearby was terrifying enough to drive her back to her feet. The thought of being torn apart and eaten alive was far worse than moving on. She needed shelter.

She left the tracks and walked down the street in front of the school. The basketball court and playground were empty. The homes appeared to be uninhabited. Kayla could have stopped at any of the houses, but instead, she kept moving forward in a mindless shuffle. She snapped back to consciousness and wasn't sure where she was. She had walked all the way down the street to Macky's Quick Mart at the entrance to Barton Harbor.

With a few infected wandering nearby, she decided to take cover in the convenience store. She made it to the front door and gave a tug on the handle. It opened. The bell jingled, and she stepped into the store.

"Hello?" Her mouth could barely form the word in her weakened state.

The store was silent, and most of the shelves had been ransacked. The cigarette shelves were empty with the exception of a few random fallen packs of Camels. The safe behind the counter was busted open. Her eye twitched and her hands trembled as she stumbled around the convenience store, looking for a way to block the door from being pulled open, but she could not think of a way.

An infected woman in bloodied scrubs approached the door from outside and smacked into the glass. She backed up and walked into the door again.

Kayla hid behind the counter and sat on the floor out of sight. Scraped up and bleeding, she hugged her knees and rocked her body, wondering what to do. On the floor to her right was a single-serve bag of cheesy puffs that she tore into, devouring it within seconds. The infected woman outside had given up and moved on, so Kayla explored the coolers for something to drink. She chugged a warm vitamin water, but as it splashed into her belly, she felt sick to her stomach.

Dizziness took over, but she pushed through it, remained focused, and found some rubbing alcohol on the shelves. She pulled off her blouse and poured some down her back. The white hot, burning pain was enough to make anyone scream, but Kayla knew better than to make noise. She clenched her teeth together and cried silently. Her calves were worse.

She changed into a Barton Harbor of Fair Haven t-shirt, then doused the fabric of another shirt with more alcohol and began to clean the dried blood from her legs. On her ankle, there was a distinct bite mark.

Kayla hurried to the bathroom to vomit. Her hands were clammy, and her vision tunneled. She sat against the bathroom wall and closed her eyes, knowing it was all over.

An hour later, she woke up even more sick than before. She vomited again and looked at her leg to see black necrotic tissue already surrounding her bite wound. Angry that God didn't take her in her sleep, she asked, "Why?"

She sobbed, but the guttural retches made her vomit more.

"Is this punishment?" she asked, looking to the drop-leaf ceiling of the convenience store.

Her head was foggy, and there was a slight pull in her head to the right, like a brick took up the right half of her brain. She focused on walking a straight path through the store, but she kept stumbling to the side.

Kayla sat back down on the floor and rested her head against the shelves. She didn't want to die in Macky's Quick Mart.

She wasn't ready for it all to end yet. She had plans and dreams. She wanted to travel, and to learn more, and to *love* more. She hadn't found real love yet, but she knew it existed.

Fucking Marcus.

She clenched her jaw and ground her teeth at the thought of him. In a fit of anger, Kayla banged her head against the shelves, screaming out. A tire iron fell into her lap. She laughed in hysteria and looked to the ceiling.

"What am I supposed to do with this?"

She looked at the poster of a man in sunglasses to her right. It was an advertisement for something blurring in and out of focus.

"You kind of look like him, you know?"

The man in the ad smiled back at her behind his mysterious shades.

"Maybe I'm immune," she told him. "Maybe the world needs my immunity."

Speaking became difficult, and her breathing more labored.

"What?" She scowled at the man in the ad, then threw the tire iron at his head. The metal bounced off the floor and landed beneath a rack of maps.

"Barton Harbor," she read the sign above the maps out loud, remembering Marcus's story about riding his bike on Barton Rd.

She stood up, but her heavy head pulled her body to the right. It took all of her focus to get to the display and pull out a map. She ran her finger down the column of tiny letters to find the barely visible words coming in and out of focus.

Barton Rd.

She found the tiny road on the map. It was not far from where she was. A wave of relief and vengeance swept over her. She picked up the tire iron and gripped it in her clammy palm. She was certain she would find Marcus there.

Before leaving, she ditched her filthy crew socks that she'd stolen from a corpse the day before, and she slid on a pair of palm tree flip-flops. She packed a plastic bag with whatever her wandering hands found: chips, aspirin, the Carroll County Realty Guide, and cigarettes—even though she didn't smoke.

Sweating and green, she flung open the door. Before she stepped foot outside, a blue car sped by so fast she couldn't follow it with her eyes. She felt drunk—worse than drunk. More like a terrible acid trip. The smear of blue seemed to stretch for miles, but it faded as she approached it. Kayla knew she was hallucinating now. She focused her energy on her map, gripped the tire iron in her hand, and prepared herself for a taste of revenge. The cheap rubber flip flops scuffed across the cement as she lumbered along, determined to find Marcus.

THIRTY FIVE

Marcus

The rain was letting up after the cold front pushed through town, bringing cooler air and sending leaves twirling through the breeze. When Marcus had found that the high school was overrun, he sprinted across the field toward the parking lot, and the infected inside the fence had been roused.

A crowd of the sick and dying souls gathered along the edge of the football field fence, following him. They fought in a brawl that put too much pressure on the fence. The joints creaked between the panels of chain links. The rickety, rusted joint snapped under pressure, and the fence opened up, spilling a deluge of the infected into the soccer fields, free to roam Fair Haven.

Marcus must have checked at least thirty cars before he found one with a set of keys inside. He had peeled out of there and watched the crowd of infected shrink in his rearview mirror. He sped down the street, passed Mackey's, and headed straight to the lake house. Despite what he had told Kayla, he knew his parents' boat was still docked when the outbreak began. But he wasn't expecting company.

Melody

The tiny round window in the lake cottage loft let in a beam of light. Specks of dust drifted through the air in a serene dance until Marcus walked through it, sending the dust spiraling out of control. He sat down beside Melody on the twin bed in the loft, while John sat on the couch below, wrapping his swollen leg.

"Where have you been?" Melody asked.

"Where have *you* been? I've been looking all over for you, and you're shacked up with some guy."

The accusation provoked her, but she clenched her jaw and explained, "I waited. You never came—"

"So, you decided to run off with this guy?" Marcus gestured toward the ladder that led to John.

"John's our neighbor," Melody snapped. "He was helping me find you."

She knew John could hear them talking, and she was embarrassed by Marcus's belligerence. She leaned back to take a breath, wondering why she bothered to argue with him. She reached into her pocket and presented Marcus's wedding band to him.

"You were at the lab?" he asked. "When?"

"Yesterday, but you weren't there." Melody held the ring out for him to take. "I found your coat, shredded. I thought...I thought you were—"

"Thank you," he interrupted with a display of heartfelt sincerity, taking the ring and squeezing it onto his finger. "I thought I lost this forever. I was attacked by one of them in the office and had to lose the coat. Greg didn't make it, M."

"I know."

"We tried to work on a vaccine, but—"

"You left me." Her conviction retracted into a dark cave, and sadness took its place.

"M," Marcus said, "I had to go. But then we were trapped. The building was overrun, and I couldn't get back to you. But you know what?"

Melody remained quiet.

"I knew you would be fine. You're a fighter."

"I'm tired of fighting," Melody said, defeat in her tone.

Marcus put a hand on her leg. "It wasn't safe to leave the lab until yesterday. We must have just missed each other. I'm sorry I left you, but this vaccine was so important."

"And?"

"Well, obviously I don't have a vaccine," he snapped, and then bit his tongue to control his temper.

"We heard on the radio that there's a safe zone—a compound at Fort Drummond working on a vaccine."

Marcus raised his eyebrows, "Fort Drummond? Military? Hope they have some real scientists there."

"If we get there, we can help."

"We?"

"Yes. You're not the only doctor here, Marcus."

"M," he said.

She cringed and cut him off before he said anything. "People were making vaccines in the 1800s before modern technology. We both know the science behind vaccines, so yes, we both can help with this. It's a lyssavirus— like rabies."

Marcus rolled his eyes. "You're not going to let this rabies thing go, are you?"

His condescending remark brought the conversation to a halt. He had always been that way. Marcus had always held himself on a pedestal while snickering at Melody's insignificance.

She despised him for it and regretted waiting for him at the house. She regretted risking lives to try to save him. Most of all, she regretted ever marrying him.

Marcus placed his hand on top of Melody's. "After I lost power, I went to the quarantine zone to find you. I thought you would be there. I was scared to death that I lost you." Marcus moved in closer and put his arm around her waist.

His touch was toxic, drifting lower toward her butt.

Melody was stiff and motionless, ready to strike when she spied a long red hair on his shirt. The same shade of unnatural red that had been on his coat in the lab. She backed away, pulled the crimson strand from the fabric, and held it for him to see.

"What's that?" he asked.

"You tell me."

He tilted his head. "That's probably from the bitch who nearly killed me. I had a real close call. Some redhead got her hands on me." Marcus told a harrowing tale of his encounter in the lab with the redhead that made him leave his white coat behind, but his words fell on distrustful ears.

Marcus moved in for a kiss. He placed his hands on her hips and glided in. She allowed her husband's warm, dry lips to press against hers, but the kiss was emotionless. She didn't love him anymore, and as he hunched his body to suckle on her neck, shame pumped through her veins.

Marcus slid his hand to the top of her pants and popped the button open, but she backed away. "What are you doing?"

"I figured—"

"John's right downstairs."

"So what?" he laughed. "You and he didn't…" His face became serious as he looked over the edge of the balcony at John, who was finishing the bandage on his leg.

John

John had heard everything from downstairs. He sat on the couch with his rifle at his side and his knife attached to his hip. His leg throbbed, and the heat radiated up his thigh. This Marcus guy was going to be a problem.

Melody climbed down the ladder, and Marcus followed.

"Before we head north, I'm making a trip down to the vet clinic for some antibiotics," she said.

Marcus sneered. "For him? No. We don't even know him."

"*You* don't know him. *I* do."

"I'm not letting you risk your life for that guy."

"He risked his for me—"

"So did I!" Marcus yelled. "I almost died trying to get to you, and I find you here with some guy…and a dog? What's that all about?"

John stood up. "The neighborhood was overrun, and Melody was worried you were trapped. We risked our asses for you."

Marcus had no response.

"But don't worry, bro. I'll go get my own meds," John said.

"Thanks, man." Marcus shot him a smug grin and patted John on the shoulder.

John would've liked to punch the guy in the face.

"*I'm* going to get the medicine," Melody said. "Not just for John. There are a lot of drugs we might need later down the road, too."

"You're not going." Marcus shook his head.

"Neither of you have a say in this!" she snapped. "You don't know which meds do what—"

"M, I have a PhD, I think I know—"

"You don't know where the keys are for the controlled substance safe. I'm going."

John smiled at her tenacity.

"I'll take the boat." Melody looked out of the screened porch at the lake and pointed to the edge of the cove. "It's right around that corner. I'll dock beyond there and climb the bank. The clinic is right there."

John sighed, "I'll go with you, Chuck."

"Chuck?" Marcus's brow furrowed.

"No," she said, eyes drifting toward his leg, and he realized he was the weak link.

"I'll go with her," Marcus cut in.

John knew that he was in no condition to travel by foot. With the prosthetic on, it was too painful. He would only slow them down, but he was afraid to send Melody out alone with this guy. Husband or not, Marcus was not to be trusted.

"If you're taking the boat, I'm coming and I can offer cover from the water."

She nodded.

He leaned on the walker and fixed the rifle strap on his shoulder.

"Or," Marcus interjected, "you wait here, and let us take that gun. You look like you need some rest."

"I'm a better shot than you," John argued.

"You don't know that," Marcus said.

Melody shushed them both. She was at the kitchen window, bent over the sink, trying to get a better view of whatever was out there.

"Quiet. Someone's coming."

THIRTY SIX

Kayla

Kayla's head filled with fluid and barely sat on top of her neck without wobbling. All of her energy and focus poured into following her map to Barton Road. She gripped her tire iron a little tighter within her sweating palm.

A few infected peppered the streets on the outskirts of town near Barton Harbor, but most of the bodies she came across were dead.

As Kayla turned down the road to the harbor, an infected man circled nearby. She readied her weak stance, but the man draped in blood had no interest in attacking her. Clockwise circling, dragging his left foot, unaware she was there.

The infected man's walk pissed her off—she clenched her jaw and fought the urge to lash out, but it was too strong. Kayla lunged at him, swinging the tire iron at his head in an outburst of rage. He crashed to the ground, moaning. The blow threw Kayla off balance, and she fell to her side. After stumbling back to her feet with inexplicable fury, she bashed him in the head again and again, until his skull was unrecognizable.

With a tire iron dripping with blood, bits of pink flesh, and sinew, she gathered her bag of supplies and moved forward.

The road ahead rocked from side to side as her flip-flops scraped along gravel.

Gravel. Marcus used to ride bikes here as a kid. Baron of Barton Road.

A closer examination of herself revealed that she had dropped her tire iron somewhere along the way. All feeling in her right arm was lost, but her plastic bag of supplies was still with her, wrapped around her left wrist, cutting off circulation.

Scattered infected meandered about the area, uninterested in her. The pain from the bite in her leg radiated up her hips and into her spine. Feverish, sweat dripped into the scratches across her back, stinging the wounds, and she didn't know how much longer she could stay conscious. She had to find that son of a bitch soon.

"Marcus," she could barely say the name aloud at first, but after a couple of attempts, she managed to yell, "Marcus!"

Kayla, sweating and trembling from the chills running through her body, shuffled forward in her search for the man who tried to kill her.

The road swayed as she called out louder, "Marcus!" The light tunneled into darkness, and she collapsed forward onto her face.

Marcus

Melody darted out the front door, leaving Marcus and John behind.

"M!" Marcus shouted and ran out after her as Melody approached a girl with flaming red hair, lying face down on the gravel.

"Leave her!" Marcus said, shocked to see Kayla all the way out here.

Melody neared the unconscious girl and inspected her from a distance, while three other infected made their way toward her.

"She's infected," Marcus said.

"No. I heard her say something."

"What did she say?" His blood rushed to his feet, and his body went calm and still as if it were readying itself for an attack.

"I think," Melody said, "she said, *help us.*"

Marcus urged Melody to get away from her and get back to the house, while John fired a shot with his rifle into one of the infected that were closing in on them. The sound startled him, and Marcus pleaded with Melody to hurry.

She refused. Melody grabbed Kayla by the hands and pulled.

John fired again, dropping another infected to the ground. "Hurry up," he shouted, resting his weight on the edge of the walker.

"Damn it, Melody! Leave her. She's gone," Marcus said.

Melody's eyes pierced him with contempt. She wasn't giving in, no matter what he said, so he let her have her way before she decided to push him into one of John's bullets.

He grabbed Kayla's feet and lifted. Together, they carried her back to the house and locked themselves inside.

"That was really stupid," he said to Melody. "Why are you always like this? Risking everything for puppies and things that don't matter? Risking *our* lives for one of them?"

Melody drove her dagger eyes into him again while he paced, eager to get moving on. He spotted the old black ammunition chest beneath the couch upon which Kayla rested. It was the chest that his grandfather used to keep old police uniforms in, the one with the pistol that got him in trouble, and Marcus wondered if it was still there.

Melody tried to relieve Kayla's fever with a wet washcloth. It was pointless, but Marcus shut up about it and let her do her thing. Melody inspected the bandage on the back of the girl's leg, and when she peeled it back, Marcus could see the arc-shape of a bite wound.

"Infected," Marcus snapped. "I told you!"

"Hey," John cut in, "She was just trying to help a person out."

"We need to get it out of here before it kills us," Marcus said.

"*It?*" Melody said with disgust in her tone. "*It's* a person! She was *talking*, calling for help."

Kayla stirred on the couch and moaned, and Marcus turned away with haste to get out of her sight. He couldn't risk going for the black chest now. If there was a pistol in there, he didn't want the others knowing when he got his hands on it.

John kept his own pistol on his hip, while Melody rummaged through the plastic bag that was on Kayla's wrist.

"What's in there?" Marcus asked.

"Not much." Melody pulled out some cigarettes, a map, and a realty book. She held it for a moment and thumbed through the pages, stopping when she spotted the listing of her grandfather's cabin. She glared at Marcus and set it down. Considering everything they'd been through, it was petty of her to still be sore over that worthless shack in the woods.

"Nothing useful."

"M, we either need to put her down, or we have to get out of here before she becomes one of them."

"I'm going to the clinic," she said.

John inspected Kayla's wound. "You said so yourself, Melody: once a person has symptoms, there's nothing that will save them. It's too late for her."

"Maybe it is," she said, "But we still need antibiotics for your leg, and we can stock up on other meds for whatever else might happen down the road."

"So, what do we do about her?" Marcus said.

"She's not gone yet."

"She may as well be!" Marcus threw his arms in the air.

"Are *you* going to kill her? Are *you* gonna stab a girl in her head when she's not being aggressive? When she hasn't fully become one of...one of them?"

John cut in before Marcus could reply. "I'll do it."

"Thank God!" Marcus sighed.

"But I'll wait until she turns."

Melody

Melody couldn't bear to take another life today, even if the girl was Marcus's secret lover.

She couldn't sit around and wait for this girl to turn into a monster. She couldn't plunge her blade into a person's head and be okay with it. Humanity was escaping her with every life she took, and she had to try something else.

"If you insist on going to the vet clinic, then I'll go with you," Marcus said, holding the keys to the pontoon boat.

John flung his backpack over his shoulder and stumbled to the side. The infection was making him weak. Dehydration and a lack of proper nutrition exacerbated the issue. Melody knew he needed to rest.

"John," she said, choosing her words tactfully. "Why don't you wait here for us? You said you'd take care of her when she—"

"Are you giving me a bullshit job because you think I can't handle it out there?"

"Do you think I'm pandering to your need to be useful?" Melody said.

"Feels that way."

"For my sanity, please stay with her, just in case. None of us should be carrying her to the boat, and even if we do get her to the boat safely, I'm not sure it's a good idea to be trapped on a boat with her. And we can't bring Harkness into the vet clinic or leave him barking on the boat."

John wanted to say more, but Melody couldn't tell what it was. He probably wanted to argue about his leg, about Marcus, about going to the clinic for drugs that were obviously just for him. Instead, he handed over his rifle to Melody.

"Come on," Marcus said, heading out the door.

John whispered to Melody, "Is he trustworthy?"

Melody nodded.

"Let's go!" Marcus called from outside as Melody and John exchanged words.

"Yes." Melody leaned in. "I trust him for this. Don't worry. Thirty minutes is all it should take."

She grabbed her backpack and turned to leave, but paused in the doorway. Marcus was already halfway down the steps to the dock when Melody ran back to John and placed the Carroll County Realty Guide from the girl's bag in his hands.

"Just in case. Page forty-eight."

John grabbed her by the wrist and pulled her in for a hug, squeezing for a full three seconds, then backed away. There was a warning in her heart that she needed to kiss him goodbye. That this would be the last time she'd see John.

John

John's entire body was weak, like his body had sprung a leak, and his life's energy was dripping onto the floor. Sharp, burning pain radiated from his knee up his thigh and into his hip. He sat in a wicker chair within reach of the girl's head and watched as Marcus and Melody pulled away on the boat. Harkness sat by his side and whimpered as Melody drifted away.

The boat went around the bend, and now he had to wait. Whether or not Melody ever returned was out of his control. He sat beside the redheaded girl, knife ready, but exhaustion drew his eyelids down.

He shook his head vigorously to keep himself awake, then decided to walk around to fight sleep. He scanned certificates and news clippings that were hanging on the cabin walls. Accolades of Marcus's grandfather, Wayne Hill, adorned the walls.

Beneath the couch sat a black chest. He had noticed Marcus eyeballing it just minutes ago and wondered what was in it that caught his attention. Just as he reached for it, the girl groaned and turned over in her sleep, letting her arm crash to the floor. John waited for her to turn; it would be any moment now. But instead, she kept breathing steadily, a rhythmic and ragged breath that lulled his heavy eyelids shut.

THIRTY SEVEN

Melody

Danger loomed in the clouds over Melody's head as Marcus drove the pontoon boat around the bend, but it wasn't just the static of a storm that worried her. She'd lied to John when she said she could trust Marcus, but she didn't dare risk dragging John along with her. He was damn-near septic with those wounds on his leg. If she didn't get some drugs for him soon, she wasn't sure how long he'd survive.

They neared the boat launch where a sailboat remained tied to the dock. Its starboard side sank beneath the choppy water, mast bobbing above the surface. Dozens of the infected staggered along the shoreline and the docks aimlessly.

Ten of them lay dead on the ground around the boat slip.

The boat's motor drew the attention of those who were still alive, and their aimless wandering shifted simultaneously toward the incoming vessel. At least six of them dropped off the dock and into the water. Some sank below the surface, and others thrashed face down and drowned within a couple of minutes. Marcus snagged the rifle and aimed at the infected, but Melody was quick to stop him.

"It'll only attract more." Melody cut the engine and let the boat drift in silence.

"There." She pointed to a wooded area beyond the docks where a pebbled shoreline was exposed. The boat passed the dock, far enough away that the infected lost interest in it. Marcus let it bump gently against the shore.

They scanned the thick wooded area that led up the hill, then made a run for it. Through the pines, up the steep, muddy terrain to the back of the veterinary hospital.

Instead of risking the trip around the building to the front doors, Melody climbed onto the dumpster out back and wedged open the small window to the bathroom. She hoisted herself up and inside the space that reeked of death. Marcus followed closely behind.

Shuffling footsteps moved outside the closed bathroom door.

"I thought you said everyone left," Marcus whispered.

"I thought they did."

He readied the rifle on his shoulder, hands trembling as someone thumped against the door.

Melody steadied her left hand over the doorknob, gripped her knife in her other hand, and looked to Marcus to be sure he was ready.

She whipped open the door, pinning herself between the door and the wall for protection as Marcus fired the rifle. She jumped out from behind the door to see Hannah with a hole in her chest.

You can't save them all, Melody had told Hannah a few days earlier. The memory flashed before her. *I can try.*

The petite, young black-haired girl had flung against the wall, but regained her footing and lunged toward them.

"Fuck!" Marcus staggered back and fired a second shot into her chest, but the girl kept coming at them.

Melody readied her knife, but she hesitated. Hannah attacked, drooling and growling, blood pouring from the bullet holes in her chest, pale skin, and blue lips.

She had stayed behind to risk her life for a dying cat.

That was how she remembered Hannah. Her kindness. Her naïve young heart. Her hysterical tears during her first euthanasia. Every memory rushed through her in that moment of hesitation.

"Her head!" she screamed to Marcus, and she backed against the wall, making room for Marcus to take another shot.

One more shot to her forehead, and her body dropped. Hannah's head cracked against the tiles. She wore purple scrubs, and blood seeped from her bullet wounds onto the floor. A bandage was wrapped around her wrist.

Melody peeled it back to expose what appeared to be a feline bite wound. Four small punctures from each canine tooth, surrounded by blackened necrotic skin.

Another light taken from this world, allowing the darkness to grow more palpable each day. It was becoming a sea of darkness, and Melody was drowning.

Marcus knelt beside his wife as she stared at the girl's body.

"Come on," he said, tugging gently on her sleeve to get her to stand up.

His hands vibrated with nervous energy, but he got Melody to her feet and wrapped his arms around her. He didn't say a word because he knew Melody wasn't one to talk about her feelings, so in this moment, she appreciated Marcus for allowing her a moment to process.

She was tired of running. Tired of fighting. For a brief moment, she considered how much easier it would have been if Marcus had accidentally shot her in the head instead.

Then her mind drifted to John. His leg would become septic if she didn't get him the antibiotics he needed, and that girl with the red hair was likely already dead.

Marcus gave her a silent nod of assurance. It was the same nod he gave her when she moved into his parents' house as a teenager. He had stood outside of her new bedroom that night and let her know that it would be all right.

He wasn't perfect by any means. Maybe he cheated on her. Maybe he was an asshole…but he was *there*, trying to be a good person, and that had to count for something.

Marcus began ransacking the cabinets, pulling out every sort of antibiotic and pain killer, while Melody stood still in the doorway to the pharmacy watching him drop amoxicillin in the bag. Whether or not she loved him anymore was uncertain—at least in the romantic sense—but there was something meaningful there. Marcus was her family.

Melody rummaged the treatment area, pulling out handfuls of syringes, bandages, sutures, and anything she could get her hands on for emergency medical care. She unlocked the safe to the controlled substances and began packing up the drugs inside. She knew tramadol was a painkiller that could be used in humans, so she put all three bottles into the backpack. Then she headed to the kennel area to be sure no animals had been left behind.

Opening the door released the stench of uncleaned litter pans. Miles the cat lay dead on the floor with an intravenous catheter sticking from his front leg, with clotted blood in the line. The rest of the kennels were empty.

After gathering everything they could use, Melody slid her arms through the straps of the backpack.

"Why don't you let me carry that for you?" Marcus offered.

"I've got it."

He tugged the bag's strap on her shoulder. "It's heavy."

She shrugged away. "I said I got it."

"You always say you got it."

"Because I do."

"It's okay to let your man help you." He closed the gap between them, leaning in to allow his breath to touch her cheek. "I missed you."

She cringed. "Let's go."

"What's the matter?"

"That girl with the red hair. Do you know her?"

"She worked in my building."

"Were you sleeping with her?"

"Whoa! For someone who's been shacking up with the neighbor for the past few days, you're awful quick to make assumptions." Marcus took a deep breath, relaxed his shoulders, and altered his tone. "We didn't even work on the same floor. She attacked me. That's it."

She could've asked a lot more questions to get to the meat of his lies, but she was too tired to try. There was nothing else to say. He always had an excuse—for being late, for smelling of someone else's perfume, for not coming home—and Melody always gave him the benefit of the doubt that he was telling the truth. She used to chalk it up to her abandonment issues, her insistence on self-reliance, and she *chose* to let him get away with it so she didn't have to lose anyone else in her life.

He held his hand behind her neck, the way he did when they kissed on their wedding day. Melody closed her eyes and recalled the moment. They were outdoors by the lake at the country club in Madison. Sunlight shone through the breaking clouds and heated her skin while the minister announced, "You may kiss the bride."

Marcus placed his lips upon hers, and they kissed. This time, they stood in the middle of the vet clinic with the stench of necrosis surrounding them, but Melody was transported to that moment years ago. Still in grad school, their dreams and lives were ahead of them. The man who had seen her through her worst hardships would be there for her forever and always, and she would be there for him.

Her lips were tinged with disgust as his lying, cheating mouth touched hers.

"We should go."

They left the vet clinic the same way they'd entered, onto the dumpsters, down the bank through the trees, but when they got to the shore, there were four infected blocking their path to the boat.

"We can cut straight through the middle of them," Melody whispered, "I'll take out the two on the left, and you take the ones on the right."

"M and M, back together again." Marcus winked and readied the rifle, but Melody placed her hand on his shoulder and pointed to the infected about 50 yards away at the docks.

"Don't use the gun."

"We'll be out of here before they can get to us."

"Please. You know this boat doesn't always start on the first try. What if we get stuck? Just use your knife, or knock them into the water."

Marcus's irritated expression quickly shifted to compliance. He smiled at her with the same scruffy smile that made her fall in love with him long ago. He gave her a nod and, for once, agreed with her. No argument and no condescending snort of derision. Melody smiled back, thinking that perhaps there was some part of her husband in there that she was still capable of loving if she could get past the spite in her heart. Perhaps she was stressed and confused about her feelings for John, but there was no time to think about it now.

Marcus and Melody moved forward, stances low, their pace brisk. Melody charged at the first infected on the left, swinging her knife at its head.

The other three infected turned to her, while Marcus shuffled far to the right to evade them all. He looped around them and hopped on the boat as Melody pulled the knife out of the man's head.

She raised her knife to charge at a petite woman in a fluorescent yellow vest while a snarling sound rushed up behind her. A limp hand dropped on Melody's shoulder, and she twisted around to see the face of a sick, emaciated man in an unbuttoned pink blouse. He lashed at her with his mouth wide open, dried blood coated his chin. She tripped and fell backward onto the ground as Marcus started the engine.

The sound of the boat distracted the woman in the yellow vest and a stocky man in his underwear who hadn't reached her yet, but the man in the pink blouse continued after Melody. He collapsed to the ground, clawing for her as she scooted back on her butt.

She scrambled to her feet while the man in his underwear lunged toward the boat. Marcus fired a shot into his chest, which knocked him down, but he squirmed to get back up.

Melody charged at the man in pink, throwing her shoulder into him to knock him off balance. Another gunshot fired into the shoulder of the woman in yellow.

The boat backed away from the shoreline.

"Come on!" Marcus yelled to her.

She stomped through the shallow water, grabbed at the ladder toward the back of the starboard side, and pulled herself on board as the man in pink got to his feet. Marcus accelerated, leaving the infected man struggling in their wake.

THIRTY EIGHT

John

John jerked upright and readied his knife, having nearly dozed off with the infected girl right beside him. His body needed more rest to heal, but that wasn't an option yet. He stood, bracing himself on the walker, and looked out over the water to where the boat disappeared behind the point.

At least twenty minutes had passed since they left. Harkness stayed at John's side like a nervous child. His soft brown ears were tucked back. John prepared his backpack so he'd be ready to leave as soon as they returned—if they returned. He turned the cottage upside-down looking for anything that could be useful.

The girl moaned, and a string of saliva stretched from her lips to the pillow as she sat up. John backed away as she looked at him with barely a spark of life in her eyes.

He didn't trust his ability to fight, considering how weak he felt, so he sheathed his knife and readied his pistol.

"Where's Marcus?" she mumbled and wiped her mouth with the back of her hand.

He couldn't believe she was still conscious.

"How do you know Marcus?" John sat down in the wicker chair near the couch and kept his pistol on his thigh.

Her voice cracked. "I kill him."

John had difficulty understanding her slurred words.

"Marcus went to get some meds. He'll be back soon."

"I'll…kill…him," she panted more clearly.

"What happened to you?"

"Marcus," she said. "He pushed me. They…bit me. Fucking Baron Barton Road," she laughed as her head bobbed like a dashboard ornament.

Poor kid. Her feet were swollen and scraped, with bits of gravel stuck in her skin. Every bit of pale flesh that was exposed was scratched and battered. Her words—*he pushed me*—was all John needed to know.

"What's your name?"

Her head looked heavy as she struggled to keep it upright. "Kayla." Drool dribbled from her lower lip in a long string, falling to her lap.

"I'm John."

A gunshot sounded out from across the lake. Kayla's eyes widened as the whizzing of the bullet cut through the air. She seemed to search for it with crazed eyes.

John recognized the sound of his rifle.

Melody would not have fired unless it was absolutely necessary. He stood to look out onto the water, but there was no vessel in sight. A shot fired in the distance again.

Kayla

The sound of the bullet was still cutting through the air in Kayla's mind.

"Marcus and my friend are out there getting medicine now," said the stranger named John.

"Your friend…dead." The sound of her own voice grew louder and quieter as if someone kept adjusting the volume. Her lips moved slowly, unable to say her words as fast as she could think them.

"Melody can handle herself. They probably ran into a couple of them." John's voice sounded like it was a mile away, even though he sat right in front of her.

"Marcus will kill." Kayla coughed, sending splatters of bloody spittle across the room.

John covered his mouth with a medical mask. "He's not going to kill his own wife."

"Wife?" Kayla's arms went limp, and all remaining emotion seemed to evaporate. She no longer felt her facial muscles, and the room spun out of control. She fought to hold onto her mind, but it was getting lost behind a cloud of random thoughts. Her parents. Her brother. The volleyball—blue and orange—her school colors. Marcus's eyes peering from between the blinds of the lab window. Those sexy bedroom eyes, enticing, comforting… evil.

The haze in her head thickened, and the room went from spinning to a violent tremor. She grasped the arm of the couch and held on for her life, burying her head as her world shook around her.

"Kayla? You're gonna be all right." When he came into focus, he was buttoning a clean shirt, adorned with palm fronds. His image seemed to jump from side to side as if she were opening and closing one eye at a time. John disappeared and reappeared before her.

"Melody will be back with some medicine soon," he said.

His voice bounced around in the blackness. *Medicine soon. Medicine soon. Medicine soon…* The man's voice repeated in the tremoring dark. It was like an earthquake opened up a void and sucked her in, and all she could feel was the tremor of a crumbling world.

"Hold on," a voice said.

Kayla believed she could hold on a little longer. She could make it until the medicine arrived. She sat upright while her head pulled hard to the right. All she needed to do was stay alive and destroy Marcus.

THIRTY NINE

Melody

Melody sat at the back of the boat while Marcus stood at the wheel with the rifle slung over his back. The gunfire had lured the infected from the marina. They rushed to the end of the docks and fell in, thrashing and sinking.

As the boat rounded the point into the cove, the tiny pink cottage came into view like a watchtower in the distance.

Marcus cut the engine, let the boat slow to a stop in the open cove, then moved to the back to sit beside Melody.

"Why are we stopping?"

"I need to shake off the nerves."

"I think we should keep moving." She refused to look at him, gazing over the water toward the cottage where John waited for them. Small holes in the clouds allowed scattered diffuse beams of sunlight to play on the surface of the water between her and John.

"What's wrong? Are you okay?" He leaned away. "They didn't get you, did they?"

She narrowed her eyes. "You were gonna leave me, weren't you?"

"No!" Marcus said. "I had to get the boat moving. I knew you could handle yourself, and you did."

Melody was frozen, a deer in headlights, unsure what her next move should be. Gray waves rocked the boat gently as they sat in silence.

Melody kept her eyes locked on the cottage while her peripheral vision kept an eye on Marcus.

"You never trust me," Marcus said, voice flat.

"You left me to die," she whispered.

"No. I told you——"

"I'm not an idiot. If you don't want me around, then say so." Her hands began to tremble. She flexed her fingers to make it stop.

Without a word, he walked to the front of the pontoon boat with John's rifle hanging over his shoulder. He stood by the wheel for several seconds and kept his back to her. "I'm sorry, M."

He pulled an orange life vest from under a seat, then brought it to her. "This obviously isn't going to work."

She took the vest from him, then set it in the seat beside her.

"Put it on," he said.

"Why?"

"Why?!" he laughed.

Her shaking hands spread up her arms into a shiver down her spine. Her teeth chattered, and her entire body now shook out of control. "Take me back to shore."

There was a look in his eyes she'd never seen before.

"Put it on!" He fumbled to get the rifle in front of him and then aimed it at her. "It was never going to work between us."

The rifle twitched with his nervous movements.

Every vein in her body was electrified with terror. Her surroundings came in and out of focus as she stared at the end of the rifle and at the deranged look on Marcus's face.

Melody stood at the back of the boat with the life vest in her hand. Her mind sprinted for a solution, but there was no way to fix this.

Marcus

Melody stood there as still as a rock, emotionless and cold, staring back at that cottage. Marcus had played all the right cards, but she still pulled away from him. The only logical explanation was that she cheated on him with that son of a bitch, John.

His chest heaved with each breath as he made his next demand.

"All you had to do was trust me. Was that so fucking hard?" He felt the sting of tears bite at his eyes, but he clenched his jaw and refused to let himself be hurt.

Melody didn't respond. She just stood there, mocking his authority, indifferent to the sacrifice that he'd made for her.

"Leave the pack of supplies," he said.

"No." She held tight to the shoulder straps.

"Don't be stupid! I'm aiming a gun at your face!"

"John needs these meds."

Marcus edged closer with the gun and pressed the cool tip of the barrel against her forehead. "Take the backpack off!"

His voice was monstrous even to himself, but it worked. She slid the straps off her shoulders and let the bag and the life vest drop to the floor of the boat, then she backed away from the gun to the ladder at the starboard side.

"Get that thing out of my face." Her words hissed between her teeth.

Melody looked at the backpack on the floor and then back at the cottage. "I'm taking some of these meds, Marcus. Some amoxicillin and tramadol."

"No, you're not."

"I'm taking some fucking drugs!" she screamed with more rage than Marcus knew she had in her.

She knelt and opened the backpack.

Rage filled every crevice of his being, and he couldn't contain it any longer. His shoulders dropped, and he sighed before squeezing the trigger and sending a bullet into her.

Melody's body was blasted overboard.

Everything happened so quickly that Marcus wasn't even sure where the bullet had hit her. Blood billowed to the surface where she had fallen in, but he could not see below the choppy surface. He pointed the rifle toward the blood and fired again, but Melody didn't resurface.

Unsure if she was dead or not, Marcus couldn't look back. If he saw her in the water struggling to survive, he might have had a change of heart. Escape was necessary, especially since John must have heard the gunfire.

Marcus stood at the helm with guilt accumulating in his gut. First Greg, then Kayla, now his wife. He threw the gun to the floor behind him as his blood pressure soared. Tears filled his eyes, blurring the world. His face contorted, and he fought the searing headache and building pressure in his brain. A clenched fist couldn't punch away the mental anguish, no matter how many times he hit himself. He wanted to puke but swallowed his sickness and started the boat. He had to get out of there before he was forced to deal with the consequences.

John

Kayla's words were incomprehensible as she mumbled on the couch.

Nothing resembling a word could be deciphered out of her saliva-strung lips. It wouldn't be long before he'd have to put her down, but after hearing those first two shots, John couldn't wait in the cottage any longer. He secured his prosthetic, and raw, wounded flesh rubbed against the padding.

"Hey," he said to Kayla, trying to keep her conscious, but her eyes were distant. She stiffened and collapsed to her side like a wooden board, then went into a seizure.

FORTY

Melody

A plume of crimson burst from Melody's arm. Before Marcus could take a second shot, she flung herself backward off the boat and into the gray water. She sank as bubbles scrambled around her body and up to the surface.

Another bullet whizzed by her, slicing a path of bubbles between her arm and her body. She pressed her wounded arm against her body and tried to swim away underwater, kicking to get out of the path of his fire.

The engine started, but stalled out.

If she could make it back to shore—

I won't make it.

The water was too rough to swim with one arm. Through the murky gray, pockets of sunlight poked through holes in the clouds. She spotted the back of the boat and struggled to kick her way toward it. Surfacing, she pulled in a quiet gasp of air and gripped the rung of the ladder with her good arm, being sure to remain out of Marcus's sight. The engine kicked on, and the boat started moving.

She held her gushing left arm tight to her body as she climbed the ladder and crept onto the boat with a watchful eye on Marcus's back.

The boat sped over small waves in the post-storm water as Melody steadied herself between the seats. The rifle was unattended on one of the seats behind her husband. She eased closer and grabbed it.

Unable to extend her left arm to aim, she did her best at steadying the gun, resting the butt of it into her right shoulder.

Her finger hovered near the trigger, and she hesitated.

Blood dripped onto the floor while everything became blurry, and her vision tunneled. Her bicep wound burned with white hot intensity, but she tried to stay focused.

Marcus turned around and tensed.

Melody kept as steady as possible. "Turn the boat around."

"You're not going to shoot me," Marcus said with a smug grin.

"Turn the boat around," she repeated, soaking wet, with a steady scarlet drip from her arm. Her body was weakening with each passing second.

Marcus turned his back on her and continued driving the boat forward.

"Last warning," Melody said, trembling behind the rifle.

Melody counted in her head, *one, two, three...* Marcus stayed true to his course. *Four.*

She aimed low and to the right of Marcus, targeting the edge of the boat to send a warning shot. She squeezed the trigger, but the bullet grazed his side. Marcus collapsed to his knees at the helm.

"Fuck!" He held his ribs and inspected his wound.

"Turn the boat around!"

Marcus stared at her, bewildered, cupping the wound on his side.

An icy feeling of disconnect glazed over her. The feeling reminded her of the day she received the orchid-colored envelope in the mail from her dad. A day when she was so terrified of the pain of loss that she didn't allow herself to feel anything.

She pointed the gun at Marcus and felt nothing for him. No love, no nostalgic fondness, nothing other than the throbbing pain in her left arm. However, another feeling crept in unwelcome—*worry* for John.

She searched diligently within Marcus's eyes to find whatever it was that she was holding on to, but it wasn't there. Shooting him would be her best option for survival. There was no reason to keep him alive right now. Her index finger moved to the trigger, and as she considered squeezing it, Marcus cranked the wheel to make a U-turn back toward the cottage.

Melody released a held breath, keeping the rifle aimed at Marcus as he held his wound with one hand and steered with the other.

Her blood dripped onto the deck, and lightheadedness began to win. She needed a tourniquet to stop the bleeding, but didn't dare set down the rifle.

"You're making a mistake," he said.

"Shut up." She worried he was right.

Her vision tapered, and her hope that she'd make it back to John faded, but Melody persevered. She pressed her wounded arm between her body and the side of the boat to create enough pressure to lessen the bleeding, but it may have been too late.

Get to John. Despite understanding that he would be all right without her, she couldn't imagine traveling without him at this point. If the past couple of days had proven anything, it was that they were good at having each other's backs.

Marcus slowed the boat as it approached the dock, but it was too late. Melody's knees collapsed beneath her weight.

FORTY ONE

John

The boat made a U-turn and headed back toward John as he stood at the end of the dock with his pistol at the ready.

His leg ached, he was weak, and the rocking boat on the water made for a difficult target. Even though he held the title of an expert sniper, it would be a damn-near impossible shot in this condition. He had about a twenty-yard effective range for this pistol under the current conditions, if he was lucky.

John was ready for whatever that pontoon boat was about to bring him. *Unless Melody is dead.*

The boat was almost to the dock, and John could see Marcus at the helm, slightly hunched—*injured.* The engine cut, and the boat eased closer.

The sight of Melody leaning against the side of the boat eased John's worries until he saw her buckle at the knees and drop to the floor.

"Chuck!"

Marcus dove to her side.

The boat bumped against the dock, and John holstered his pistol so he could tie it to the post.

"What happened?" John shouted as Harkness jumped on board to greet Melody.

"They got on the boat!" Marcus said. "She's infected. Stay back."

John froze in disbelief. Harkness licked at Melody's arm, and she opened her eyes.

She locked her gaze on John as he was about to climb on board. She shook her head at him with a panic-stricken face—a warning—as Marcus lifted the rifle from the floor.

He reached for his pistol, but Marcus had already fired a shot into John, center mass.

Melody jumped to her feet as John felt the jolt of pressure against his chest. He fell overboard, and his head smacked against the dock.

Melody

Melody roared a guttural, animalistic sound that erupted from her core. She charged at Marcus, plowing into him swiftly, fiercely. Marcus was thrown off-balance and overboard into the shallow, choppy water.

"John!" she screamed.

His body floated face down, thumping into the dock post, unresponsive.

"Get up!"

Harkness barked as Marcus got to his feet in the shallow water. There wasn't enough time to make a decision. She untied the boat from the post, hoping John would come to and climb aboard, but his body remained lifeless.

She wanted to puke, but she moved to the front of the boat and started the engine.

Marcus stomped waist-deep toward the shore, readying his rifle on his shoulder.

"M!" His voice was gritty with fury.

Harkness stood on the back of the boat barking, while Melody looked to John's body once more as it floated face down. She shoved the throttle forward and pulled away from him.

"Get up," she demanded under her breath, waiting for movement, but there was no sign of life.

Marcus scrambled on shore and aimed at Melody. The bullet whizzed through the air, missing her.

She ducked below the seat and kept the boat moving forward. Her eyes burned with tears, but this time, she could not keep herself from crying. Heart-wrenching pain overpowered the throbbing gunshot wound to her arm.

Marcus fired again.

"Fucking bitch!" His voice grew distant.

Melody cut the engine in the middle of the cove and dropped to the floor for her backpack while Marcus screamed at her from the dock.

Tears and blood spilled onto the boat's deck.

The bungee cord that she'd collected from the house that morning made a decent tourniquet. She pulled it tight using her free hand and her teeth.

Violent tremors rocked her body as she opened the bottle of tramadol for pain relief. Without knowing the dose, and without caring if it was right, she popped three pills in her mouth.

Marcus fired again, unaware she was too far out of range. He shouted obscenities across the lake that she struggled to hear now. She looked back, hoping to see John climbing to shore, but instead, she saw the girl with the flaming red hair right behind Marcus on the dock.

About twenty others were in pursuit. A mass of infected rolled, slid, and stumbled down the slope toward the sound of Marcus's yelling, but he was too focused on Melody to notice them.

The redheaded girl scuffed her feet along the dock with her focus locked on Marcus. She collided into his back and swung her arms in a frenzy, clawing and biting until they both fell.

Marcus screamed out as she tore into him, and two other infected threw themselves on top of the pile. The mound of bodies thrashed. They wrestled and entangled themselves on the dock, and Marcus's screams became lost in the chaos.

Melody watched in horror as her husband was torn apart, but her attention pulled toward where John had fallen into the water.

She couldn't see him anymore. She pictured his body sinking, tangled below the surface in the weeds.

Infected bodies from Barton Road tumbled down the bank and, one by one, dropped into the water around where John had fallen. Many of the infected were too weak to get back to their feet once they'd fallen to the base of the hill, and the rest dragged themselves onto the dock and tumbled over the edge.

She couldn't watch any longer. The icy glaze took over, and Melody collapsed to the floor of the boat and stared to the gray sky, seeking some pinpoint of light—some little bit of hope to grasp onto—but there was no hope left.

FORTY TWO

Melody

She drove the boat up the lake and dropped anchor for the evening. She'd be safe on the water overnight. The day's storm had moved far to the south, and the clouds broke apart, exposing patches of clear sky. She and Harkness dined on a can of mixed vegetables while the sunset cast orange and purple light across the water, but she had trouble finding beauty in the vista.

It's the living that's the hard part.

Maybe it was too hard to keep going. Maybe she could pop a few too many painkillers and slip away peacefully on the water. Melody pulled her pale orchid envelope from her pocket and decided it was time to read her father's last thoughts.

She carefully ripped open the seal of the soaking wet envelope and pulled out soaked, yellow paper. The paper was haphazardly torn at the top, like her dad had ripped it off the legal pad with no more care than one would rip free a grocery list. Messy handwriting looked back at her:

Dear Melon Bee,
If you're reading this—well, I guess you know what it means if you're reading this.
I'll be gone.
I love your mom.

I love her with so much of me that when she died, too much of myself died too. I'm a shell now, and I choose to quit.

But you know what? I have loved. I have loved in a way that people dream to be able to love. And I have lived. Really truly lived a full life, but I can't keep going anymore now that half of me is missing.

Be strong, Melon Bee. I know you will be, because you're far stronger than me.

Days will come that are so hard that you want to give up, but don't. Don't quit life until you've lived—truly lived. Even when you're 101 years old, don't die until you've enjoyed life.

I'm not saying you'll get to do all the things you want to do, but you will get to experience sunsets and the stars at night. You'll get to experience love and friendship and all the things that make life worth living for.

Don't let the crap that happens to you in life keep you from living. Live with a fire in your heart and a fire under your ass and fight like mad.

I love you…More than I could ever say or prove.

-Dad

Harkness wiggled himself up against her and whimpered, curling into a bundle. Melody clutched the paper against her chest and squeezed the orange vial of tramadol in one hand. She wadded up the note with spiteful rage and nearly chucked it overboard, but instead curled into a fetal ball and cried harder than she'd ever cried before.

Then she tucked her note back into her pocket and pulled herself together. She dressed her bullet wound, looked back across the lake, and whispered a heart-wrenching goodbye to her dad, to her husband, and to John.

FORTY THREE

John

Before John had been shot in the chest and left for dead, he waited for Melody to return. Kayla stiffened and went into a violent, grand mal seizure. He aimed his pistol at her head, but right before pulling the trigger, her body settled down. She sat upright and stared out the window with the vacant expression of a corpse, but she was still aware—still *human.*

While Kayla was upright, he dragged the black chest with gold clasps from under the patio couch. Marcus had his eyes on it earlier. A quarter-inch layer of dust on the lid fell off in damp clumps. An empty gun holster and a neatly folded police uniform sat on top. He pulled out the contents—certificates and awards, a baton, handcuffs—all of which John stuffed into his pack.

At the bottom of the memorabilia was a faded vest.

"No shit," he said.

He stood up to look out the window toward the pontoon boat that now moved away from the cottage, farther out into the lake.

He didn't know what the hell was going on out there, but he knew two things: he didn't trust Marcus, and he needed Melody to be okay. John picked up the 1980s-era Kevlar vest and strapped it beneath the palm-frond button-down shirt.

John left Kayla on the porch and ran to the canoe leaning against the tree as sharp stabbing jolts of pain shot from his leg.

Another shot fired from the boat as it moved away. Countless scenarios played through his mind as to who was shooting and why.

With every ounce of strength he could muster, he flipped over the canoe and pushed it through the grass. Each heave sent the canoe a bit closer to the edge of the slope and a wave of excruciating pain and nausea through his body.

He knew he'd never catch up with her by rowing, and he didn't know whether or not Melody was even on that boat, but he had to do something.

He recalled the boat with the red lightning bolt, but with the flood of infected wandering the gravel road, he didn't dare try when time was of the essence.

But then the pontoon boat made a sudden turn and headed back in his direction.

John met them at the dock as they pulled in.

After John was shot in the chest, his head smacked against the wooden dock, knocking him out. He wasn't sure how long he'd been in the dark, but he pulled his face from the water and sucked in a deep breath. His head swam in a disorienting fog while Melody's boat pulled away without him. Gunfire blasted above as Marcus shot at her from the dock. John stayed low and close to the dock posts.

He eased toward the bank, careful to stay out of Marcus's line of sight. However, before he could emerge from the water, countless infected poured down the slope toward Marcus. Uncertain of his strength and not confident enough to take on so many of the infected, even with his pistol (which was now wet), John tucked himself quietly along the water's edge.

As he hid from Marcus and the infected, Kayla stumbled down the hill.

An infected man dropped into the water in front of John, then another. John remained still, with his knife at the ready, as Melody stared back toward him in the water, unaware he was alive.

As more infected splashed into the lake around him, he protected himself with quick and covert attacks.

Then, as if the universe didn't think things were hard enough, Melody drove the boat away without him.

He waited for an opportunity to get out of there and follow her, but the infected kept coming. Each second that passed was another second longer that it would take to catch up with her.

Barton Road filled with the infected that had busted through the fence from the quarantine zone. They wandered around the lake cottages, and many skidded down the bank into the water.

John waited over an hour before the infected became sparse enough to make it out alive. By then, there were bodies floating, several lay dead on the bank, and many had wandered off. The sky had darkened, and John eased out of the water and climbed the hill toward the cottage.

In unbearable pain, John managed to disengage two slow-moving infected on his way to the screened porch, then he snuck inside without attracting any others.

He peeled the Kevlar vest from his body and inspected the bruising on his chest.

The sky blackened, and the moaning of infected outside the lake cottage was enough of a deterrent to keep John from rushing after her blindly.

He took some more Tylenol and decided he would have to wait until morning to get moving. His chances of finding her were bleak, but he had to come up with something.

Melody and Harkness were long gone. They had to be clear on the other side of the lake by now. Even if he could remove the red lightning-bolt boat from the side of the house down the street, and even if he could get it to the water, he wouldn't be able to track her in the dark. John had no idea how to get to the cabin where Melody was heading.

FORTY FOUR

Melody

The next day brought cool, autumn temperatures, and Melody drove the pontoon boat toward the marshy outlet that fed into the foothills of the mountains. Occasionally, she would spot the dark silhouette of a figure stumbling along the shoreline, but more often, she saw inanimate bodies on the docks and in the backyards of lake homes.

She pulled into the swampy cove of state-protected wilderness, where there were no inhabitants for miles. The engine cut off, and the boat drifted through lily pads and calla plants in the shallow cove.

Before leaving the boat, Melody had found half a jar of Skippy in the storage compartment, along with some moldy bread that she tossed overboard. She changed her bandages, popped another painkiller, and used her fingers to eat peanut butter out of the jar.

She sat on the floor while Harkness licked the peanut butter from her hand. Blood stained the edge of the boat where Marcus had been shot. Trauma from the past few days had turned her blood as stagnant as the swampy water around her. She worried if she cried again, she might never get up and leave the boat. She might've lain there forever, allowing the mosquitoes to feast on her body, so the infected could not.

"Be strong," she repeated her father's words.

She walked all day with her arm bandaged in a makeshift sling. Her head swam within the thick haze of a slight opioid overdose. Harkness followed along.

She crossed the ankle-deep swamp, climbing from each grassy patch of earth to the next to keep her feet out of the black muck as often as she could. She trekked through the densely wooded foothills that laid between the two main routes through the forest, avoiding the nearby small towns.

Melody hiked in a trancelike state, even walking along the road for a short time with the steep faces of each mountain on either side of her. She came across more dead bodies than she did the living, but nothing fazed her.

"Here we go," she said to Harkness as they left the pavement for a dirt road. "It's a long way up."

Two miles up the road, they turned onto an ATV trail, and after another mile, an even smaller dirt trail blocked by a cattle gate. It was in one of the pictures taken by the realtor for the ad. Melody had argued that it wasn't even part of her grandfather's land, but the realtor insisted it was a good shot of some rocky prominences that might help the sale. Her drugs began to wear off, and she realized how close she was to the cabin.

The throbbing in her arm returned, and the harsh reality of her pain and loneliness settled in. On the third trail turn, the trees changed from the half-naked oak and walnut trees to a dense-packed forest of pine. The trail narrowed and wound up the side of the mountain.

It was silent, except for the sound of evergreen needles crushing beneath her feet. No wandering infected came up here. No dead bodies. The air smelled of pine, like Dad had just dragged in a fresh-cut Christmas tree.

Melody paused at the fork in the narrow ATV trail and cut to the right along an overgrown path, nearly obstructed from view by the summer's growth.

She climbed the steep hill, but the cozy log cabin didn't come into view until she cleared the fallen branches that had blocked what was going to be the driveway someday.

She was home.

The oak trees surrounding the cabin had shed most of their leaves into a blanket of yellow. She climbed the front creaking porch steps. The realtor, in an effort to stage the property, had hung a sign above the entrance that read *Live, Laugh, Love*. A single nail held it in place, and she imagined that nail being driven into her heart.

She wedged open a window and climbed inside.

The cabin was adorned with furnishings that the realtor had towed in by four-wheeler, hoping to improve the ambiance. A cozy, lightweight leather couch was situated before the fireplace, a rocking chair, and some canisters on the counters. The stone kitchen oven reminded her of her grandfather's venison stew, and it beckoned her to light a fire.

She cleaned herself up first, using the fresh spring water flowing through the manual pump outside, but once she was settled in for the night, an overwhelming sense of loneliness encompassed her.

She sat down on the back deck overlooking the small lake far down the side of the mountain slope.

In her hands was the wooden *Live, Laugh, Love* sign that she'd pried off the front of the cabin. With the blade that John had given her, she scratched over the word *live* and carved the word SURVIVE above it.

She struggled to understand the point in surviving any more.

Life was too hard—it was always hard—and she couldn't think of a good reason to keep fighting like her dad had told her to do.

The daylight faded yet again, and the first stars were shining through the twilight overhead. Melody would have preferred to die in peace, right here under the stars, and she had the opioids to do it.

FORTY FIVE

Melody

Melody sat on the back deck of the mountain cabin and held her dad's crumpled note to her chest as if her heart could absorb the words into her soul. The whispering thought of suicide popped in and out of her head, but survival spoke louder.

She was always just surviving, and she hadn't *lived* yet.

She needed to stay alive a little longer and give life a chance, but her dad's words of advice had no clue what the world would become.

The stars of the Summer Triangle were still overhead in the early twilight autumn sky. Melody's eyes were tired, but she craned her neck back and looked to the stars.

The sight made her heart float for a moment, defying the weight that crushed it a second earlier. There they were—her stars—her dad's stars, unwavering in their glow. Her constant through life's storms, always there, behind the clouds, waiting to shine through.

Harkness wiggled beside her and rested his jowls in her lap, creeping his paws up in a poor attempt to sneak his sixty-pound body into her lap.

She let out a laugh and invited him up, and her laugh turned into tears as he licked her jawline.

There were little things that she would miss if she didn't keep living, like the companionship of a dog and the beauty of the stars. Despite the state of the world, there was still joy to be had.

Whether Fort Drummond would stand long enough to find a vaccine or not, whether mankind fades into non-existence, there would still be stars in the sky and sunlight through the trees and puppy kisses.

Melody ran her fingers along the letters of her *Live, Laugh, Love* sign, unsure if she was destined only for survival. Or perhaps she needed to find a way to make living worth it, despite the world around her.

Maybe that was her dad's point: that life would be what she made of it. And what about *love* and *laughter?* Perhaps she would be destined to experience those with nobody other than Harkness.

"That wouldn't be so bad, would it?" She scratched behind his ear as he snored in her lap.

Harkness jerked himself upright and growled, looking toward the side railing. Melody rushed inside at his warning.

As she locked the door to the back deck, there was a thump on the front door.

Her exhaustion would not win today. She tiptoed to the front door.

A voice called from the other side. "Chuck?"

At the sound of his voice, Melody's heart felt like it took flight, twirling up in a spiral, like the autumn leaves blowing from the trees. She rushed to unlock the door.

John stood with an overstuffed backpack, prosthetic limb strapped to the side of it, standing on her front porch. He braced himself upright on the aluminum walker.

She stared at him with her mouth agape, and Harkness danced in a figure eight between them.

"How?" she asked. "I saw—"

John exposed the top of his Kevlar vest beneath his buttoned shirt, and Melody ran her fingers along the edge of it.

He handed her the Carroll County Realty Guide that Melody had placed in his hands the day before. It was folded back to the listing of her grandfather's cabin.

"Page 48, just like you said."

Melody threw herself at John in an embrace that could not bring her close enough to him, pinning the walker between their bodies.

"How's your arm?" John said.

"Fine."

"That's a long way to travel with only one good arm."

"I'd say the same thing about your leg."

"I have to admit it wasn't too hard. A lot of them are already dead." John shifted his weight on the walker. "That boat with the red lightning bolt. I borrowed it. It didn't take long to get in the water. Then I used maps and this realty guide to find the property. Once I got to the dirt trails, you left a hell of a foot trail to follow. Your footprints look like a drunken pirate stomped up the mountain."

"I took a lot of drugs."

John shifted his weight again with a wince. "That's why I'm here. You still have those meds?"

"So, you're just here for the drugs?"

"Why else would I be here?"

Melody smiled.

"Don't flatter yourself, sweetheart," John said, letting himself inside.

Melody treated John's leg and started a fire, and Harkness curled onto the floor near the heat while they sat on the couch.

John eased closer, nuzzling his face into her neck. His scruff had softened with another day's growth. It brushed against her skin, and she welcomed his touch. He wrapped her within his arms and laid her down as the stone fireplace popped and crackled.

"You're not going to punch me this time, are you?" he asked.

"We'll see."

His chest heaved, and the orange light of the flame danced across John's crow tattoo, creating an illusion of the birds flapping their wings, trembling with excitement to take flight.

John placed a gentle kiss on her dry, cracked lips. She wet them with her tongue as he moved down her neck and collarbone to her arm. He ran his fingers along her bandage, into the crook of her elbow, and along the inside of her palm, as if exploring every crease, healing every bruise and bullet hole. Her aching, wounded body softened at his touch and, suddenly, the throbbing of her bullet wound was overpowered by the throbbing ache in her heart.

John hovered over her, planting kisses, until all of the throbbing in her body moved to the space between her legs. Melody lifted her pelvis from the couch and pressed against him.

Within the heat of the firelight, their bodies entangled, clothes melted away. Gooseflesh rose hairs to attention. Toes curled in ecstasy, and they were safe within each other's embrace. Melody's sore body tensed and writhed as currents of primal pleasure surged through her veins. For now, they were the only two burning-hot stars in the universe, revolving around each other, dancing within each other's powerful gravity.

She wished she could stay hidden away in that cabin forever, tucked within the comfort of John's company, but she knew better. Life had never been that easy.

Later that night, Melody sat in the lounge chair on the back porch while John approached with two cups of hot tea.

She took the steaming cup within her palms with a smile. "We have tea?"

"It was in a canister in there. There are jars of spaghetti noodles, rice, and some herb-infused oils."

"The realtor brought them in for staging."

"We can make the little bit of food we have last a few days. Longer if we need to."

They sat beneath the naked trees, sipping tea while they still had some tea to enjoy, and they looked at the stars splattered across the black canvas above.

John held Melody's hand and smiled, and her heart filled with contentment and something resembling love.

The cold weather was moving in, and soon they were sure to be encased in snow, with nothing but a small fireplace to warm themselves. Their supplies would run out, and the struggle to survive would continue.

Melody sipped from the warm cup and released a sigh, knowing the storm would never quit. They would listen each day for news from Fort Drummond on the crank radio, and they would wait. The spread of LV01 was sure to wax and wane, and the storms would keep coming, testing Melody's strength, but she would survive. She would fight like mad, like her dad told her to, with a fire in her heart and under her ass, and she would survive. Even more importantly, she would stick with John and Harkness for as long as she could, and she would laugh, she would love, and in turn, she would live.

MORE BY RED LAGOE

Bloodstains by Gaslight

In Excess of Dark

Impulses of a Necrotic Heart

Nightmare Sky: Stories of Astronomical Horror

Dismal Dreams

Lucid Screams

ABOUT THE AUTHOR

Red Lagoe is a horror writer who resides in Coastal Virginia. She grew up on 80's slasher movies, Tales from the Crypt, and Alfred Hitchcock presents. As a dabbler in amateur astronomy, she enjoyed being the curator and editor of *Nightmare Sky: Stories of Astronomical Horror*. Red also worked as a staff writer for Crystal Lake Publishing's *Still Water Bay* series. In addition to writing, Red loves creating art using traditional fine art mediums like paint, ink, and charcoal, and she is the owner of Death Knell Press.

www.ingramcontent.com/pod-product-compliance
Lightning Source LLC
Chambersburg PA
CBHW071302250626
47159CB00004B/1279